Puzzle Girl

Rachael Featherstone was born and raised in Woodford. Her path to writing was a little unorthodox. After reading Mathematics at Oxford University, New College, Rachael went to work in research.

When Rachael's mother was diagnosed with terminal cancer in 2012, Rachael decided to take a chance, quit her job, and fulfil a life time ambition to write a novel. She went back to university and completed a Masters in English Literature and had several short stories published.

Rachael now lives in Hampshire with her husband, Tim and daughter Elodie.

Puzzle Girl

RACHAEL FEATHERSTONE

ﬃ CANELO

First published in the United Kingdom in 2018 by The Dome Press

This edition published in the United Kingdom in 2022 by

Canelo
Unit 9, 5th Floor
Cargo Works, 1–2 Hatfields
London, SE1 9PG
United Kingdom

A CIP catalogue record for this book is available from the British Library.

Print ISBN 978 1 80032 647 7
Ebook ISBN 978 1 80032 229 5

Look for more great books at www.canelo.co

Printed and bound in Great Britain by Clays Ltd, Elcograf S.p.A.

1

I dedicate this book to my mum who always believed in me and taught me to follow my dreams.

I love you and miss you.

Prologue

Every story has a beginning, middle and an end, and tonight, my story begins. Finally doors that seemed super-glued shut are opening. Tonight I won't just be 'Lovable Cassy', I'll be 'Cassy, the next big thing'. 'Cassy, the woman who—' My phone beeps and I quickly unlock it to see a new email from my boss.

> From: Thomas Samuel
> Sent: Fri 19:20
> To: Martin Robertson; Cassidy Brookes
> Subject: Dinner at Lola's
>
> Arranged to have drinks before Patterson dinner so aim for 8pm.

I forward the message to Seph, he'll have to meet me at the restaurant. I don't have time to weigh up the pros and cons of the three different clutch bags on my bed. I just grab the little black one – black does go with everything – and shove my phone, purse and lipstick inside.

As I shut the front door of my apartment, I hear the one opposite open.

'Looking sexy, Princess.'

'Don't call me that,' I say and slap Dan on the shoulder. Dan is, to all intents and purposes, my surrogate brother.

'Sexy or Princess?'

'Both,' I say. 'I'm going for the cool and sophisticated look.'

Dan and I even look like we could be related. We both have dark hair, fair skin and small curved noses. Our eyes are different though. Dan's are dark brown but mine are lighter with a swirl of green.

'Where's Seph?' he asks.

'Meeting me there. Don't pull that face.'

'Just remember it's not about him. This is your big night.'

I grin. It is my night for a change. Don't get me wrong, I understand that Seph has a demanding job as a lawyer, but it will be nice to have him on my arm for once.

'Wish me luck.'

'You don't need it,' Dan says and gives me a hug.

'Now go before you're late.'

I hail a taxi as soon as I reach the main road.

'Lola's, Shoreditch, please.'

I still can't quite believe what I'm about to do. I've been working my way up the ladder at Holywells, a leading digital marketing agency. I have a wonderfully diverse set of clients but I'm yet to get that star client that puts you on the map. Until tonight that is. Tonight I will be meeting my idol, the God of digital marketing, who transformed social media from being a place of chit-chat to a professional enterprise. Within five years of founding MediaTech, it outgrew the ranks of traditional marketing agencies and now develops its own bespoke social media products. And now MediaTech are interested in bringing Holywells on board to run some of their platforms. It's like a dream come true. With MediaTech on my CV I could go – and do – anything. I could even start my own business one day.

My hands are shaking with anxiety and excitement in equal measure. I would usually do some sort of puzzle to help me relax but tonight I want to stay completely focused. Instead I take a few deep breaths and pull out my notebook – I never go anywhere without my notebook – and read over my talking points for the dinner. We arrive at Lola's at 7.50 p.m., I thank the driver and pay. Even from the outside, Lola's has a smell that makes you salivate. The most exclusive restaurant this side of London, newly awarded a second Michelin star. This night really couldn't be more perfect.

The porter greets me with a friendly smile and helps me take off my coat. I feel like I'm walking on velvet, the carpet is softer than cashmere. I can see the maitre d' waiting to greet me. I begin the short walk towards him and suddenly I'm filled with nervous energy again. I take another deep breath and say my calming mantra in my head.

I am a strong, professional woman.

I am a calm, professional woman.

I am a calm, successful woman.

'Good evening, ma'am.'

'I am a confident, successful woman.'

'Indeed, ma'am.'

Did I really say that out loud? My cheeks get that prickly sunburn feeling and I'm definitely blinking too often.

'Do you have a reservation?' the maitre d' asks. He has a look on his face that makes me think he may have asked me that already.

'Err, yes,' I say and tug at my skirt, my cool, sophisticated look well and truly evaporated by my own body heat.

3

I flick my hair back and say as confidently as possible, 'I'm with the Holywells party.'

'This way please.'

OK, so as beginnings go, this one is not as good as I hoped but I'm determined that this night is going to be a success. I follow the very polite maitre d', who didn't so much as smirk at my embarrassing introduction, through to the bar. Mr Samuel and his wife are already here. Mr Samuel, one of Holywells' senior partners and head of my department, is the very best kind of boss and mentor: innovative, fair, intelligent and just a little bit eccentric. Try to imagine Elton John in his mid-forties wearing a polo shirt and Rupert the Bear's yellow checked trousers and that's what he looks like most Fridays before he goes off to play golf with clients. He has a soft smile and is always surrounded by an aroma of peppermint that puts me at ease.

'Ah, Cassidy, you remember my wife?'

'Very nice to see you again, Mrs Samuel.'

'Please, call me Veronica. And where's your other half?'

Before I can reply, Martin arrives along with a blonde of the fashion-model variety. I expected no less. Martin and Veronica greet each other like old family friends.

'Cassy,' he says and nods his head in greeting, 'this is Isabella.'

'Hello, Martin, Isabella,' I say.

Isabella whispers something in his ear and then heads towards the ladies' room. My fake smile was obviously too convincing because Martin has taken a few steps towards me.

'It's nice to see you've let your hair down for a change.'

'Is that your way of saying I'm uptight?'

He's only been here two minutes and already I feel like I'm having an allergic reaction. The side of Martin's mouth crinkles into a smile.

'It was a compliment. I'd almost forgotten your hair had a natural curl.'

Something in Martin's gaze almost fools me into thinking he's genuine, but then I remember who I'm talking to. Martin is my colleague, or 'my peer', as the professional world would say. Every day he comes into the office wearing a new pair of cufflinks like a mark of his alpha male status. There is never a jet-black hair on his head out of place. I admit that his pristine, tailored, slim-fit suits bring out the best in his physique (not that I would *ever* swoon over him the way the other office girls do). He has the George Clooney gene; he's even the same height. Women of all ages seem to be drawn to his dark brown eyes and his soft smile that says, 'you can trust me'. I used to think it was just women, but not even the firm's partners can withstand his charm. They treat him like a chip-off-the-old-block.

'Oh my God, he's here,' I whisper to Martin.

A shyness comes over me that I haven't felt since my first date with Seph. Gregory Patterson, the most influential social-media expert in the country, is walking over to us with a beautiful woman on his arm who makes even Martin's latest conquest look ordinary.

'Greg, so wonderful to see you again,' Mr Samuel says and shakes his hand enthusiastically.

'Likewise.'

'Let me introduce you to two of the company's rising account directors, Martin Robertson and Cassidy Brookes.'

I shake his hand feeling almost giddy. I think I mumble something about it being an honour to meet him but I seem to be having some sort of outer-body experience. Opportunities like this don't usually come so early in a marketing career. The *Mad Men* wining and dining element is usually just for partners and senior staff, but with Anabelle, the Head of Accounts, on maternity leave, Martin and I have had more opportunities. We talk business for around twenty minutes, enjoying the best cocktails I've ever tasted. I make a few good points but I can't help but be a bit distracted wondering where Seph is. He should have been here by now.

'Well,' Mr Samuel says when the conversation reaches a natural pause, 'shall we make our way over to the table?'

I decide that it's best not to mention that Seph is yet to arrive. I hope he's OK. I hate the way my mind rushes to the worst conclusion but I can't help it.

'I must say, you are making me feel special bringing me here,' Gregory says as we are shown to our table. 'I'm impressed you got a reservation at such short notice.'

'Ah, well, I can't take the credit for that,' Mr Samuel says. 'Martin arranged it. I think he's better connected than I am.' Everyone laughs as I feel a little piece of me die inside.

Seph's empty chair is threatening to give me palpitations. I discreetly pull my phone out of my bag and send him a quick text under the table. One of the advantages of working in the tech business is that using a smart phone blind becomes second nature. The waiter pours each of us a glass of pink champagne and I feel my bag vibrate on my lap. I pull out my phone and read the text from Seph.

I stare at my phone. I go in and out of the text message app five times. He definitely sent it. It's definitely the correct date and time. How… How could he think this is the right time for a joke? Unless it's not a joke. My mouth goes dry.

'A toast,' Mr Samuel says, 'to endless possibilities.'

The bottle probably cost a week's wages but I can barely taste it. My heart is thumping with fear. My mind is whirling and I can barely keep up with the conversation.

'Ah, well perhaps we should get Cassy to test you. Cassy?'

My eyes slowly pass over Mr Samuel's face. I am vaguely aware that I need to respond.

'Cassy is our in-house quizmaster,' he remarks to Gregory. 'She revived the Holywells' tradition for pub quizzes when she joined. Cassy, I'm sure you can think up a brain teaser to test Greg.'

I blink hard. I can hear the words Mr Samuel is saying but I can't seem to join them into a sentence.

'Greg was just telling us that he is a puzzle fanatic like you, Cassy,' Veronica adds and gives me a look of encouragement.

'Puzzles, yes,' I say. 'I do love puzzles. Holywells participates in a monthly pub quiz.'

Oh God, I think that's what Mr Samuel just said. I instinctively raise my hand to my forehead. This is all too much to process.

7

'Cassy? Is everything OK?'

'Fine, thank you.'

I need to talk to Seph.

'So… do you have a particularly nasty brain teaser for—'

I push my chair back from the table. Mr Samuel looks at me with surprise.

'I might just go and give Seph a quick call to make sure he's on his way.'

I stand up but my legs falter beneath me.

'Wow,' Martin says, holding me tightly by the arm, 'those cocktails seem to have gone to your head. Here, allow me to escort you.'

'Ah, such a gent,' Gregory says. The others all smile but I don't seem to remember how.

'Cass, what's going on?' Martin asks as soon as we're out of earshot. 'You're off your game.'

'I'm fine,' I say and yank my arm back, my senses slowly coming back to me. 'I just… need to make a phone call. You can drop the knight in shining armour routine.'

Martin holds his hands up in surrender and walks back to the table. As soon as he's out of sight I call Seph's mobile. It rings out. I try again. Three more times in fact. I call Dan and it goes straight to voicemail.

'Dan? Are you home? Wherever you are, can you go round my flat? It's Seph. He sent me this weird text and I think he might be…' I take a deep breath. 'I think he might be leaving me.'

I can barely believe what I'm saying. Seph, boyfriend of seven years, would never do something like this. It just has to be miscommunication. I stand outside Lola's for another few minutes but I know it is going to look odd if I wait much longer. I'll just have to go inside and act like

I need to use the ladies'. I briefly return to the table and give a feeble reason to be excused again. Almost as soon as I enter the bathroom my phone vibrates.

> **From: Seph Mobile Fri 21:13**
> Don't try to contact me. This is the best way. Bye

I barely have time to process the words – they all seem to be moving around like I'm trying to solve a conundrum – when my phone starts flashing Dan's name.

'Hi,' I say, my voice nearly failing me.

'Hey, hun.' Dan's tone, a little softer than usual, is all I need to confirm that this nightmare is really happening. I sink to the floor, my knees crunched up to my chest. I can see my pathetic reflection in the floor-length mirror on the far wall of the bathroom and watch myself taking shallow breaths as Dan talks about something. I see mascara tears running down my reflection and instinctively lick my lips. They're salty.

'Cassy? Are you still there? Cassy? Cassy!'

I snap out of my daydream and stand up. 'I'm here,' I say and brush down my dress. 'Can you keep Seph at the flat until I get there? I'll be about twenty minutes.'

I wipe my eyes with a paper towel and patch up my mascara. What's that saying from *Grease*? *It's no use crying over spilled milkshake.* Well, this milkshake hasn't toppled over yet.

'You can't walk out on dinner,' Dan says.

'Yes I can,' I say determinedly. 'This is more important. *Seph* is more important. I have to speak to—'

'Cassy, Stop! Please, hun, just stop… He's already gone.'

I don't remember getting home. Martin put me in the taxi I think, probably thrilled to get rid of me and have Gregory all to himself. It seems like everyone wants to get rid of me. Except Dan. He tucked me into bed almost as soon as I got home. He said I could sleep at his but I wanted to sleep in my own bed, so he offered to stay in my spare room instead. He didn't think I should be alone. It's late now. Maybe even early morning. My head is pounding and my pillow is cold with damp. I must have been crying in my sleep. I pull myself out of bed and walk to the en suite, there's a sour aftertaste in my mouth that I want to get rid of.

The sight of my toothbrush brings tears to my eyes. It looks so lonely in its little holder. After a sharp intake of breath to steady myself, I reach for the toothpaste. Oh my God, he took the toothpaste. I don't believe this. *I bought the toothpaste!* What kind of man – no, what kind of *animal* – does that? I walk out and slam the en suite door shut. All the fear and sadness that has been engulfing me suddenly turns to rage. But then just as quickly it turns back to sadness. I throw myself back onto the bed and begin to cry.

'Cassy? Are you—' Dan doesn't finish his sentence. He lies down on the bed next to me and pulls me in close.

'I just don't understand why.'

'It's OK, Cassy. Everything's going to be OK.'

'No it's not,' I say. 'It's over. He's gone.'

I lie in his arms, letting the words process, and I whisper, 'The end.'

One

The sunlight seems to have once again found that impossible-to-get-rid-of gap in the curtains and the sound of my alarm clock soon adds to my torment. With my eyes still closed, I fumble for the snooze button. My hand hits something tall, cylindrical and cold but, like an arcade claw machine, I grab nothing but air. Half a second later I hear the dull thud of glass hitting carpet. I peer over the edge of the bed, my eyes squinting to adjust to the light. It's a bottle of Merlot. Thankfully empty, although I don't remember finishing it.

I pick up my phone and start to sift through the overnight emails. Then I catch sight of the time. I double check my alarm clock.

How many times have I pressed snooze?

I meant to get up extra early today. I sit up straight and then quickly hold my head. I think I may have drunk that whole bottle of Merlot on my own. My eyes start to focus on things in the room: my suit hanging on the wardrobe door; the empty space next to the wardrobe where Seph's muddy golf clubs used to hibernate and the wonky hook on the back of the bedroom door where his football calendar used to hang. I really do need to make buying a new calendar a priority. I quickly pick up my notebook and add it to my most recent to-do list.

I gather my strength and walk to the kitchen. The toaster pings and I let out a cry of shock.

'Morning, Princess. I'm making toast,' Dan says, popping his head above the counter. I hadn't noticed him crouching down by the fridge. 'Don't you have any butter?'

'Second shelf, behind the yogurt.'

I sit down at the breakfast bar and hold my head in my hands. Scattered scenes from last night replay themselves. 'It would have been our eight-year anniversary,' I remember telling Dan. 'Eight years.'

'I know,' he'd said. 'Thank God you only wasted seven and a half years.'

'Do you have any jam?' Dan is asking me now.

I shake my head and a vision of Dan tucking me into bed last night comes back to me.

'I don't have time for toast,' I say, my body finally kicking into gear. 'I need to get to work. I've got that meeting remember?'

'Why do you think I'm up this early,' Dan says and smiles at me, almost sympathetically.

Neither of us has mentioned the meeting since I first told him about it last month. MediaTech had been deliberating for some time over whom to partner with and had finally narrowed their agency choices down to us and one other firm. With Anabelle still on maternity leave, Mr Samuel had asked Martin and me to each come up with a strategy to swing the decision in the firm's favour. I hadn't known quite how to react when Mr Samuel had approached me. It had been a chance to redeem myself for the disastrous client dinner early this year but also a reminder of how brutally Seph had dumped me in the same number of characters as a single tweet – I'd counted, twice.

Dan had been the one to encourage me to take this second chance, just like he'd been the one to pick up the Seph-shaped pieces of my heart. 'This is a perfect opportunity to prove to yourself that you've moved on,' Dan had said to me when I told him. 'And show all of them what you would have shown them at that dinner if not for an inconsiderate, egotistical—' I'd stopped him then. But Dan was right. This was a second chance that few people get in their careers. Spurred on by this thought, I quickly begin to gather up the things I need to take with me and put them in my bag. Usually I do this in the evenings but last night was an exception. I shower and get dressed so quickly I consider sending a timesheet to the Guinness Book of Records.

'Weren't you planning to get up *extra* early today?' Dan asks, mockingly, when I return to the living room.

'Yes, thank you for that wonderful insight, Daniel.'

'It's called irony,' Dan says as I rush past him.

'What is?'

'You, Miss Organisation Extraordinaire, running late.'

'I am not running late,' I retort.

'Oh right. So err, why exactly are you galloping around the flat?'

I pause and let myself catch my breath.

'Because I'm not as early as I would like to be,' I say.

Dan laughs. 'You've been doing so well since the moron left as well. I bet this is the first time you've been running late in what, six months?'

'Six months, six days and eleven hours to be exact but who's counting. And I am *not* running late.'

13

Dan sighs. 'Y'know what I keep asking myself? Are you actually counting or just freakishly good at maths?'

I stop and look at him.

'Let's go with the maths thing,' I say.

Dan looks like he wants to say something but decides against it.

'I'm fine,' I say. 'I'm just stressed about this meeting. I really need it to go well.'

'It will,' he says and gives my shoulders a quick massage. 'As long as you don't miss it because you're running so *late* that is.'

I give him a friendly slap on the arm and head to the door just as Dan starts singing, 'Ironic' by Alanis Morrissette.

As soon as I get into the corridor I realise I've forgotten something. I rush back inside and walk over to Dan. I kiss him gently on the forehead.

'Thanks for staying over last night.'

'Anytime, Princess. Now go before you miss your own meeting.'

–

I am definitely not late. However, I am significantly behind schedule and consequently have successfully missed my regular DLR train, my backup DLR train and my backup, backup DLR train. That said, the DLR seems to be running behind schedule today as well, with trains every fifteen minutes rather than every seven, so it's not entirely my fault that my pocket-sized journey planner is looking like it would have been more useful as toilet paper.

The DLR platform is lined with businessmen and women, most tapping away frantically on smartphones and looking a little impatient. The board has said the next train will be arriving in three minutes for the past ten minutes and I can feel my leg beginning to twitch. Soon I really will be late. It's not long before the marketing manager in me takes over and I find myself cross-examining each billboard ad in turn. The latest film whose title catches the eye brilliantly. The Richard and Judy book club selection that uses its patron's stamp of approval so effortlessly. Then I reach an empty billboard and my mind goes into overdrive thinking about what I would advertise on it.

A good piece of brand advertising lasts a lifetime, that's what Mr Samuel always says. 'Keep Calm and Carry On' is a prime example. Does it only make people remember the Second World War posters? No. Why? Because it resonates with people today. Now we all have our own personal version of the Keep Calm family. Mine's easy: 'Keep Calm and Do a Puzzle'.

The red and blue train draws into the platform; the brakes let out a loud, piercing screech. I walk into the front carriage and sit in the front row, by the window. The same as every weekday morning. The same as I did the very first time I got on a DLR train with my gran at the age of five.

A small burst of excitement still erupts in my stomach as I sit in the 'driver's seat' of the DLR. I remember the first time I saw the Passenger Service Agent open the control box, the buttons reminded me of Liquorice Allsorts but I couldn't understand why there was no steering wheel.

The other commuters pile on behind me. Many are trying to juggle their morning coffee in one hand and the *Financial Times* in the other while also holding on to one of the aqua-blue hand rails. Most of the women are wearing trainers and have shoe-carrying-enabled handbags. Some are even applying make-up as the carriage jolts up and down sporadically, a skill I wish I had. For England, it's a pretty nice morning, but for mid-August it's fairly underwhelming. Nevertheless, inside this now sardine-packed carriage the temperature is rapidly approaching 'surface-of-the-sun'.

> *The next station is Canning Town. Change here for the Jubilee line.*

It still bemuses me that so many people choose to live close to Canary Wharf and then commute into the City. Why would they choose to live in the middle of a sterile, colourless nowhere only to commute into the culture-filled city that is London?

Obviously I am one of these people. But I did have a reason to move east. The law firm Seph works for is based right in the sterile heart of Canary Wharf. But I have to admit, even though Seph's gone, I don't want to move. Living by the London Excel Centre has been a lot better than I expected. It's an up-and-coming area. It's even got its own little Tesco Metro now. And it's also cheap enough for Dan to rent the flat opposite. It's like we're in *Friends*! He's like a mixture of Joey and Chandler. I'm Monica except, instead of being a chef, I'm a marketing strategist and, instead of cleaning, I make lists. I'm forever making lists, they help me to focus and prioritise.

> *The next station is East India.*

A voice comes through the speakers to let us know we are going to be sat here for a couple of minutes and within seconds my leg is twitching. I stare at the winding tracks ahead as if somehow, if I stare hard enough, I can magically make the train move. I decide to look over my notes to take my mind off the time.

I unzip my bag and pull out my note –

Oh my God, I've forgotten my notebook!

This *cannot* be happening. Not only have I *never* gone a day since secondary school without a notebook, today of all days I *really, really* need it!

The next station is Blackwall.

It's too late to go back for it. My lungs are starting to hyperventilate the phrase, 'need notebook, need notebook'.

I take several large, deep breaths. I need to look for the silver lining. Although this situation doesn't seem cloudy so much as tropical storm.

OK. OK. There is a sliver of silver lining, I suppose. I do, after all, have a back-up copy of my notes in the office. I take out my phone and go to the virtual notepad. It hasn't got my notes but I can make a new list, which will have to do for now. The battery hasn't got much charge left I notice, but it should last until I get to work.

The next station is Poplar. Change here for services towards Canary Wharf.

I start to run over today's pitch in my head. I begin with a short clip which will be used as an advert for the new MediaTech platform. It has a voice-over that I pretty much know by heart. It's a satirical mash-up of some of the more famous advertising voice-overs of recent years.

17

It goes: 'Everyone has secrets, don't they? Things they dare not share with the outside world. But the truth is the internet knows most of them. Ever noticed how the ads running down the side of social-media platforms become more and more aligned with your personal preferences? Almost like Internetland knows just what you want? That's because it does. Internetland has been tracking you. Someone, somewhere, has your Internetland travel path. Remember, it's not just a travel path, it's your travel path and it's time you claimed it back.'

The next station is Westferry.

I look out of the window as we leave Westferry station, although I don't remember reaching Westferry station or the announcement for that matter. My leg is twitching again. There's no more prep I can do before I reach the office so I turn to my best stress-busting technique: the free newspaper, or more accurately the crossword in the free newspaper. It's amazing how a puzzle can transport you out of a stressful situation. You can forget about everything that's going on in your life. The social media posts drop off your radar first, then the people around you and the scenery, until finally the only thing you can see is the small black-and-white grid in front of you.

The next station is Limehouse. Change here for C2C services.

I'm halfway through the crossword and I get stuck. I slam the paper down on my lap with such force the man next to me makes eye contact. The frustration of the clues, the fact I've forgotten my notebook and being late suddenly all seem too much. I can't keep my mind off what happened at Lola's. Mr Samuel didn't say much about what happened after Martin had helped me into the taxi but I can guess how it must have looked. What must Gregory Patterson think of me? I'm lucky I'm being allowed to stay on the account.

The next station is Shadwell. Change here for trains to Tower Gateway.

This is my chance to make amends for running out on that dinner. If I can demonstrate that my marketing project will increase the forecasted online traffic and consequently the revenue streams of the proposed MediaTech platform, the Lola's dinner will become a distant memory. If I screw it up… The thought triggers my right shoulder to jar. The knots in my back feel like golf balls under my fingers as I try to smooth my tensed muscles. I remind myself that it is important to think positive thoughts.

The next station is Bank where this train termin-ates. All change.

I spring to my feet and shuffle forwards to get as close as I can to the doors. I glance at my watch. I had been aiming to get into the office for 7 a.m. and prepare until 10.30 a.m. But it's already 8 a.m. and the train is only just reaching Bank station.

I get ready for my daily game of Underground Army, a game I made up to help keep me sane. It stops me killing tourists or fellow commuters as I tackle the assault course that is getting-out-of-Bank-station during rush hour.

I hang on to the hand rail as the train jerks into the station. The long, dull beep starts and the doors slowly begin to open. Commuters pile off like a swarm of ants, oblivious to the other commuters around them. The woman in front of me is trying her best to wheel off a pushchair and carry her suitcase at the same time. Travelling with a child in rush hour must be the worst.

'Here, let me help you,' I say.

I take the suitcase and prop it up on the platform while she manoeuvres the pushchair over the gap between the train and the platform edge.

'Thank you,' she says to me, still looking a little flustered. 'I think I'm going to wait for the crowd to go first,' she says and sits down on the platform bench.

'No problem,' I say and then quickly jog towards the archway that leads to the escalator to make up for the precious seconds lost.

I dodge my way through a group of early-bird tourists who are gathered around an Underground map looking puzzled. The escalator is in sight. I nudge my way through the crowd that has gathered at the bottom waiting to ascend at a snail's pace up the right-hand side.

As a child, I used to run up the stairs. But in three-inch heels and a suit-dress, the safer option is to power-walk up the left-hand side of the escalator. I quickly reach the top and then hastily weave through the crowd to get ahead for the next set of escalators. Why the engineers could not have just built one long escalator, I don't know.

Finally, after a few tortuous minutes, I reach fresh air, a little smoky and fumy as it always is in the City. A gentle breeze cools me down from the sticky, claustrophobic heat that the Underground generates. I used to switch to the Central line at Bank and go two stops to Chancery Lane before making a short five-minute walk to the office off Hatton Garden but since the break-up I've been walking from Bank. I've made a conscious effort to get fit, both physically and mentally, to clear my mind of negativity and feel good about myself again. The walk from Bank to Hatton Garden is a mile and adds about ten minutes to my journey but not only do I find the walk therapeutic, it is also like a mini victory at the start of everyday and a reminder that life after Seph – my life after Seph – is better.

I was about a week into my new regime when I realised that Exit 1 was the most efficient exit. The first couple of days I'd used Exit 3 to the Royal Exchange, one of my all-time favourite places, but then I realised you spent the first five minutes after escaping the Underground navigating your way across two sets of traffic lights. I begin to weave my way through the stream of Londoners and tourists and my thoughts soon turn to my presentation as I start my brisk walk down Poultry. *Everyone has secrets, don't—*

A woman shrieks. There's a long, continuous beep from a car horn and the treacherous screeching of brakes. I freeze. A cyclist veers off the road and onto the pavement. It's heading right for me.

'Look out!'

Two

I can't move.

My right foot and the pain centres in my brain are the only parts of me that are not frozen. I press my lips together to stop myself from screaming.

'Give her some space, everyone.' A man is kneeling down beside me. I think he is the one who pushed me out of the way.

'Here, let me help you up.' He offers me his hand but I shake my head. I don't even want to *touch* my foot let alone attempt to stand on it.

The cyclist had been coming straight for me when this man had saved me. We'd fallen over together in a heap. I'd landed awkwardly on my right foot.

'Where does it hurt?'

'It's my ankle,' I manage to say at last.

'OK. I'm Pete. I'm a personal trainer and physio. Are you OK for me to have a look at it?'

His eyes look filled with genuine concern but my independent, I-don't-need-anyone's-help attitude kicks in.

'It's OK, I can do it,' I say and lean forward to wrestle off my shoe, its three-inch heel only hanging on by a strip of suede.

It was a bad idea.

I let out a small cry, winning a collected round of murmurs from the bystanders who have circled around me. I try to stand up, putting my weight on my left side and leaning on Pete's arm for some support. It still hurts but I'm just going to have to suck it up. I have a meeting to host. I have a spare pair of shoes under my desk so there is no need to panic.

'I think you should get that looked at,' Pete says.

'No, I'll be fine,' I say and try to look pain-free. 'Thank you so much for what you did for me, I—'

'It was nothing. Anyone would have done the same.'

I only manage to take half a step before my foot gives way beneath me.

'You're not fine,' Pete says, coming to my rescue for the second time. 'There's an NHS walk-in centre around the corner from here, let me take you.'

'I can't. I have to get to work.'

'It could be broken.' My eyes widen. 'Or just a sprain,' he quickly adds. 'Either way, you need to see a doctor. I'm sure it won't take long and I can take you.'

Frustratingly, I don't think I have a choice. I can't walk.

'Is it really just around the corner?'

'It's just the other side of the Royal Exchange. Here, take my arm.'

We set off – Pete acting like my personal bodyguard, shielding me from all the tourists who think this is some kind of circus act.

'What happened to the cyclist anyway?' I say, mentally cursing Boris Johnson for introducing the 'Boris bikes'.

'The wanker just cycled off, didn't even glance back,' Pete says and I feel his arm tense, 'Excuse my French.'

I gesture that there is no need. It was lucky no one got seriously injured. How the car didn't hit the cyclist in the first place I'll never know. We cross over the two sets of traffic lights I'd been trying to avoid and we slowly progress down Threadneedle Street. My right foot feels remarkably warm and I have a horrible feeling that it's swelling up…

–

'It's just in here,' says Pete, opening the door.

Pete was almost right. Under normal circumstances the centre would probably be a five-minute walk but it has taken us about fifteen as a result of my hobbling. Despite my frequent trips down Threadneedle Street to visit my gran, who lives near Leadenhall Market, I'd never noticed the NHS walk-in centre before. Both outside and in, it is pretty unremarkable.

The ground floor looks like any regular doctor's surgery but on a bigger scale. Straight in front of me is the large waiting area fitted out with plastic school chairs but there are a few more comfortable armchairs towards the back. To the left is a corridor which leads to the nurse's room and a machine to self-test your blood pressure. To the right is a corridor that leads to the doctors' consultation rooms and a flight of stairs. According to the sign, floor one is for counselling, the dentist and careers advice.

There are only a few other people waiting, most staring at posters or looking pensive to avoid making eye contact with anyone else. I hop to the nearest seat, wincing as my foot touches the floor, and watch as Pete explains the situation to the receptionist. She reminds me of the deputy headmistress at my old primary school. She is a pale, thin-faced woman with bobbed hair, blonde except for the grey roots. She is wearing a blue and green flowery, ironed shirt. I'm pretty sure my mum bought the same one from Marks and Spencer in the January sale last year. I'm guessing they are around the same age as well, mid-fifties.

I can only catch snippets of the conversation from here. Operation… Scan… Hospital… That's enough scary words for me. My meeting is in under an hour. I haven't got time for this.

'It's not broken,' I call out from the chair. 'I bet it's not even a sprain. I really need to get to work.'

'We can't advise that you leave, Miss?'

'Cassidy Brookes.'

'We can't advise that you leave, Miss Brookes, without being seen,' says the receptionist. She walks over and hands me an ice pack. The cool, blue bag instantly soothes my now slightly podgy foot.

'I'm sure it will be OK now,' I reply.

'It's Threadneedle's policy that you should be seen in an event like this,' she says. I can hear the excitement in her tone as she recites the centre's protocol. I can always recognise a fellow rule lover, but in this particular case I really couldn't care less about her protocol.

'You're probably right,' I say and flex my facial muscles into the biggest smile I can, as if somehow smiling at her will make us best friends and move me to the top of the waiting list. She doesn't smile back. I can see Pete fidgeting by the entrance.

'If you're all right, I'll be on my way,' Pete says.

'Yes, of course. Thank you again, for everything.'

I wish I could stand up and shake his hand but I dare not try. Instead I just smile and watch him walk away. I sigh to myself, it's not every day you witness such 21st-century chivalry. Perhaps if he hadn't spent most of the walk here talking about his Crossfit-champion girlfriend I might have thought fate had brought him to me. I lean back in the plastic chair; I cast my eyes over the posters on the wall.

Are you over 65? Sign up for a flu jab this September.
It could be a stroke. Act F.A.S.T!
Are you stuck in a rut?
Book an appointment with our careers advisor.

After a ten-minute daydream about how I could help the NHS increase health awareness through social media, I notice my left leg is bouncing and my fingers are playing Mozart's 'Rondo alla Turca' on an invisible keyboard. Oh, this is stupid, I don't have time to sit here twiddling my thumbs. Maybe I should just go? My foot is starting to feel a bit better now that I've got the ice pack on it. The receptionist isn't looking; this is my chance. I pick up my bag and head for the door.

'Argh!'

'Whoops!'

'Sorry,' I say, unable to move. My entire body has turned hot and prickly. I only managed two steps before collapsing into the arms of an incoming patient. He caught me in between the several designer clothes bags he is holding in each hand.

'Are you all right?' he asks and helps me to stand up straight. It is only now that I register how attractive he is.

'Yes, sorry. I'm fine, I was just…' I can see the receptionist watching me out of the corner of my eye. 'I was just… moving to a more comfortable seat.'

'Here, let me help you.' He steers me towards the far corner of the waiting area. 'Here you go, no chance of anyone accidently bumping into your foot from all the way over here,' he says.

Despite my best efforts, I slump down in a dead-cushioned, stale green-coloured armchair in a very ungraceful manner and curse myself for not having met this guy under better circumstances. At least the armchair is more comfortable than it looks.

'Tha—'

'Oh, here you are,' says a light, high-pitched voice coming from behind us. A twenty-nothing-year-old girl, who seems to be one of the nurses, comes bouncing over to us and plonks a big wet kiss on his cheek.

Barely 9 a.m. and already I've seen two knights in shining armour, both loved-up, it must be a record. Since Seph left I seem to be seeing couples everywhere – maybe there always were this many happy couples in London and I never noticed when I was part of one myself. For the first few months after the break-up, seeing couples upset me. I missed Seph. But now when I see a happy couple I feel more depressed than upset. I've passed the rebound stage. I want to move on. I'm ready to meet someone else. But any guy I think looks half decent inevitably has a beautiful girl hanging off his arm.

'Come on,' says this guy's beautiful girl and tugs at his sleeve. 'I need to try these on before the patients arrive.' Her eyes are now fixated on the bags he's carrying.

What is this, a healthcare centre or a shopping mall?

I shouldn't snap. Not even in my thoughts. I know jealousy will get me nowhere.

'Excuse me,' he says to me and then obediently follows her out of the waiting area and around the corner to the consultation rooms.

Talk about having a well-trained puppy dog for a boyfriend.

I sigh loudly. I know there is a puppy out there for me somewhere. I just need to be patient. *Ha. Patient. In a doctor's surgery. Ba dum dum tss. Oh God, shut up. Even my jokes are lame.*

I sigh again and I suddenly sense several pairs of eyes glowering at me. 'You'd sigh as well if you were in my shoes,' I feel like saying. A little ironic laugh slips out before I can help it as I think of my beautiful Dune shoes that I threw into a street bin on the way here. I roll my shoulders back and close my eyes. I need to put all this into perspective. Some people in this waiting-room might be really sick. I should be grateful that all I have is a swollen ankle.

OK, I'll give it another ten minutes. If I still haven't been seen by then I'll have to call the office and tell them I'm running late. God it's going to look so unprofessional. In need of a distraction, I turn to the worn-out stack of battered-looking magazines that is within arm's reach. They are all six months out of date and unappealing. Although one near the bottom has the familiar blue and yellow chequered jacket of a puzzle book. Indeed, it is a puzzle book. I rummage through my handbag for a pen.

All the word searches are done, as are the Sudoku puzzles, most of them incorrectly. I search through for my favourite puzzle – the cryptic crossword. I have always loved them, ever since I was a kid. Surely that one won't be completed, it's not the most popular puzzle.

OK, I am officially vexed. Why would anyone know-ingly write in the wrong answers, words that are not even the right length, in pen, in a puzzle book that doesn't even belong to them?

There are no puzzles left at all, I realise, after a more thorough flick through the book. The only thing left is on the back inside cover. A blank sheet of squared paper, like you get in maths exercise books at school. 'Make Your Own Crossword Competition'. The deadline has long passed but it sounds like a good challenge. Besides, I've always found crosswords to be very therapeutic.

Make Your Own Crossword

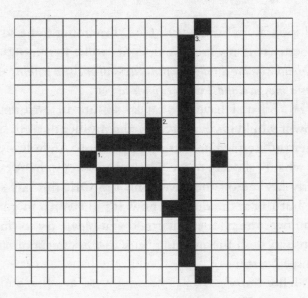

Across

1. The man responsible for putting morons on bikes. *(7 letters)*

Down

2. What kind of animal dumps his girlfriend and steals her toothpaste? *(5 letters)*
3. What should a decent person do if they can't do cryptic puzzles but insist on completing them? *(6,2,6 letters)*

I draw my grid. Both 'loser' and 'Johnson' have an 's' so I make them overlap and I overlap the 'n' in Johnson with 'answer in pencil'. That takes up about a third of the grid and I start to colour in the squares around the answers. With so many blacked-out squares the crossword looks a little lonely, mirroring its maker I suppose. At least it helped me to vent my frustration in a more constructive way.

I look at my watch. Oh God. I'm going to be so late. I'd better ring my creative designer to let her know.

Hello, you are through to the voicemail of Sofia Jenkins, please leave a message and I will get back to you.

'Hi, Sofia. I have had an ab-sol-ute nightmare. You know it would have been Seph and my eighth anniversary yesterday? I ended up getting a bit drunk. Anyway – that's not what I called up to say.' I let out another sigh. 'A cyclist nearly ran me off the pavement. I'm OK, this guy saved me, but I'm at the doctor's now. It's too much to go into detail over the phone, but could you please try to find an excuse to push the meeting back to this afternoon and if you see Martin—'

'Hello, Cassy.'

'Martin! Hi there.'

'Should my ears be ringing?'

'Oh, I was just leaving a message for Sofia to say, well to ask her to tell you, that I have been held up with an emergency and not to worry and that I will be in shortly and that I am still fine to host today's meeting.'

'I see. Well I got the message.'

'So it seems. Anyway must go.'

Oh crap. Now I really am in trouble. He hopefully didn't hear the whole of that message. What was he doing at Sofia's desk when she wasn't there anyway? I will just have to hope that on this occasion he doesn't do anything manipulative…

Oh, who am I trying to kid. I need to get to the office now! I hobble over to the reception desk as fast as my foot will allow.

'Excuse me.'

'One moment please.' I lean on the counter unable to stop my fingers tapping.

'Actually I was just going to say—'

Before I can finish my sentence she gets up and walks into the back office out of sight. I wait for a *moment*. Moment is one of the words on my 'loathed words' list that I began in one notebook and now is continued in about another five (I get through a lot of notebooks). How long is a moment exactly? Inevitably the only answer I can think of is too bloody long!

'I was just going to say,' I repeat when the receptionist finally reappears, 'that I think I won't stay to see the doctor after all.'

'But it's Threadneedle's policy that—'

'I understand that,' I say with a tone of desperation creeping in. 'However… it's just not fair.'

'Not fair?'

'On all these other patients who have been waiting longer than me. They must be running late for something too.'

'Well, Dr Danes is ready for you now so the only thing delaying the other patients is the fact that we're having this conversation. Here you go,' she says and holds out a pink slip of paper.

I take it from her, too defeated to do anything but mutter, 'Thank you.' I can feel everyone's eyes burning the words 'queue jumper' on my forehead as I hobble off to the doctor's room. I think the thought of ruining somebody else's schedule is actually more painful than my foot.

I give two rather feeble knocks on the door of Dr Danes' consultation room.

'Hello, it's Cassidy, isn't it? I hear you've had a tough morning.'

I don't know whether it's her caring motherly voice, the stress of my upcoming meeting or the throbbing in my right foot but I suddenly burst into tears.

'Take a moment,' she says and hands me a box of tissues.

I think this is what they call post-traumatic shock. It's like I'm not really in the room as Dr Danes asks me to lie down on the examination bed. I'm vaguely aware of her pressing on my foot as she feels the ligaments and measures the inflammation. She asks me to flex my foot which surprisingly I can do without much pain. Then she gets me to sit up and says, 'The fact you can still move your ankle without too much discomfort suggests it is not a sprain, but there is a lot of inflammation and bruising so it will be painful for at least a few days and I would like you to come back in twenty-four hours for a check-up, or sooner if the pain worsens significantly.'

In some sort of daydream-like state I must have left the room and got a leaflet with the centres' opening times from reception because I'm now standing on Threadneedle Street, my arm outstretched, waving the flyer at an approaching taxi.

'It'd be quicker to get the tube, love,' says the driver when I flop onto the back seat and tell him I want to go to Holywells just off Hatton Garden.

'I've hurt my ankle, broken the heel of my shoe and need to give a presentation in less than an hour.'

The driver has already stopped listening by the time I get on to explaining the morning's events in detail. The traffic isn't great but I'm in the office twenty minutes later.

—

'Ah, Cassidy, glad you could join us. Martin filled us in. You really didn't need to come in today.'

Mr Samuel is standing by the doorway of meeting room 5 – the meeting room where I am supposed to be delivering my presentation to the senior partners in six and a half minutes time – something is making me uncomfortable. I hadn't expected anyone to be here yet, partners turn up late to meetings, never early. I had been planning to have a quick practice run through of the presentation.

'Oh, I'm fine, Mr Samuel,' I say, doing my best not to look wrong-footed. 'Besides, I'm looking forward to our meeting.'

'Oh, there is no need. Martin just took us through the plan. He thought he'd take the pressure off you, given your circumstances.'

WHAT! Martin did what?

'But... But the meeting isn't supposed to be for another five minutes?'

'A slight hiccup in my calendar meant I needed to rearrange. I'd been on my way to tell you when I bumped into Martin who explained your situation, and kindly offered to take us through the strategy himself. It's a very good idea the two of you have come up with.'

I don't believe this. This was my presentation. *My* idea. *My* ingenious social media strategy that was going to repair my reputation with Gregory Patterson. Martin had *nothing* to do with it. I thought Martin might try to sabotage my meeting, but I never thought he would claim my work as his own!

'Cassidy? Are you all right? You look very flushed. I think Martin is right, you should take the rest of the day off.'

'Honestly, Mr Samuel, I'm fine. I'd love to go through the project in more detail—'

'Don't worry about that. Martin has us all well prepped. We've given Martin the go-ahead to do a trial run on a select few clients.'

You have got to be kidding me! I furiously try to think of a way to salvage the situation while Mr Samuel makes small talk with me as he walks me back to the main floor.

'Sofia?'

'Yes? Oh, hello,' Sofia says, abruptly stopping what appears to be a giggling contest with a few of the other creative designers.

'Please can you order Cassidy a taxi home? She isn't feeling up to an afternoon in the office.'

'Of course,' Sofia says and then mouths, 'What's going on?' to me as she makes her way back to her desk. I shake my head. I can't bring myself to explain. Clearly she never got the voicemail. Martin must have thought he hit the jackpot when Mr Samuel needed to rearrange my meeting. Such a perfect opportunity to take the credit for my work while simultaneously looking like a supportive work colleague. God knows what he actually told Mr Samuel and the others had happened this morning. Surely Martin didn't fill them in on *everything*.

'Cassidy,' Mr Samuel says before clearing his throat and continuing in a hushed voice, 'break-ups can be very…

emotionally distressing. And it takes time to… to heal. A long time sometimes…'

Well, now I know. What a git. So I got a bit nostalgic last night. There was no need to make it into a big deal. The last thing I need is Mr Samuel thinking I'm fragile!

'I don't want you to worry about work,' Mr Samuel continues. 'Martin said he is happy to cover your meetings today.'

I bet he did. Men. They are all, without exception, pigs. Damage limitation is the only option.

'Thank you, Mr Samuel, I appreciate it. See you on Monday.'

Mr Samuel nods and walks away, leaving me alone in my office to ponder what just happened.

'Cassy? Your taxi will be here in five minutes. Are you OK?' Sofia asks, walking into my office. She's wearing a figure-hugging, knee-length dress in her signature colour, purple. She waits for me to fill the silence but I don't.

'What the hell happened, Cassy? Why did Martin end up doing the meeting?'

'It's a long story,' I say with a loud sigh and hope she'll take the hint. I don't think I can bare to relive this morning's events.

'I was late today too,' she says, changing the subject. 'I had quite an eventful evening last night.'

Didn't we all, I think to myself. Oh God, she clearly wants to tell me about it, she's hopping around on the spot like a seven-year-old waiting to go to the funfair.

'Why, what happened?' I ask in the most animated voice I can muster.

'Joey proposed!'

'Cassy? Cassy? Are you all right?'

Sitting in the taxi, holding the phone to my ear, I can picture the concerned frown on Dan's face, three lines across his forehead, chewing the inside of his right cheek. Dan really is my rock, my best friend and my surrogate twin. I had to ring his flat four times before he picked up today. His monotone voice told me that I had interrupted him playing a video game but he quickly sprang into action as soon as he had detected the 'my-life-is-ruined' tone in my voice.

'What is it? What's wrong?'

'I don't know where to start,' I say and wipe my eyes.

'You could always try the beginning.'

The beginning. Where should that be? The bit where a cyclist nearly killed me? The bit where Martin decided to steal my work? Or how about that fact that my creative designer who is three years younger than me and has only been with her boyfriend a year has got engaged before me? I can't seem to find the words.

'Where are you now?' Dan says, quietly.

'In a taxi,' I reply. 'Just coming to Commercial Road. Mr Samuel gave me the day off to recover from the "emotional distress" that Martin so thoughtfully told him all about.'

'What happened? Did the meeting go badly?'

'I didn't do the meeting. Martin did.'

'What? Why? And what the hell does *emotional distress* mean?'

'Mr Samuel knows I got drunk last night and why.'

'What? But how?'

'Martin.'

'God, what an arse!'

Somehow Dan sounds even more livid than I feel.

'Don't worry, Cassy. I'll make my way over.'

'What, the whole five metres over you mean?'

'Is that a smile I can hear down the phone?'

'Yes… and tears.'

'It's going to be OK, Cassy. See you in ten.'

Home, sweet home, I sigh to myself, pulling my key fob out of my bag and stumbling into the reception lobby. All my remaining energy sapped away the second I got out of the taxi. I just want to hibernate in my flat and the next time I emerge into reality I want all of the problems from this awful nightmare to have evaporated. I walk over to the lift and sigh even louder. How long can it take to fix one bloody lift? It's been weeks! Suddenly a loud crash and several swear words echo down the stairwell. I look up. It's Dan. He's doing some kind of freak circus balancing act with what appears to be the entire contents of his flat.

'What on earth are you doing?'

'Moving in,' he replies casually.

'Oh right.' Hang on. His words coil through my ear to my brain for processing. 'What exactly do you mean *moving in*?' I grip hold of the cold, steel banister and start limping up the stairs towards him, peering up to see if it is some kind of strange Dan-world joke.

'You're going through a tough time,' he says, his voice full of concentration, like he is walking a tightrope. 'Moving on takes a lot of effort. So it's only right that I, your most trusted and noble friend, move in.'

'Firstly,' I say when I finally reach him – it's amazing how much harder it is to hop up three flights of stairs than it is to walk up – 'I have moved on. I'm over him. And secondly, what do you mean tough time? I'm allowed to get drunk every once in a while.'

'I should hope so, I don't want to live with a party pooper.'

'But—'

'Being over someone and moving on are two different things.'

'But—'

'You're lonely, Cassy.'

I swallow hard.

'Now help me move this armchair, will you?'

—

By 5 p.m. I'm curled up on my white leather sofa in my red Forever Friends pyjamas, hugging a mug of hot chocolate and watching Dan play a soon-to-be-released alien-killing video game. The living room has been transformed into a bachelor pad. Dan's hi-tech gaming equipment is stacked high next to the TV and the leads cover the cream carpet like a spaghetti matrix. Dan lived for video games when we were growing up so I guess I shouldn't find it surprising that he now gets paid to test games for a living, but I struggle to see the thrill in shooting computerised aliens for hours on end.

I keep thinking about what Dan said, about there being a difference between being over someone and moving on.

Until yesterday I really did think I'd done both but the non–anniversary brought back all the emotions I'd felt when Seph walked out on me. When we first broke-up, I'd just wanted him back. I remember asking Dan if he'd help me get Seph to see reason the day after the Patterson dinner.

'Are you *nuts*?' he'd said and looked at me as though I'd just asked whether stealing from a crippled child is morally acceptable. 'The guy is a total moron,' he'd said slowly, like he was trying to communicate with a foreigner who didn't speak English. 'I can't tell you how many times I've wanted to kick him out. Cassy, this is the best thing that has *ever* happened to you.'

I'm still not 100 per cent convinced it is the *best* thing that has ever happened to me. Even if breaking up with Seph was the right path, surely there would have been better ways to separate. Seph didn't just walk out on me. He stole my confidence. I'd felt so secure, so settled, and then suddenly all my plans for the future had been taken from me with no warning and no explanation. I'd blamed myself and sometimes I still do. Maybe I was too focused on my career, perhaps I did neglect him. Dan would go mad if I ever told him that. His thirty-minute outburst the day after the Patterson dinner left me in no doubt about what he thought of Seph.

'He was your Achilles heel,' Dan said. 'In every other way you are so independent, but he consumed you. I bet we could count on one hand the number of times you were allowed to spend an evening without him in the past few years.'

'Well, couples tend to go out as couples,' I argued back.

'Couples are not supposed to be chained together, committed people are allowed to have their own lives too.'

'I do have my own life!'

'Cassy, if you weren't with him, you were making a list of the things you needed to do for him when you were with him.'

'So what? I liked things to be perfect for him, for us.'

'He demanded you had things perfect and that's not the same thing.'

'What are you talking about?'

Dan then listed every habit and action of Seph's that had made him want to hurl. Everything from the way Seph chewed his food to how he said my name. It was a fairly substantial hatred I'd come to realise. One that, as my friend, Dan had felt necessary to shield me from until the break-up. I sort of wish he had shielded me for a while longer. I hadn't been ready to hear all that. At least not the stuff about Seph taking away my independence and confidence. Even now, six months later, I'm still trying to get my confidence back.

I've been on a few dates but they've fallen flat. The spark hasn't been there or we've had nothing in common. And the dreaded thought has crept into my mind more than once:

What if Seph was the only chance at love destiny is going to give me?

I know Seph wasn't Mr Right. Deep down, I do know that. But part of me still wants him to come back. Part of me still thinks there's a chance he'll walk back through the door. I need to believe that. Otherwise I have to accept that he fell out of love with me, that he decided I wasn't good enough. My thought twists fate – the intercom starts buzzing.

'I'll get it,' I shout from the hallway.

Seph may not be Mr Right but that doesn't mean it wouldn't be nice if he wanted me back…

Three

There should be a law against buzzing the wrong flat number, or at least a fine. I could have been trying out for the women's 110-metre hurdles the way I had rushed to answer the door yesterday, cack-handedly hopping (rather than jumping) over cardboard boxes in the hallway (my right foot is still very painful when I put pressure on it). The finale was my attempt at a long hop–jump to the door. I'd got myself all worked up about fate bringing Seph back. (I blame it on the stressful day.) I'm not entirely sure what would have happened next. Would I have welcomed him back with open arms or slammed the door shut in his face? Of course it wasn't Seph at the door and there was no Olympic gold medal either.

'Pizza delivery for Smith,' came the unbroken voice of a young teenager, through the intercom.

'Wrong flat.'

'Flat 13?'

'No, this is flat 31,' I replied bitterly, and wondered how secondary-school maths had gone so far downhill.

I hadn't bothered to wait for an apology, I had just sloped off to my room to curl up on my big, lonely bed and tried to forget about the day.

I must have fallen asleep eventually because now my room is being lit up by sunlight and I can hear Dan's snoring, or heavy breathing as he calls it, coming through the wall. My stomach is rumbling. I drag myself out of bed and make my way to the kitchen. I used to go to Tesco every Saturday morning and make Seph a special breakfast, but my shopping habits have become lax since the break-up. Staring at the lengthy food list on the fridge door, I don't need to open it to know there's nothing inside to eat.

There's a knock on the door and I'm pleased to say my heart doesn't flutter in anticipation. There's no way Seph would miss his Saturday driving range session. I fasten my dressing gown and hobble over, my foot still feeling sore and bruised. It's probably one of the neighbours asking me to join the neighbourhood watch again. There's a second knock.

'I'm coming,' I call out and quicken my pace.

I almost fall head first, tripping over another box of Dan's games. He's really taking this moving in thing seriously given it's only temporary. I assume he knows it's only temporary? The past few days have simply been a blip.

'If it's for me, say you don't know me,' comes Dan's sleepy voice from the spare room.

I try to smooth down my hair as much as possible and wipe away the sleep from my eyes. I take a deep breath, smile, and open the door. A tall, thirty-something man with dusty-coloured hair is standing there. He's wearing an off-black suit and shiny polished shoes. I find myself wondering if this is destiny's way of saying there are plenty of fish in the sea. Then I see the wedding ring.

'Good morning,' he says and gives me an estate-agent smile.

'Morning,' I say, coolly. I really haven't got the patience for this. I'm not in the mood to discuss my rental opportunities or for a request to donate to charity or for a chat with a Jehovah's Witness or anything else for that matter. Maybe I should make a sign that says, 'If you're not Prince Charming, don't bother'.

'I was looking for your neighbour. Daniel Douglas?'

'I can't say I know my neighbours too well, sorry.' I try to act as natural as I can but the nerves in my eyelid start to twitch like they always do when I attempt to lie. I start to close the door but he jams it open with his arm.

'Well, if you happen to see him before I do, please tell him to call Ralph urgently,' he says and holds out a business card. I snatch it out of his rough-looking hand and give him my best get-the-hell-away-from-my-door-or-I'll-call-the-police glare. He takes a step back and I slam the door shut.

'What was all that about?' My hand is actually shaking a little as I toss the card at Dan.

'Nothing important.'

'If you're in some kind of trou—'

'He's just some guy I owe some gaming work to, no biggy, just couldn't face talking to anyone this early on a Saturday.'

'It's one o'clock in the afternoon?'

'You can talk. You're only up because you thought it was lover-boy come home with his tail between his legs.'

'Oh shut up.'

'Whatever. Aren't you supposed to be going to the doctor's?'

I roll my eyes. Going to that walk-in centre yesterday only added to my crap situation. I'm now not only boyfriend-less but possibly strategy-less too since Martin is trying to claim my idea as his own.

'I noticed you're still limping, better to be on the safe side with these things,' Dan says, sensing my reluctance.

'I suppose you're right.'

'I'm always right, Princess,' he says and yawns.

I hate how he always calls me Princess. He only does it because he knows it winds me up. He tricked me into thinking our year 8 school prom was fancy dress and I turned up as Belle from *Beauty and the Beast* (not in her fblue tunic but the golden, embroidered gown in the final scene). He's called me Princess ever since.

I take a long shower and brush some of the tangles out of my hair before I leave. It's a deceptively bright day; I wish I'd worn my jacket. Despite being a Saturday, with little chance of getting squished by travellers on the DLR, I still sit in the front row so I can make a quick escape at Bank station. That said, I have made a small adjustment to my list of things to avoid doing on the DLR to Bank.

List #89: Things to Remember when Travelling by Train

- Don't make eye contact with <u>anyone</u>.

- Don't talk to anyone unless there is an unattended bag.

- Avoid attracting obese people to sit next to you by taking up slightly more than half the space on a two-person seat.

- Don't smile (you run the risk of being classed as an Underground Nutter).

- Where possible, avoid carriages with:

- People with large suitcases.

- Teenagers wearing headphones who are bobbing their head up and down.

- *Check for moronic looking cyclists the moment you leave the station.*

Given the fact that my foot tends to throb when I put pressure on it, I decide against walking up the escalator and instead take my time, gliding up slower than a milk float on a dual carriageway.

When I eventually emerge from Bank station, I am greeted by the bubbling excitement of City tourists over-powering the drilling at the roadworks on Cornhill and the diesel revving of black cabs. If I were a tourist I'd definitely go to Bank. Of course Big Ben, the Houses of Parliament and the London Eye are cool landmarks of the capital but they're on every London postcard going. The Royal Exchange on the other hand, or the Bank of England, have just as much English heritage and beautiful architecture. I'm preaching to myself for so long I almost forget where I'm supposed to be going. The Thread-needle Walk-in Centre seems much closer to the station today.

'Hello and welcome to the Threadneedle Walk-in Centre. How can I help you?' asks the receptionist.

'Hi, it's Cassidy Brookes? To see Dr Danes? I've come for a check-up? I twisted my ankle yesterday?' I can hear myself finishing every sentence with a high note, questioning even my own name. Why does that happen whenever you have to explain to a receptionist why you are in their building?

'Hello again,' she says. I can see her eyes register that it is the annoying girl who didn't want to follow protocol. 'Please take a seat and the doctor will be with you shortly.'

I make my way over to the waiting area and sit in the same armchair as before, right at the back, away from all the germs.

The doctor will be with you shortly.

I know what that means. With nothing better to do I decide to add a few more questions to my 'Make Your Own Crossword' from my last visit. I pick up the crumpled puzzle book from the stack of old magazines and quickly flick through to the right page.

Oh my God.

Someone has actually done my crossword!

Across

1. *The man responsible for putting morons on bikes. (7 letters)*

2. *What kind of animal dumps his girlfriend and steals her toothpaste?* ~~(5 letters)~~ *(5,5 letters)*

3. *What should a decent person do if they can't do cryptic puzzles but insist on completing them? (6,2,6 letters)*

I agree with you, anyone who uses pen is a loser, but perhaps in certain areas there is an alternative answer?

'What do you mean *your* crossword?' Dan says and switches off his video game.

I can barely get my sentences out as I fill Dan in on every last detail. 'I've been like this the whole way home,' I say as I start hopping around with the curtains wide open so the whole world can see. 'Everyone on the train must have thought I was either on the verge of wetting myself or I had taken some sort of recreational drug overdose.'

'So what did—'

'I didn't even moan when a guy with a huge duffle-bag barged past me in his hurry to beat me off the train!'

'But what—'

'God, I feel amazing. I feel like opening the window and shouting it out.'

'But—'

'Hmm. Maybe that is going a step too far. I think it's just the stark contrast of yesterday's down-in-the-dumps to today's super-cool-puzzle-mystery. Not that it's much of a mystery. It's hardly surprising there was someone else as bored as I was in the waiting-room. But it's the *way* they answered it—'

'Cassy!' Dan grabs hold of me, clamping my arms to my sides. 'You need to breathe, slowly. Good. Now, are you calm?'

I nod.

'So, tell me, what did you write back?'

'I didn't,' I say and flop down on the sofa to avoid the risk of heart failure from too many one-legged star-jumps.

'*You didn't!*'

'Well, what was I supposed to do? Put a tick and say well done?'

Dan picks his controller back up, shaking his head.

'Why? Do you think I should have written something back?' I poke him in a pointless attempt to distract him from aliens.

'I – did – not – say – that,' he replies in an I'm-trying-to-concentrate kind of voice.

'But you are thinking it, aren't you?'

I stand up and walk in front of the TV, hands on hips. I simultaneously hear the 'game over' music and a sigh from Dan.

'Well, I probably wouldn't have been sad enough to invent my own crossword.'

I open my mouth to interrupt and go over my ordeal again, but Dan's eyes tell me that may not be wise.

'However,' he continues, 'if I *were* that sad, and if someone *did* reply, I would probably...'

Congratulations. You've been given a bonus life!

'What?' I ask as Dan hurriedly picks up the controllers again and starts tapping away.

'Hang on, this is the last fighting scene in the level.'

Dan manically presses at his controller, ordering a hunky-looking solider to shoot loads of evil aliens. I really can't see the fascination myself. Sitting as patiently as I

48

can, I make a mental note to do a manicure this week, my cuticles are awful.

Excellent work! You've reached the bonus round. Be sure to collect more ammo.

'Sorry, what was I saying?' Dan asks, clearly not interested now there are no more aliens to kill.

'Should I have replied to him?'

'How do you know it's a man?'

I shrug my shoulders. 'Hunch. So...'

'Maybe. So what did the doc have to say?'

'It's not sprained,' I say, giving up on getting any sensible response about the puzzle book. 'But she said it will be tender for another day or so because of the bruising.'

I flick through an old copy of *Hello* magazine lying on the table. I haven't bought any mags recently. Not since I had to cancel all the subscriptions. A few months before the break-up I'd started subscribing to one or two, OK maybe a few, wedding and bridal magazines. Before you say it, it wasn't to drop hints. There had been no need. One morning when Seph had been running late for a client golf day, he'd asked me to fill up his water bottle and put it in his bag and as I put it inside I'd seen it. A small red velvet box with the words 'Marry me' imprinted on the front. I didn't look inside although I knew it would be his grandmother's ring. He'd told me before that he had inherited it and that her initials were inscribed on the inside but he'd never shown it to me. He'd kept it at his mother's house. So when I saw the box in his golf bag I knew it wouldn't be long before he proposed. Well, actually, I suppose I didn't know because he never got around to proposing.

Maybe that's why Seph left? I find myself thinking. Maybe he got cold feet about getting engaged? I read somewhere that for some men cold feet can sometimes happen even before they propose and that you are supposed to be supportive.

'I hope your pensive look has nothing to do with the moron,' Dan says, throwing me a quick glance as he annihilates another load of aliens. Moron has become Dan's name for Seph since the break-up.

'No,' I say back, rather defensively. I know he can't read my mind, but sometimes I do feel like he has a Cassy-mind cheat book.

'Have you eaten?' I say, hoping food will coax him away from the subject of Seph.

'You ordered us a pizza half an hour ago.'

'I wasn't even home half an hour ago.'

'I know. But I guessed your password – which I have now changed to moron – and ordered it from your Hungry House account.'

'On my credit card I assume.' Is it bad that I'm not at all surprised?

The doorbell rings and annoyingly my heart flutters.

'That will be it now,' Dan says.

Of course. It's far more likely to be the pizza than Seph. The smell of melting cheese, sizzling ham and juicy pineapple soon makes me forget all about the moron. Dan pauses his game. Blissful silence at last. We tuck in, no need for plates or knives and forks. Dan picks off all the pineapple and gives it to me and I pick off all the mushrooms for him. If someone was looking through the window at us they'd think we were a young married couple. It occurs to me that I haven't seen Dan's (latest) other half for ages.

'So how's Luke?'

'Dead.'

'WHAT?'

'Dead to me at least.'

'Dan, that's not funny,' I say with a stern look, before turning it into a concerned frown. 'So when did this happen?'

'About a month ago.'

'*A month!* You never said.'

'You've had enough going on,' he says nonchalantly and takes a large bite of stuffed crust.

God, I feel awful.

'I'm sorry. I've been a pretty rubbish friend lately.'

'What do you mean lately?' he says with a Cheshire cat grin. I lob a bit of pineapple at him and we laugh. 'Feels like old times, doesn't it?'

It does. I can't remember the last time we did this. I've shut myself away since the break-up, buried myself in my work. And before the break-up I spent the evenings making sure everything was perfect for when Seph got home from work. He didn't really like me going out too much. He said I was out at work all day so the evenings were his. I thought it was sweet. It showed how much he loved and missed me. Looking back now, it was borderline controlling. The more I've been thinking about Seph and me, the more I feel like I'm reading about someone else's life in *Cosmopolitan*, 'How My Boyfriend Treated Me Like Crap But I Still Loved Him'. Dan's right. Breaking up was the right thing to do. But why did it take Seph dumping me for me to realise it?

'Tell me I'm going to start feeling better soon,' I say and lean my head on Dan's shoulder.

'You just need a distraction,' Dan says.

'Like what?'

'Erm… what do you reckon this mystery guy meant in that last clue?'

'I don't know really, he said something like… "You're right, pens are for losers, but perhaps there is another answer".'

'Freak. Sounds like a clue from one of those cryptic puzzles you are always doing.'

I sit up straight, suddenly full of energy. 'You think?'

'Maybe.' Dan shrugs.

Think, Cassy, Think. What did he write exactly? *I agree with you, anyone who uses pen is a loser, but perhaps in certain areas there is an alternative answer?*

Of course it's a cryptic clue! That's why he didn't fill the answer in, how did I not realise it sooner? I *have* to solve it.

–

'Come on, sleepy head. Bedtime.'

For a split second I think it's my wedding night and Seph is carrying me over the threshold. Then I realise that Dan has picked me up off the sofa and is clambering over the boxes in the hallway to my bedroom. I must have fallen asleep trying to solve the clue.

'What time is it?' I say (in yawn language rather than English).

'Two o'clock in the morning.'

'What? Why didn't you wake me up sooner? It's going to ruin my sleep pattern.'

'Well, you only just started snoring.'

'I do not snore,' I say defiantly.

'Whatever, Princess.'

Trust me, I'm no princess. Any peas resting under my firm mattress definitely turn into green slime when Dan flops me down onto my bed with a thud.

'Sweet dreams,' he says and blows me a kiss from the doorway.

The room instantly darkens and the emptiness is deafening. I don't know if I'll ever get used to sleeping in a double bed alone. Dan thinks I need a distraction from my singledom but what distraction could ever be big enough?

List #577: List of potential distractions

- ~~Go on holiday~~ need to keep my eye on Martin so he doesn't steal any more of my ideas!

- ~~Learn to drive~~ walking is part of my new fitness regime.

- Join a gym (again).

- Get a new hobby.

- Get a new boyfriend?

- *Solve cryptic clues by mystery man?!*

Four

I've cracked it!

I agree with you, anyone who uses pen is a loser, but perhaps in certain areas there is an alternative answer?

'Alternative' is an anagram indicator for the clue's original answer, 'answer in pencil'. If I rearrange the letters it spells, 'winner in places', which is the opposite of a loser in certain areas. Genius!

I can't believe I didn't realise it was a cryptic clue sooner. I yawn loudly. It took me six hours to solve it in the end. Six! I don't think I've ever taken that long on one clue before. Still, I might now be able to switch off and get some sleep!

–

It's no use. I can't get back to sleep. My thoughts keep drifting back to the puzzle. It was pretty ingenious to turn my clue into a cryptic one. I wonder who wrote it. I reach for my notebook. I need a list. I need to think about this logically.

Firstly, it needs to be someone who went into the walk-in centre on Friday. (Isn't it great how tiredness makes you state the bloody obvious?) Although, that is an important point, it means I can narrow it down to... a patient, a doctor, a cleaner or... a workman. I quickly form a list of about ten potential suspects.

I begin to work my way through the list, starting with the least likely so I can cross them off. It's always nice to see a list get shorter.

There was nothing noticeably *wrong* with the centre on Friday. The place was fairly dingy and dim but the lights were working. It wasn't particularly warm but it was a cold day for August and I very much doubt an NHS centre can afford to turn on the heating in summer. Even if there was some maintenance work going on, despite the stereotypical workman having lots of tea breaks, replying to a crazy lady's puzzle doesn't really fit their image. Therefore... highly unlikely to have been a workman.

Next.

Unlike a workman, a cleaner may well have taken the time to look at the magazines in a kind of, do-I-need-to-clean-these, sort of way. But surely they would have thrown it out? All the puzzles are done. Not to mention all the other tattered magazines were still there on Saturday so it hardly seems likely that someone sorted through the crap recently. So... could be, but doubtful.

A doctor. This is much more like it. Maybe it was a young, sexy, lonely, single doctor who is new to the centre and looking for love. Maybe he spotted me in the waiting-room but was too nervous to speak to me so decided to see what magazine I was reading instead. I like this idea. Definitely possible. The fact I didn't notice him is irrelevant. I was in pain. Doctor stays on the list.

Please don't tell me that the happy chirping I can hear is from a bird perched on a tree outside my window and that a ray of sunshine is due to shine through the window any minute now. God, I haven't slept yet! Or if I did it wasn't for very long. I'm going to have to get to the bottom of this.

OK. So that just leaves… a patient. Realistically this seems the most likely but it leads to so many options. Man, woman, old, young, sick, really sick? Knowing my luck, it was a gay nineteen-year-old. Or a woman. Still, maybe she has a really hot brother? Or it could just be my One. The One. The man of my dreams, finally free to find me now that the moron is out of the picture. My true love, ready to sweep me off my feet. Oh, bloody hell, Dan was right. I should have replied. Now I'll never know who it was. I throw the notebook onto the bed. I don't need a list, I need a plan.

–

'What the hell are you doing?' Dan groans from under the pillow.

'I can't sleep and the light is going to start coming in through the window soon,' I reply, snuggling in next to Dan.

'And that's my problem how?'

'I hasten to point out that you are currently residing in *my* spare room,' I say in my best posh English accent, 'and, seeing as you're awake—'

'I wasn't before an elephant climbed into bed with me.'

'I'm going to ignore that. Besides, it's your fault I'm awake. I solved that clue like you told me to. It's 'winner in places', it's an anagr—'

'Spare me the details, please?'

'Anyway,' I say, a little put out he doesn't want to hear how I solved it, 'I was thinking, I should have replied.'

'Cassy, you solved the puzzle, congratulations. Now forget about it,' Dan says and pulls my lovely duck-feather pillow over his head.

'But I need to know who wrote it.'

'No, you don't.'

'Yes I do. Beside it will take my mind off Se—'

'Don't start going on about him again.'

'Well, I need *something* to distract me, you said so yourself.'

'Yes but, when I said you needed a distraction, I didn't mean get obsessed about a puzzle-loving weirdo.'

'Puzzle-man.'

'You've named him?'

'What if he is the man of my dreams?'

Dan groans again.

'We could have a secret love story in cryptic code,' I say dreamily.

'Don't be so stupid!'

'It's not stupid!'

'All right, whatever. So why don't you go and write a message back in the morning, then? Notice that it is not morning yet.'

'The walk-in centre isn't open on Sundays.'

'Monday then.'

'But I can't go back again.'

'Yes you can. Just walk in.'

'Ha ha. You're so funny.'

Dan tips an invisible hat on his head. 'Say you forgot something.'

'Like what?'

'I don't know, your earring?'

'Dan, that's a great idea,' I say, tickling him through the duvet.

'Oh, Cassy, go back to bed and let me sleep.'

Sleep is out of the question. I have a list to complete and only twenty-eight hours before I can go to the doctor's and write my reply. I need to get started!

List #578: Who is Puzzle-man?

- ~~Workman~~ highly unlikely to bother to read puzzle (or understand it).
- ~~Cleaner~~ magazine stand was still dirty on Saturday.
- Doctor POTENTIALLY!
- ~~Old patient~~ wouldn't have been so quick minded.
- ~~Young patient~~ wouldn't bother with magazine when has a phone to text mates.
- Gay patient...
- Married patient maybe.
- Female patient NEW BEST FRIEND.
- ~~Really sick patient~~ too sick to be bothered to do a puzzle.
- *Man of my dreams!*

Monday morning, I find myself standing in a queue at the reception desk at Threadneedle Walk-in Centre, wide-eyed and ready for action. Even at 8 a.m., the coughing and spluttering coming from the waiting-room undermines the benefit of any antibacterial cleaning that might have happened overnight. I contemplate by-passing the queue but just as I'm about to make my move, the protocol-loving receptionist notices me and her eyes flicker to the sign on the desk.

All patients using the GP Surgery must report
to reception to sign in.

I guess I could just pretend to be using some other service within the walk-in centre but I don't want to make this lie any bigger.

'Are you sure you left it here?' the receptionist asks, peering over the rims of her glasses, when I reach the front of the queue.

'Yes, quite sure. I think I must have dropped it while I was waiting. Do you mind if I go and check?'

She nods, but her squinting eyes tell me she doesn't believe me.

God, I just had a horrible thought. What if Puzzle-man is *her*? No. It can't be the receptionist. She would definitely have thrown the magazine out if she had noticed all the puzzles were done. Oh God, what if she *has* noticed all the puzzles are done and she's thrown it out already?

I hurry over to the armchair, which conveniently isn't visible from the reception desk. I pick up the puzzle book and quickly flick to the 'Make Your Own Crossword' page. I write in my answer – which fits perfectly. He really must be a genius, he even kept the (6,2,6) letters correct! OK, so I guess that's it?

Although… I should probably leave him a message so that he has something to reply to. That's assuming he comes back to the centre. God, I sound like a crazy person. What was I thinking listening to Dan? I mean, who cares that someone filled in my puzzle. It was probably just a bored patient like me. Some guy with nothing better to do while he waited. But then… he did go to the trouble of leaving me a clue. Surely he'll want to know if I solved it? Maybe I should leave him a message.

Crap. I didn't think about this part. I was concentrating so hard on getting here and finding the puzzle book that it didn't occur to me to plan a response. What the hell am I supposed to write?

> **To: Dan Mobile Mon 08:40**
> Hi Dan, what shall I write in the puzzle book?

This is hopeless. Dan won't be up for another four hours. Oh God. I can hear the determined sound of heels plodding along the floor. It's the receptionist. She's coming to check up on me. I grip the pen; I need to write something, *now*.

'Miss Brookes? Did you find it?'

—

That was *so* close. She almost caught me but I managed to shove the puzzle book away in time and get the hell out of there (with my imaginary lost earring in tow). It was sort of exciting, sneaking around like that, and I can't help but smile wryly to myself as I walk to the office.

It takes me longer to reach Holywells than I had anticipated. My limp isn't too noticeable but I still have to tread lightly on my right foot. I cross the lobby and press the button for the lift, still on a high from my walk-in centre antics. I guess I will have to come up with another excuse to go back there to see if he replies again. I've no idea what excuse I can use. 'I lost the other earring' isn't going to cut it. I am going to need a cunning mind to help me and there is no one better than my Jennifer Aniston look-a-like creative designer, Sofia. At exactly five foot she is a good six inches shorter than me but her high heels usually make up most of the margin. Sofia is the only other person in the office who is immune to Martin's charm and, being the two most senior women in the team, we have to stick together. But God, I was so rude to her on Friday. I totally freaked out when she told me she was engaged. It was all too much to take in. I have some serious making up to do…

'No, *I'm* sorry,' Sofia is saying to me a few minutes later. 'If I had known it was your anniversary I would never have told you like that.'

'It wasn't your fault. Although I am surprised you hadn't heard – Martin seemed determined that the whole office should know about my *emotional distress*.'

'Oh, Cassy, I am sorry. If I hadn't been late, he'd never have heard that message and the meeting—'

'What's done is done.'

'You're not going to let him get away with it, are you?'

'I haven't decided what I'm going to do yet, but you'll be the first to know, don't you worry.'

Out of the corner of my eye I can see Sofia playing with the hem of her lilac shirt and then gazing at her engagement ring. She obviously wants to show it off, but I can't quite bring myself to look at it. I can still remember the butterflies I felt when I found the little box in Seph's bag. I thought I'd be wearing a ring by now.

'Here, I got you this,' I say, and hand over the engagement card and the how-to-plan-your-dream-wedding book I'd bought Sofia after my visit to the walk-in centre on Saturday.

'Ah, thanks, Cassy.'

'My pleasure. And congratulations again. I'm sorry I didn't seem more excited last week.'

'I know the engagement must seem like it's come out of the blue,' Sofia says, still looking a little guilty.

'I was a bit surprised,' I say. 'In a good way,' I quickly add. 'I hadn't realised things had got so serious.'

'Yeah,' she says and smiles, unable to hide her happiness. 'I mean, we started living together ages ago and—'

'I didn't realise.'

Sofia shuffles uncomfortably in her seat.

'I hadn't wanted to tell you. You had so much going on with Seph and everything. I just thought, well… my relationship would be the last thing you'd want to hear about.'

I wince. It's just like Dan all over again. Everyone's been trying to shield me from what's been going on in their love lives and I've been too self-absorbed to notice.

'You seem far more together now,' she says. 'It's just, I know I never met Seph, but the way you spoke about him, I thought you'd never get over it.'

'I think part of me thought that too. But,' I can feel the smile creeping back to my face, 'I've found a distraction.'

Sofia is mesmerised as I recount the Puzzle-man saga.

'And then,' I say dramatically, 'the receptionist comes over.'

'So did you get to write something?' Sofia gasps.

'Well—' I stop mid-sentence, distracted by the sound of laughter. Martin. He is standing on the other side of the office, apparently having a cosy chat with Mr Samuel and some of the other partners. From my mediocre lip-reading skills, I reckon it has something to do with golf and how they should get together sometime.

'Hello? Earth to Cassy.' Sofia is waving her arms in front of me. 'Who are you goggling at?' She leans over to follow my gaze.

'Cassy! You haven't got a thing for Martin, have you?'

'Very funny,' I whisper. 'Come on, I want to know what he's up to with Mr Samuel.'

'Don't tell me you have a crush on Thomas?'

Her comment sends the testosterone-filled office into spasm and suddenly there are six pairs of boy-blue eyes staring at me from behind their multi-coloured desk cubicles. I glare at them to mind their own business. As I should be doing, I know – very hypocritical of me. We're all part of the food chain. I was once in their shoes, now I'm wearing more expensive shoes, but wishing they were even better.

When I started on the graduate scheme there was a 50:50 male–female ratio (unlike the 90 per cent male office I'm now working in). It was me, Rebecca, Chloe, Josh, Harrison and… Martin of course – how could I possibly forget the bane of my life? The days were varied and we had a laugh: the six of us in our adjacent cubicles as we rotated through creative, tech and account management. We looked up to those who had made it to an office, like Martin and I now have. We all tried to slog up the ranks but one-by-one people had dropped out. Rebecca went to do a Master's degree. Chloe chose tech as her speciality and was so good at it she was poached by a competitor; the last I heard was that she'd been offered a partnership, unheard of at our age. Josh went travelling. And Harrison realised that if his daddy was a large-enough client to get him a place on a prestigious graduate scheme without him even having a degree, then he was probably rich enough to not need to work. That just left Martin and me. We both went down the account management route and established our own list of clients, reporting to Anabelle. She is due back from maternity leave next month so I don't have long left to demonstrate that I'm ready to be given more responsibility. Hence, I really need to know what Martin is up to.

'All I'm saying is, Thomas is both your boss and a married man. I really don't think it's a good idea,' Sofia is saying to me, unable to stop laughing at her own joke. Has she really been going on about Mr Samuel the whole time my mind drifted down memory lane?

'All right, enough now,' I say and cast another anxious gaze over at the graduates. The last thing I need is for someone to overhear and get the wrong idea. 'And since when did you get on first name terms with Mr Samuel anyway?' I ask, changing the subject.

Sofia smiles and shakes her head. 'Cassy, you are the *only* one in the office who doesn't call him Thomas.'

'Hardly,' I reply, less certain than I would like as I sift through my memories of people saying hello to Mr Samuel.

'If you say so Cass-id-y.'

'Cute.' I pull a face I haven't made since I was three years old. Can I help it if I like to be professional?

'Anyway,' Sofia carries on in her I-want-to-gossip tone, 'did you manage to reply or not?'

Puzzle-man. I almost forgot about him.

'Oh, I wrote something about how it is nice to find someone on the same wavelength for a change and how most men never show any creativity or thoughtfulness,' I say.

Sofia looks quite let down.

'What? Was that the wrong thing to say? Oh God, I've screwed it up, haven't I?'

I should have waited for Dan to text back. Although, he *still* hasn't bothered to reply to my text.

'It's just a bit…'

Sad.

That's what she wants to say.

'Keen,' she decides upon.

'What would you have said then?' I say petulantly.

'I don't know. It's not really something I'd—' She changes her mind about what to say next. 'Maybe, "I can see you've met the same species of loser as me or maybe you're one of them?"'

Hmm. That would have been a better thing to write. At least then I might have been able to confirm if it was a guy. It is a guy though. I'm sure of it. I store the thought and take a deep breath. Martin is walking over to us.

'Good morning. And how are the two most beautiful girls in the office today?'

'Hello, Martin,' I say coolly. His fake charm won't work on me. I still haven't decided on the appropriate retribution for him stealing my work on Friday. I know the correct thing would be to take him into an office, sit him down, explain how I feel about the situation and work out how to resolve it. But those things only work in the How-To books. Definitely not with a ruthless, egocentric pig like Martin. No. I need to be smarter than to show my cards to him.

'You and Thomas seemed to be having a nice cosy chat over there,' Sofia says. I try to send secret brainwaves to tell her to shut up. Martin looks at me quizzically. I smile lightly and look away as if uninterested.

'Actually,' Martin says, 'that's why I came over. Tom and I are going to catch a round of golf today.'

Tom! Not even Thomas! Since when? Still, this is my chance.

'So you won't need to join me for the afternoon meet-ings,' he adds to Sofia.

Account directors tend to invite a creative designer to their client meetings, in case the client wants to bounce new strategy ideas, but I'd had no idea Martin had been taking Sofia. She is more experienced than necessary, unless he's taken on some new big clients I don't know about.

'Don't worry, Martin,' I say, 'I'll cover your meetings.'

'No need to trouble yourself. None of them are urgent,' he says.

'Oh, but please? I want to thank you for covering for me on Friday,' I say with the most angelic smile I can produce.

What can he say to that? Nothing.

Ha. Round two goes to Cassy!

From: Cassidy Brookes
Sent: Mon 18:20
To: Jonathan Davies
Subject: Strategy Meeting at Holywells

Dear Mr Davies,
It was very nice to meet you today in Mr Robertson's absence. If you have any further questions please do not hesitate to contact Martin or me.
Kind regards,
Cassidy Brookes (Account Director)

PS: I have left your son's thank you card on Martin's desk. I'm sure Martin will be delighted to know the free tutoring he gave Ben secured his place at university.

—

From: Cassidy Brookes
Sent: Mon 18:25
To: Amelia Hislop
Subject: Strategy Meeting at Holywells

Dear Mrs Hislop,

It was very nice to meet you today in Mr Robertson's absence. If you have any further questions please do not hesitate to contact Martin or me.

Kind regards,

Cassidy Brookes (Account Director)

PS: I have forwarded on your daughter's contact details to Martin but I was unable to find out if he is single at the moment.

—

From: Cassidy Brookes
Sent: Mon 18:35
To: Christopher Rills
Subject: Strategy Meeting at Holywells

Dear Mr Rills,

It was very nice to meet you today in Mr Robertson's absence. If you have any further questions please do not hesitate to contact Martin or me.

Kind regards,

Cassidy Brookes (Account Director)

PS: I'm sorry that I wasn't able to discuss the latest twenty-twenty cricket game at the Oval with you. I will most definitely send you on any complimentary tickets I come across for the next match.

From: Christopher Rills
Sent: Mon 18:35
To: Cassidy Brookes
Subject: Re: Strategy Meeting at Holywells

Cassy,
Thanks for the meeting. Would you mind telling Martin I'd like another one when he's back?
Cheers, Chris

PS: Here's the link to the golf website I was telling you about www.golffordummies.co.uk

Yesterday was a total disaster.

After fifteen minutes of, 'You really don't have to,' and 'I insist,' Martin had reluctantly accepted my offer to cover his meetings, in part because we both saw Mr Samuel walking towards us and neither of us wanted him to see us squabbling like school kids. Sofia emailed me Martin's schedule once I was back at my desk and as soon as Mr Samuel and Martin were en route to play golf, I opened the file. I nearly fell off my seat. Martin had as many meetings scheduled for Monday afternoon as I had for the whole of last week. I went over to see Sofia immediately.

'Hey, what's up?'

'Could you give me access to Martin's full calendar, not just today's, please?'

'I'd better check with him.'

'He won't mind. It will make it easier to sync our workloads. Part of the new Patterson strategy we're trialling together.'

She bought the lie.

Ten minutes later I felt like vomiting and not just because I felt like a cow for lying. Martin had seen nearly twice the number of clients as I had in August. Maybe I'm losing my game? I hadn't realised Martin had taken on so many new clients.

Things seemed to get worse as the afternoon went on. In between meetings (in which every single client told me how much they missed him and didn't I follow football, golf or cricket) I noticed he had re-opened communication with over twenty clients. Just skimming through the correspondence made the pit of my stomach rumble. Even after I'd eaten my way through a large bar of Galaxy I still couldn't shift the feeling. That's when I had noticed the names – Mrs S Azar... Mr F Allegro... They were too familiar. So I cross-referenced with the department client list. Martin had been reaching out to *Anabelle*'s clients and started to form relationships with them! Now, on the one hand, it could be called taking initiative. On the other hand, Martin is an opportunist snake. All the hard work had been done by Anabelle. He was just calling them up and having a thirty-minute meeting without needing to do any paperwork. No wonder he'd been able to get more meetings than me! Round three to Martin.

I look at my reflection in the office lift. My fringe is finally long enough for me tuck it behind my ear. Getting a fringe had been my knee-jerk reaction to breaking up with Seph. Doesn't everyone say, new haircut, new woman? I hadn't had the guts to cut my hair short or dye it blonde, so I'd decided on a fringe. Anyway, it was a disaster. It made me look about sixteen.

The lift dings and the doors begin to open. I adjust my skirt and correct my posture. *Today is a new day*, I tell myself, *and things can only get better*. I step out of the lift and instantly feel at home. The smell of freshly printed presentations mixed with coffee beans gives me a warm feeling inside. I start to make my way over to my office on the far side of the floor, passing the graduate pods and Sofia's vacant desk on the way. I'm just about to step inside when I hear footsteps behind me.

'Ah, Cassidy, just in time.'

'Mr Samuel, good morning. How are you?'

'Excellent. In fact, I can't keep this news to myself any longer.'

Before I can probe further he turns and claps his hands.

'Excuse me, can I have everyone's attention please?'

Silence sweeps through the office just as Sofia appears from the kitchenette.

'I have some very exciting news. MediaTech have decided to host an industry-wide digital-strategy conference and they have asked us to partner the event.' Murmurs break out and Mr Samuel holds up his hand. 'Fitting the Holywells culture, this event will be pioneering for the industry as it will be for employees *and* clients. We will use it as a platform to launch the firm's new alliance with MediaTech as well as increase our market presence. The conference will take place in three weeks.'

I glance over at Martin, he doesn't look in the least bit surprised. No doubt he was told all about this when he was playing golf yesterday. Excited murmurs fill the office again and Mr Samuel beckons for Martin and me to come over to him.

'There is something else the two of you should know,' he adds quietly. 'Anabelle informed me today that she has decided not to return to work so that she can focus on her family and the new baby.'

My heart is beating so loudly I begin to feel self-conscious. I know what's coming next.

'As a result, the role of Head of Accounts will soon be available and we would like to fill the position in-house. In other words, we want one of you to take over. Now you've both been working on the MediaTech account but once our alliance is made official at the conference we will want someone to lead the partnership. I'd like you both to think about what you could bring to the role and you will both have a chance to pitch to the partners. We'll announce Anabelle's replacement at the conference but, for now, let's keep this between ourselves.'

Five minutes later I'm sitting motionless at my desk, trying to digest Mr Samuel's bombshell that the promotion will be announced in three weeks. I stare down at my to-do list, feeling sick. It might be short but it certainly isn't easy to complete. I need to find and secure a lot of new clients to wow the partners and I need to do it fast.

'How is my partner in crime on this fine Tuesday morning?' Martin's voice makes me jump, I hadn't heard him come in. I seriously think he must get his shoes designed specifically for creep-effectiveness.

'If you mean me, I'm fine, thanks for asking and my name is Cassy or actually Cassidy to you.'

'Lighten up, Cass. I was just coming over to say thank you for covering my meetings while I was out with the boss yesterday.'

I wonder how many times I'm going to have to listen to him rubbing it in about how he's pals with Mr Samuel. Ten? Twenty?

'I hope you coped OK. I know it must have been a lot more work than you are used to.'

I dig my nails into my hand to stop myself from gouging his eyes.

'It was nothing.'

Eventually the loathing-imbued silence pushes him towards the door.

'Shame about Anabelle. Well, I'd better get back to the grind and start working my magic.'

His entire vocabulary makes me want to hurl. Especially after what happened yesterday. He may be a chauvinistic pig, but he is right. He does have a bigger workload than me and, more worryingly, he has more clients than me. I bang my head onto my desk so hard that my pen holder falls over. This is going to be a long day…

–

The stars in the sky look like tiny teardrops in an endless void when I eventually make my way to Bank station. I feel like a graduate again, leaving the office at 10 p.m., wondering if I've done enough or if I should go back and work through the night. I contacted thirty-three clients in total. Some have already replied asking for a catch-up meeting which has left me feeling a little better but I can't shake the feeling that I've been looking at this all the wrong way. Winning a few new clients isn't going to change anything. What I need is to win a super-duper corporate client. A big FTSE-100 company that will double my money under management and blow Martin's client list into insignificance. I need a client like Lockley & Co., a multinational enterprise with billions of pounds at its disposal. If I could somehow get Holywells to act as the lead digital agency for the Lockley & Co. franchise,

I'd win hundreds of new mandates for the firm in one go. But how? That is the million – actually billion – dollar question.

Maybe I should be taking a step out of Sir Lockley's book. He started his career in a grocer's at fourteen. No qualifications – just a shop boy. After he'd managed the store for a year he started his own supplier business and it grew and grew until he was selling everything from Granny Smith apples to iPads. He invested in so many different ventures along the way and went from strength to strength. He sold a few companies and merged the rest to form Lockley & Co. What a man. No wonder the Queen knighted him. I'd love to start my own business one day. But being promoted will do for now.

I feel utterly exhausted as I sit on the DLR. I don't even bother to get my favourite seat. I really don't think I can handle any more calamities this week.

From: Cassidy Brookes
Sent: Tues 10.15pm
To: Lorella Beaumount
Subject: Meeting with Sir Lockley

Dear Lorella Beaumount,
My name is Cassidy Brookes and I am an Account Director at Holywells. We are a leading digital marketing agency with experience catering for 360 media strategies. We are currently launching some new initiatives that I believe would be invaluable to Lockley & Co. (please see the attached presentation).
I would be delighted to discuss the initiatives with Sir Lockley in more detail.

Please could you let me know if it would be possible
to set up a meeting with Sir Lockley in the next few
days/weeks?
Kind regards,
Cassidy Brookes (Account Director)

Five

I knew I should have let the phone go to voicemail. I should have known there was only one person in the world (other than Dan who is currently demolishing another Cassy-credit-card pizza) who would call me at 11 p.m. for a 'quick chat'. It is never just a quick chat either. Even though she says it is. Even after I explain I am having a tough week in the office and need an early night. I think it must be some kind of subconscious parental punishment for me leaving home.

'Rebounds can be a dangerous business,' Mum is saying to me now, having run through major but completely insignificant updates on our entire extended family. 'Many clever women have gone wayward after a break-up, believe me, dear. I've had my fair share of wayward moments.'

'Too much detail, Mum.'

'All I am saying is, you need to stay sensible.'

'Yes, Mum.'

'Are you eating right?'

'Yes, Mum.'

'Plenty of vegetables?'

'Yes, Mum.'

'Which ones?'

'Carrots.'

'No, she's not,' Dan shouts, jumping into life from the sofa, trying to add to my misery. 'She's eating loads of takeaways.'

'Oh, is that Daniel?' Mum asks, her voice instantly lighter and excited.

I think Mum loves Dan more than me. I don't mean that in a jealous way. God, if anyone deserves to have some parental affection it's Dan. His mother died when we were in primary school and his dad never recovered. I still don't know the ins and outs of what went on, but by the time we were fifteen something needed to be done. I'll never forget the look on Dan's face when my mum confronted him. 'Now, Daniel,' she said, her tone as low and serious as when we accidentally graffitied the school wall. 'I've spoken to your father.' Dan's pupils had dilated so much you couldn't tell his irises were chocolate brown. 'He's agreed that you can come and live with us, if that's OK with you.' Dan nearly pushed Mum over when he hugged her, it was the first time I had seen him truly happy.

I hand him the phone, glad to be off the hook.

'Hello, Ann,' Dan says in his innocent boyish way. I leave them to it and make my way over to the kitchen on tiptoes, having to concentrate to avoid tripping over wires and game controllers. They talk long enough, thankfully, for me to stick a ready meal in the microwave and eat it watching today's *Eastenders* on catch-up. As the 'duh, duh, duh' of the *Eastenders'* closing theme tune starts I detect a devious edge in Dan's voice. Glancing over at him I get a nervous twinge in my stomach. He is definitely up to something…

'We'd love to go.'

I knew it! What has he got me into this time? It had better not be the wedding of a long-lost cousin.

'Tomorrow night at seven.'

Dan is nodding and winking at me. I'm surprised Mum wants to do something tomorrow, she usually goes to yoga on Wednesdays. Oh dear God, no! I snatch the phone from him.

'Sorry, Mum, I don't think I can make it. I'm doing the office pub quiz on Thursday night so I really should stay late and work tomorrow, sorry.'

'Oh but, darling, yoga will do you the world of good.'

'You didn't tell me you had to work late,' Dan butts in. He must have run into my bedroom and picked up the second phone to join the call. Sneaky git. 'You have been so stressed lately, yoga is the perfect thing for you. Ann, you do have the best ideas.'

'I'm sure work won't mind you leaving a little early given everything that has been going on,' Mum is saying as I march into my bedroom and make silent death threats at Dan. 'I could always call—'

'No, it's fine, Mum.' The last thing I need is my mum calling work for me. What does she think it is? Playgroup?

'Excellent, darling,' she says in her teacher's voice, like I've just got an A in an exam. 'I'll see you both tomorrow. Love you both.'

'Oh come on, Princess,' Dan says when we are both back in the living room. I glare at him but he looks totally un-phased, in fact, he looks smug. 'You're the one who keeps saying I need to get out of the house and stop playing video games.'

'Indeed,' I say through gritted teeth. Don't get me wrong. I know people say yoga is great for the mind, body and soul. But it's not for me. I just know.

Dan and Mum have saved me a space near the front when I arrive at the church hall on Wednesday evening. Mum is impossible to miss, dressed in a matching magenta combo of cotton three-quarter length trousers and a short-sleeved T-shirt. I edge my way across the yoga-mat-covered floor, being extra careful not to tread on anyone's bare feet. Everyone seems to be fixated on something at the front. Dan. He is looking extra sexy tonight, wearing silky black trousers and a loose white vest that his rippling muscles shine through. How he does it without ever stepping inside a gym I don't know. If only he wasn't gay.

'Good evening, ladies,' says a light, airy voice from the back of the hall. 'Oh and gentleman.'

Turning around, I feel like I have been transported to the backstage of a luxury magazine photo shoot with a model posing as 'The Woman Everyone Wants To Look Like In Heaven.'

'Don't mind me,' Dan says with a little snort to follow. Is that a smitten glint in his eye? Maybe bi-sexual after all?

'My name is Letitia Sunshine.'

That can't be her real name surely. I glance at Dan but he is too mesmerised to notice me. I watch as Letitia walks gracefully through the class. I guess it *could* be her real name. She has such a warm, angelic glow about her I think I could believe anything she tells me. She lays down her navy-blue mat at the front of the hall and with one easy, free-flowing movement, positions herself into the classic yoga position, her feet resting on her knees and her back perfectly straight. To my horror everyone in the room has copied her, Dan and Mum included. No one told me this was an advanced class. I pull my right foot onto my left knee and ferociously tug at my left foot but to no avail. Out of the corner of my eye I see the edge of Dan's mouth twitch.

'Let us start by engaging with our breathing,' Letitia says calmly. 'Eyes closed, everyone.'

I feel a bit ridiculous but at least no one can see me wobbling about. I try to reposition my legs but it's no use. I am going to have to just sit cross-legged like I did in primary school. The room seems to breathe in unison, everyone's chest expanding and then making a collective exhalation, loud enough to blow out a fire. If there was a fireplace, I mean. It's actually quite cold in here.

I puff along with everyone else. It is far harder than it looks. My lungs don't seem to be big enough to suck in air for that long. After a while my body begins to relax, my muscles unclench.

'OK, everyone, now slowly open your eyes.'

I feel a pinch of anger as my eyes start to refocus on the room and we all stand up. Like she has somehow invaded a private conversation I was having with my inner self.

'OK, everyone, now we've done the warm-up—'

That was just the warm up?

'—let's get started with some gentle Hatha positions.'

A what position?

'First, the Tadasana.'

–

The next thirty minutes are the most strenuous and humiliating of my adult life to date. I didn't know the human body could contort itself into those positions. Mine definitely can't.

'Just relax, darling,' Mum whispers as she performs the Utkatasana perfectly. Dan's grin is now a permanent feature.

'OK, everyone, let's move into the Garudasana, or the Eagle pose.'

I watch as Letitia demonstrates at the front; my muscles tense in fear. I'm not sure if I can even attempt this one. I try to hook my left leg around my right calf and bend down to the floor with my left arm over my right. Or is it supposed to be my right arm over my left? I stumble to the floor. Letitia notices. How could she not? She comes over to me and places her soft palm on my shoulder. I feel like she just passed on some of her wisdom to me. A kind of psychological warmth fills my body and my muscles instantly relax.

She shows me some easier poses and I manage those.

'OK, everyone, let's finish how we started.'

I still can't do the yoga cross-legged position but I do think my back is a little straighter. The breathing thing is so surreal. It is as if my body is breathing through me, rather than for me.

'How did you find your first class?'

I open my eyes to see Letitia's perfectly petite, ballerina figure peering down at me.

'Was it that obvious?'

She smiles and I suddenly feel like I want to hug her. 'Your mother gave me a heads-up before the class.'

Ah. Of course she did.

'You did very well though, truly.'

She looks too pure to lie so I shall take that as a genuine compliment.

'Another excellent class, Letitia,' Mum says when she and Dan join us.

'Thank you I—'

Some of the other class members are beckoning her.

'Don't let us keep you,' Mum says. 'We have to be off.'

Letitia nods, but I'm almost sorry to see her walk away.

'Come on, Cassy,' Mum says and holds the door open for me.

'I'm so bloody tired,' I say once we step into the crisp night air.

'Language, Cassidy! So what did you think then?'

'It wasn't what I was expecting. Letitia was nice…very graceful. How old do you reckon she is?'

'Forty-two,' Mum says.

'No way!'

'She most certainly is. I asked her after class once.'

'Well, all I can say is, if I look as good as her when I'm thirty, I will have done well.'

'So, Princess,' Dan pipes in, 'yoga not so bad after all, eh?'

–

OK. So maybe I was a little too judgmental…

Yoga is awesome.

I ache like never before but at the same time, I am reborn. I really can *feel* my breathing and there is a bounce in my step as I make my way out of Bank station the following morning. My ankle is well and truly recovered and I reach Hatton Garden within fifteen minutes. The queue for coffee is long and I would normally skip it, but not today. Waiting in line outside Starbucks I take a deep Kapalabhati inhale. I instantly regret it. The diesel fumes of a nearby bus mixed with cigarette smoke from the man standing next to me fill my lungs. But nothing is going to dampen my new, refreshing outlook on life. I do a forceful exhalation and all is well again.

The queue moves fairly quickly, we all shuffle forwards like a line of military prisoners and I'm soon inside the overheated café. Most of the tables are taken, some people setting up camp for the day with their laptops and paperwork spread out over a four-person table. What jobs allow you to work from cafés? I should make a list for potential career changes. Surely they can't all work for themselves? It would be nice to work for myself one day though. 'Brookes Advisory', I smile.

The boy on the till looks too young to have finished school. Apart from a few spots he doesn't look as if he's reached puberty. I wonder what his story is. He catches me looking at him. I smile. Well OK, I beam. I'm happy and I think it is only right I share it with the world.

'Can I have… a tall skinny latte with hazelnut, please?' Not my usual double espresso – but it seems fitting for my mood. 'So… Adam? It is Adam, isn't it? I know sometimes you share name tags.'

The woman behind me has stopped texting on her phone to look at me. She thinks I'm babbling, but I don't care. I can babble if I want to.

'Yeah,' the boy grins, 'it's Adam.'

I smile and resist the urge to turn around and gloat at the lady behind. That would not fit my new Cassy Brookes image.

'So are you just fitting in a shift before school?'

'Yeah, I'm doing AS at Cathedral College down the road.'

'Wow. That's impressive. I hear they only take really bright people,' I say and give him my, *I'm-so-impressed* look.

I didn't even realise there was a sixth-form college nearby but I feel good about encouraging a young person to continue their education. I wonder if they have some sort of mentoring scheme I could sign up for?

Adam hands me my change and then leans forward as if to whisper something in my ear. Maybe he wants me to give him some more encouragement. I lean forward too, although the stupid counter is so wide there remains quite a large gap between us.

'Listen,' he says, loud enough that everyone can hear. 'My parents won't be home for a while so I could always bunk off today and y'know... maybe you could teach me some biology instead.'

I take a step back as Adam winks at me. The queue behind me sniggers and people on nearby tables have looked up from their morning papers. My cheeks feel like they are melting under the heat.

'I was just being polite... Obviously I'm not interested in you. You're a kid... It would be paedophilia... Although not technically... I don't think.'

Cassy. Shut. Up.

This really could not get any worse.

'Everything all right, Cassy?'

Oh my God. It just did.

'Cassy?'

Maybe if I don't answer he'll think I'm someone else.

'Cassidy Brookes!'

The café is dead silent except for the sound of the milk for my latte frothing. Every customer has stopped drinking to watch the action. I. Want. To. Die.

'Ah, Cassy, it is you.'

I feel a firm hand pat me on the shoulder. There really is no way out of this is there? Play dumb. It's the only option.

'Martin, hi, how are you this morn – And Mr Samuel, hello.'

Please, someone, shoot me now. What are the chances that after five years of going to the same coffee shop before work, the one day something like this happens, your boss is standing in the queue behind you? *And* that he is getting coffee with the person who takes pleasure in humiliating you?

'Good morning, Cassidy,' Mr Samuel says. He doesn't quite make eye contact, obviously as embarrassed for me as I am for myself. He must have heard everything.

'Lady?'

I turn to see Adam holding out my takeaway coffee. He's nodding at the cardboard cup holder and I realise he's written his number on it.

I take the coffee from him and bow my head to avoid eye contact.

'See you in the office, Cass,' Martin says, the happiness singing from his glistening white teeth.

I just nod. There are no more words. I shuffle past the rest of the queue and escape as quickly as possible. So much for breathing posi-bloody-tivity into one's life. I *never* want to recall this moment *ever again*.

-

I'm still livid when I get to my office. Why did Martin have to call me out like that? My computer bleeps as I sit down at my desk. It's a message from Martin. He has cc'd me on an email about some course on how to

84

influence people that is being run by our Learning and Development team:

What football match? So now Martin is a friend of the family as well as on nickname terms with Mr Samuel. Also, why is he asking on my behalf, like he is my superior or something?

'Before you say anything, I was just being nice.'

'Martin!' I jump so high out of my chair, my thigh knocks into my desk and my glass of water tips over.

What is it with me and drinks today?

Martin grabs a few tissues off my desk and begins to mop up the puddle forming on the floor while I quickly salvage my paperwork.

'Are you OK, Cass? You seem a bit on edge?'

'I'm fine.' Not.

'I just wanted to check you saw my email about the course?'

'I did.' I gesture at my empty glass and Martin follows me out of my office towards the water tank.

'I think it will be really valuable,' he continues.

'I have no doubt,' I say, unable to manage any kind of smile. 'Anyway, I'm sure you need to get back to—'

'So, how's single life treating you?'

His question catches me off guard. His eyes have softened, almost as if he has a genuine interest in my personal life.

'It must be hard getting back into the world of dating,' he says.

'It's not. I mean, I'm not.'

My cheeks begin to burn. A couple of the graduates are heading our way. This conversation needs to end now.

'Besides,' I say briskly, 'it's none of your business.'

Martin holds his hands up in surrender. John and Charles are only a few steps away from us now. 'I was just trying to be a friend. After what happened at Starbucks—'

'Nothing *happened*,' I whisper, 'and I'm not looking to date anyone.'

'No?' John interjects, inviting himself into the conversation. 'I heard you looked ready to get back on the horse in Starbucks this morning.'

I glare at Martin. 'You told them that?'

'Actually it was Sammy from tech support who told us about the woman who hit on the Starbucks barista,' Charles says.

'Martin just confirmed it was you,' John adds.

I bet he did. I dare not make eye contact with Martin in case my look really does kill him. Instead, I take a large deep breath and put on my politest smile.

'John, Charles, I don't know what you're both going on about. All I did was order a coffee.'

'So you weren't hitting on a teenager?' Charles sniggers and I feel my face redden.

'Of course I wasn't,' I snap.

Martin walks away. I bet he's enjoyed every minute of this conversation.

'So, I guess, what with me being twenty-one, I'm a bit too old for you, Cassy?'

'Oh shut up, Charles. It was a misunderstanding and I'd appreciate it if you didn't spread rumours.'

'Absolutely.'

I nod and turn, but I hear him quietly say 'not' to John. I *hate* Martin. Why couldn't he have kept his big trap shut? Just this once. I will throw myself off the top of this building if he gets promoted instead of me. All right. I won't actually do that. But inside I'll be dying a slow and painful death. I can see him on the other side of the office, having a good laugh with some of the tech guys.

He's probably filling them all in on the Starbucks incident.

It wasn't like that, I want to scream, but I don't. It will only make matters worse. I just need to put this in perspective. I mean, in the grand scheme of things it's not that important. They'll all just have a quick laugh at my expense for an hour or so and then I can put this whole ridiculous nightmare in my mental dustbin. I bet that by lunch time this will be old news.

–

It's 1.30 p.m. before I build up the courage to leave my office and go to the Holywells cafeteria. The smell of chicken tikka fused with vinegary fish and chips fills the corridor. Inside, the seating area is packed, all the comfy garden furniture style sofas are taken and so are most of the school hall dinner tables. Holding my grey plastic tray and a five-pound note, I join the shortest queue for sandwiches and wraps.

'What will it be?'

'Could I get a chicken wrap, please?'

'No problem. Would you like a smile with that?'

'Sorry?'

'It was a joke. You look pretty down.'

'Oh yeah. I've had a bit of a bad morning, that's all.'

'We all get those. Hey, I heard a good story today that will make you laugh – proper cringe worthy.'

No. It can't be.

'Apparently some sad old woman who just got divorced hit on a guy young enough to be her son in Starbucks this morning.' He laughs.

Even the cafeteria staff know!

I hate, hate, *hate* Chinese whispers. I am *not* divorced! I am *not* sad or old and I did NOT hit on him.

'Err, here's your change,' he says, no longer smiling, just looking embarrassed for me instead. If there had been a silver lining it was that my name seemed to have got lost in translation but I think the disgusted look on my face has given that game away. Someone get me out of here, please!

My wrap falls apart on the plate as soon as I sit down at my desk to eat it. Even food is rejecting me. I stand up and close my office door.

'Argh.' I've had enough of this stupid day.

'Are you OK, Cassy?' Sofia asks, poking her head around the door with genuine concern on her face.

'It's not true,' I gasp.

'Oh, I know,' she says, a little sheepish, her eyes filled with pity. 'It's just, well, now the guys have told everyone, it doesn't really matter if it's true or not,' she sighs, 'does it?'

I bang my head on my desk.

'Sofia, I know it's not your job, but would you mind going over to the kitchenette and making me a tea? I can't face overhearing any more gossip today.'

Sofia smiles at me sympathetically. I'm too ashamed and upset to care. I take some deep breaths and try to feel at one with my breathing. But it's no use. The magic of yoga has deserted me. The more deeply I try to breathe the more I see red.

'Are you still going to come to the pub quiz tonight?' Sofia asks when she returns with my cup of tea.

I take a determined swig.

'Yes I am,' I say, slamming the mug down, 'and I'm going to kick Martin's arse.'

From: Lorella Beaumount (on behalf of Sir Lockley)
Sent: Thur 4.59pm
To: Cassidy Brookes
Subject: Re: Meeting with Sir Lockley

Dear Miss Brookes
Thank you for your email and the detailed proposal you attached. I'm afraid Sir Lockley has no availability for the rest of this month but I will forward this information on to him.
Regards,
Lorella Beaumount (Executive Personal Assistant)

Six

Pub quizzes are my Achilles heel. Doing any kind of puzzle – a crossword or a Sudoku – is good, but a pub quiz is something else. The public display of admiration you get for figuring out a difficult clue is better than having an orgasm. Nothing in five years, not even glandular fever, has ever stopped me from making quiz night. I'm first to the table; always in charge of the answer sheet.

The quiz Holywells takes part in each month is at The Queen's Nose, a small pub just around the corner from the office. From the outside it looks like a pub-to-avoid: damp and full of pervy old men. The inside is not much better but there is no denying the atmosphere it has on the third Thursday of every month. The place is packed as men and women, all suited and booted, crowd around the wobbly oak tables. The tiny stage has a wonky microphone stand on it and a large whitewashed chalkboard on the wall behind it. Each team name is written up on the board in a different-coloured chalk.

Holywells signs up as two teams each month: the Perfect Partners versus Jolly Juniors. Mr Samuel is the captain of the Perfect Partners and I'm the captain of the Jolly Juniors. There are five rounds: film and music; the picture round; sport; general knowledge; and finally my favourite round which is made up of ten cryptic clues. The Jolly Juniors are five months undefeated, the record since the tradition began.

As usual I arrive first at The Queen's Nose. I order a sneaky double vodka on the rocks which I down before anyone else arrives. Even quiz night hasn't completely been able to numb my embarrassment about the Starbucks kid. I'm ordering a double vodka and lemonade as Martin and the graduates arrive.

'No Sofia?' I ask, adding four pints of lager to my drinks tab.

'No, she said to tell you she was sorry but Joey wasn't feeling well and wants her home early.'

'Simon and Lucas can't make it either,' Mr Samuel informs us a few minutes later when he and some of the other partners arrive. 'As two of our team members have been called into a client meeting we think it is only fair one of you joins us this month to level the teams out.'

Yes. This is my chance to impress. If I play with the partners I'll have a whole evening of networking. Besides, I am the natural choice. It's a well-known fact that I am the cryptic-clue guru and I'm pretty hot on most of the other rounds too.

'We'll have...'

'I'd love to—'

'Martin—'

Wait, did they say Martin? Everyone is looking at me.

'I'd love to... be captain of the Jolly Juniors again,' I say in a hopeless attempt to look less pathetic. The conversation moves on which gives me time to drown in my own misery. Of course they were going to pick Martin. He's in their pocket, wiping their arses most of the time already. Is it too soon for another drink?

'And so into the final round and it's neck and neck between the Perfect Partners and the Jolly Juniors.'

'Come on, Cassy, think. You've been totally off your game tonight,' John is saying.

'And by that he means you're totally hammered,' Charles pipes in.

'Am not,' I say and suppress a burp. 'OK, team, we can do this. Last round come on.'

By the third cryptic clue it's apparent that I should no longer be the person writing down the answers, my hand seems incapable of doing what my brain tells it to. John takes over and I sit back and look blankly at my empty glass.

'OK, everyone, the final results are in.'

'Is it over already?'

The graduates are shaking their heads and laughing, though I'm not entirely sure why.

'In third place is… The Rock Stars.' Cheers break out from behind us, my heart starts to beat faster. Please let us have won.

'I can announce that we have a tie for first place between the Jolly Juniors and the Perfect Partners.'

'What?' I scream and get to my feet. John helps me back onto my seat.

'Ahem. In the event of a tie we move to sudden death. There will be one more cryptic clue for each team. The first to decipher it wins. OK, listen carefully folks, here it comes. *You won't find acrobats at this university.*'

I put my hands on my head. *Acrobats, acrobats, dancers? Circus? This university? Warwick, LSE, Cambridge, Oxford. Dancing LSE, Circus Oxford. That's it!*

'Oxford Circus!' Martin calls out.

'Coooorrect! Perfect Partners are our winners.'

—

'Lighten up, Cass,' Martin says, putting his arm around me ten minutes later, 'you didn't think you were the only one who rocks at cryptic clues, did you?'

Before I can reply, Mr Samuel bounces over and hands us both a drink. He raises his glass and says, 'Here's to you, Martin. We might have to make you a regular on our team.'

'To Martin!' the other partners chime in. I attempt to sip my drink without choking on it. Martin looks over at me and winks. If I didn't know better, I would say he won the pub quiz just to annoy me. There's nothing else for it but to go to the dark side. I must get revenge on Martin.

List #92: Reasons I hate Martin

- He calls me Cass even though I've told him to call me Cassidy.

- He is unethical, insensitive, arrogant and stupid.

- He took the credit for my MediaTech strategy.

- He told Mr Samuel I'm emotionally distressed.

- He stole Anabelle's clients before she announced she was leaving.

- It's his fault everyone thinks I'm divorced and hit on a child.

- *He thinks he's God's gift to women, marketing and pub quizzes*

List #581: How to Stop Martin getting Promoted

- Ask him nicely to back off.
- Tell Mr Samuel Martin stole my idea.
- Send an anonymous email to Mr Samuel saying Martin stole my idea.
- Hold a gun to Martin's head and get him to confess that he stole my idea.
- Blackmail him into giving me half of his clients.
- Get him to resign.
- Sabotage his account list by telling the clients he is dead?
- *Kill him?*

I've been sitting in my office with the blinds closed and my computer screen dimmed but even after four paracetamols my headache won't go away. Sipping a mug of hot water and lemon, I can barely focus on the new emails in my inbox. None of the corporations I've approached are interested in Holywells revamping their social media strategy.

In need of a distraction, I open my browser and do a google search for 'Puzzle-man' and 'Threadneedle Walk-in Centre'. I'm about to turn the screen off completely, afraid my head will never recover from this hangover, when something catches my eye. It's an advert for the free careers' advice service the walk-in centre offers. That might be a good excuse to go to the centre. It might even be something I need. I follow the link and it takes me to a downloadable questionnaire. I print it off and shut down my computer. If I'm not going to get any actual work done, I may as well work on my professional development. Holywells takes its employees' personal development very seriously. I know they encourage us to explore this through the Holywells online portal for learning and development but surely I get brownie points for finding the questionnaire on my own? I hardly think it matters that I stumbled across it while I was thinking of reasons to go back to the Threadneedle Walk-in Centre and that the questionnaire is really a means to get an appointment with an advisor that will allow me to check the puzzle book. Besides, I do desperately need some careers advice – if it's the kind that helps you destroy your smooth-talking, smart-arse, bum-licking, smarmy rival.

–

The questionnaire wasn't particularly long but it took me two and a half hours to complete. After background questions that were basically a summary of my CV, there were three questions: What career aspirations do you want to have attained in a year? What career aspirations do you want to have attained in five years? What career aspirations do you want to have attained in ten years? For each question you had to state the reason you wanted it and any obstacles you may encounter.

The first was easy. I want to make Head of Accounts and my obstacle is Martin. I had to use an extra sheet of paper to explain the situation fully. Five years wasn't too hard. If all goes well I should be a partner and about to drop down to working part-time to look after my two children. The obstacle being that the moron has dumped me and I'm not sure how I can ask Puzzle-man if he wants children. (I took out the bit about Puzzle-man before I finalised it.)

It was the third question that had me stumped. Being a housewife or a homemaker doesn't seem like me, given that the most I can cook is a chicken hotpot and a Sunday morning fry-up that is below-par and not a birdie according to Seph. Don't get me started on cleaning. So if not that, what do I want to be doing in ten years? Making partner is the furthest I've ventured in my mind. And I don't think I want to be at Holywells for my entire career. That's when I felt a little twinge in my stomach. I tried to shake it off but it wouldn't go away. The more I thought about the question, the stronger the feeling got. I do know what I want, it's just that I think of it as more of a dream than a possibility. I want to start my own business. Exactly what, I don't know, though it would definitely involve helping people in some way. The list of obstacles I came up with took up a side of A4 paper front and back. My hand was shaking as I wrote the biggest obstacle on to the form. *I'm afraid to fail.*

I leave the office around noon to grab some lunch from a café that happens to be on Threadneedle Street, so it makes perfect sense to pop in to the walk-in centre on my way with my questionnaire.

'Hello, again,' the receptionist says, not looking particularly pleased to see me.

'Hi. I was hoping to book an appointment with the careers advisor,' I say and hand over the questionnaire that could pass for a novella.

'OK. We'll contact you and let you know the date of your appointment. It usually takes about three weeks.'

'*Three weeks.*'

'Yes. I'm afraid we only have one careers advisor at the moment so the wait time has increased. Is that a problem?'

'No, it's fine. Thanks,' I say and make a hasty exit.

I walk back to the office feeling very annoyed with myself. I've totally wasted a morning and now I'll have to work late on a Friday, my pet hate.

Three weeks is far too long.

I'll have to think of another excuse.

Seven

When I finally arrived home on Friday evening, an A4 envelope was waiting for me. I say it was for me – it was addressed to me – but it was from Moonpig and it was the birthday card I'd spent hours designing for Seph. I'd completely forgotten about it. Moonpig had done a special offer at the beginning of the year and I'd gone crazy designing cards for everyone's birthdays.

I forced myself to open it and look at the mosaic of pictures of the two of us. There were no signs in the photos that anything was wrong with our relationship. Whatever had changed must have changed later. I ripped up the card right there and then and threw it in the bin. I spent the rest of the evening racking my brains for different reasons to go back to see the doctor. That's when Dan had intervened.

'Will you stop that?' he yelled through our adjoining bedroom wall and gave it a hefty thump for good measure. At the time, I wasn't exactly sure what it was I was supposed to stop doing. I was only writing a list. I heard him stomp out of his room.

'Will you stop that bloody pacing?'

'Dan! You can't just butt into my room at one o'clock in the morning. What if I'd been naked?'

'You're not.'

'I might have been.'

'Well, it would have been more traumatic for me than you, Cassy, trust me.'

'Oh, whatever.'

'Whatever yourself. Just lay off the floorboards all right? Some of us want to sleep at night.'

'I was only walking slowly.'

'You were pacing.'

'I was writing a list.'

'Well don't. Either go to sleep or get out,' he demanded and pointed in the general direction of the front door like he had just found me trespassing on his private property.

'Number one, it's my flat and I can pace if I want to. Number two, I'm on a roll and I won't be able to sleep if I don't finish it.'

'Am I bothered?' Dan said, doing his best Catherine Tate impression. We both stood still, arms folded, trying to stare each other out. Dan caved first with a loud tut of defeat. He stomped off again, this time into the kitchen. I heard the contents of a cupboard being thrown onto the work surface and shortly afterwards Dan stomping back into my room where he proceeded to throw a jar of Horlicks at me.

'Knock yourself out,' he'd said and slammed my bedroom door like the mature seven-year-old he is. In the few seconds that I contemplated whether or not to make a mug of Horlicks, Dan managed to fall into a deep snore-ridden sleep. I was thinking about storming into his room and ranting that I couldn't sleep with his constant snoring when I had my eureka moment.

Sleeping pills. It was the perfect excuse for me to go to the Saturday drop-in session at the Threadneedle Walk-in Centre. A stressful job with a promotion at stake and a broken heart is surely enough to win some sleeping pills. Right?

–

My notebook is stuck to my cheek when I wake up on Saturday morning. There is a splodge of drool over my *How to stop Martin getting promoted* list. I flick to the next page, Martin can wait until Monday. Today is about Puzzle-man. The plan is simple: go to Threadneedle Walk-in Centre; ask to see the doctor; check the puzzle book; ask the doctor for sleeping pills; and drop the prescription on the way out (that way I have another excuse to go back).

Squinting through the sunshine to look at the time on the clock, I see it is 8.30 a.m. I'm almost certain the walk-in centre opens at 9 a.m. on a Saturday. If I aim to get there at 10 a.m. there is bound to be a backlog of patients (but not so many that my dodgy-looking green armchair will be taken). I think I will give make-up a miss today; a few bags under my eyes will help my case. OK, let's get this show on the road.

–

No make-up was a mistake. Looking at my reflection in the DLR window I look like a bedraggled hag and I'm sure the woman sitting next to me thinks I'm a dirty stop-out, on my way home from a one-night stand, she keeps giving me The Look. This whole thing seems like a dumb idea now. I mean, there is no rational reason even to go back. So someone did my crossword. What is the likelihood they will have replied again? How many serial doctor-goers are there in the world? More to the point, how many serial doctor-goers do I want to talk to? I feel stupid. I look stupid. My reflection looks stupid. Yet... What if he really is the man of my dreams? Doesn't every heroine in every good romance story have to take at least one insane leap of faith to meet Prince Charming? Maybe this is mine.

The next station is Bank where this train terminates. All change please.

The journey seems to have only taken seconds. It's a little bit too early on a Saturday morning for tourists, thankfully, and I have a nice, pleasant journey to the walk-in centre.

9.45 a.m. Early as usual. Still, I may as well go in now I'm here.

I can hear the receptionist chatting away before I even get through the door. I wait as she hands some paperwork to an elderly lady (who reminds me very much of my gran). I have one final run-through of what I am going to say as the elderly lady starts to make her way slowly over to the waiting area.

'Hi there,' I say and beam like a clown.

The welcoming smile the receptionist was wearing a moment ago seems to have become forced.

'Ah, it's Miss Brookes, isn't it?'

'Yes, that's right. Good memory. What's your name?' She blinks.

'Sorry, I wasn't trying to be funny, I just thought it might be nice not to have to keep referring to you as "the receptionist".'

Her expression is saying the same thing my inner voice is, how often do you need to refer to the receptionist, you weirdo.

'It's Janet.'

'Ah, that's a lovely name, my great aunt—'

'Please take a seat in the waiting area and the doctor will be with you shortly.'

Janet is so eager to get rid of me she doesn't even ask me to confirm my address. Not that I mind. I haven't even started lying and I'm already getting a nervous sweat, a twitching eye and a gaggle-mouth.

Crap! The gran look-a-like seems to be steering herself towards my armchair.

'Sorry, excuse me,' I say as I dodge past a few of the incoming patients. I slip around the other side of the waiting-room – if I'm quick I'll be able to cut her up.

She's closing in.

I'm going to have to make a dive for it.

'Oh sorry, dear,' she says, looking up from the floor as she gets to the chair. 'Do you know, I didn't even see anyone was sitting in that chair? I thought it was empty. My eyesight is not what it used to be. I had better book another appointment at the opticians soon.'

I feel my body heat with shame.

'No, actually, I just beat you to it but please, you sit here,' I say and stand up.

'Oh, don't worry, dear. I like the look of this one more.'

The lady sits in the armchair next to me which does look a lot more comfortable, thankfully, and is closer to the consultation room. I attempt to wipe the layer of guilt from my mind by sifting through the stack of magazines for the puzzle book. I think back to the message I wrote last time. A silly comment about how thoughtless most men are and how it was nice to find someone on the same wavelength as me. Puzzle-man might not think we're on the same wavelength of course. In fact, my pitiful comment might have scared him off. Guess I'm about to find out. I see the familiar cover, crumpled and creased, worn and torn. Except – as I pick it up the cover falls away and reveals a shiny, new, latest edition of the puzzle book inside. It's a little smaller – must be due to cost-cutting in the recession, less paper, same price. The top, right-hand corner of one of the pages is folded over. I open it up and that childhood excitement on Christmas morning rushes through me.

It opens up on a page of 'Letters from Readers.' There's a scribbled comment on the top:

> *I hope you approve of my attempt to show I'm one of the rare thoughtful specimens of the inconsiderate sex (and for your chance to show you are worthy of writing in pen when doing a cryptic puzzle!)*

Ha. Proof that it's a man! The writing isn't joined up, so maybe I can rule out an elderly man (no doubt they would have been forced into good handwriting techniques at school). The 'i's have that annoying thing where the dot is a circle rather than a dot. That surely means he is my generation or younger. It's too neat and accurate for a child, thank God. I give myself a mental slap around the face to shake off the thought of the Starbucks incident.

I search around in my bag for my notebook. I look at the list of potential puzzle-men and cross off the unlikely choices. This new evidence really does increase the probability that he is a twenty-something-year-old. He may actually be my knight in shining armour!

'Mrs Dryer?' Dr Danes calls.

'That's me. Lovely to meet you, dear,' says the lady next to me.

That means I must be next. I turn my attention back to the puzzle book. He's underlined a couple of the things in the letters and I start to do the same.

> Dear Rosie,
>   On behalf of my husband, I wanted to thank you for last month's excellent puzzle book. He said it gave him the <u>most peace and quiet he's had in years!</u>
>   Avid reader, Shirley

To improve my insight into what women want, would you rather a 'super loser' or a guy who makes you do puzzles all day?

Anything beats super loser, why are you a puzzle-loving kind of guy?

> Dear Rosie,
>   I tried out the 'Make your Own' cross-word and had so much fun I want to do more! Any plans to run another competition? Would love to see mine in print!
>   Jessica

Shall we send in ours?

Somehow I think we'll lose!

'Miss Brookes?'

Time's up. I quickly fit the crumpled old cover back on and stash it near the bottom of the pile of magazines. OK, back to business. Act tired.

'Hello again, Cassy,' says Dr Danes as I step inside her consulting room. 'Back so soon? Is everything all right with your foot?'

'Sorry? Oh yes. My foot is fine.' I'd almost forgotten about the cycling incident, so much seems to have happened since then. Dr Danes looks at me with that weary-but-understanding doctor's smile that makes you want to tell them your whole life story and list every ailment, even though you know you only have a five-minute slot.

'How can I help you?'

'Oh, it's nothing too serious. It's just, well you see, I'm here because I'm having trouble sleeping.'

'Oh?'

'Yes. Well you see…'

And then I let loose and the five-minute rule goes out the window. I tell her all about Martin and how he bulldozed my meeting. I even tell her about the Starbucks guy who I wasn't hitting on. I tell her how badly I want the promotion but that Martin has more clients than I do because he stole all of Anabelle's and is a moral vacuum. Her eyes are filled with so much concern and compassion I just carry on pouring my soul. I tell her about Seph, about how he stole my toothpaste and how I'm worried I'll never find somebody else. I tell her that even as I am telling her all this, my chest is getting tight, my palms are starting to get sweaty and my heart is pounding so hard I think it might explode.

When I finally stop for air, she gives a small considerate sigh, takes off her black Specsavers glasses and looks me straight in the eye.

'Cassy, how long have you been feeling this anxious and paranoid?'

Anxious?

Paranoid?

I'm not anxious. I just want things to go well. And I'm definitely not paranoid. Martin *is* out to get me. I know it. He probably wants the promotion just to stop me getting it.

'I'm not,' I say. 'There's nothing really *wrong* with me. Everyone reacts to being dumped and screwed over at work like this, don't they? It's normal, isn't it? I think I'm just tired.'

'Yes, given the circumstances, I'm not surprised you are finding it hard to wind down. You seem to have a lot of stress and pressure in your life at the moment.'

'I thrive under pressure,' I say instinctively. That's what I always tell people. It even says so on my CV.

'It's not uncommon for people, during particularly difficult periods of their lives, to become a little anxious. And that can cause sleep deprivation and in some cases a mild paranoia. Although people can feel uncomfortable talking about it, almost one in three people suffer from some kind of mental—'

'I'm not mental!'

'I wasn't saying you are.'

Bloody hell. I only wanted some mild sleeping pills.

'But I think, from what you have told me, you may benefit from some cognitive behavioural therapy.'

This is my punishment for lying, isn't it?

'I really don't think I need to see a shrink.'

'It's not psychiatry or counselling, it looks at how you behave in certain situations. Why don't you take a look through these leaflets and if you want to discuss it further you can arrange another appointment. In the meantime, I'll give you a two-week prescription of Zopiclone.'

'Thanks,' I say, my hand visibly shaking.

There's nothing wrong with me. I mean, I know loads of people use medication to cope with the rat race but I'm coping just fine. I only came here today to ask for sleeping pills so I could reply to Puzzle-man. Which reminds me, I have a mission to complete.

The reception area is quiet. Janet has her back to the front desk. Clutching the prescription in my right hand I walk over to the door. I stop. An elderly gentleman is making his way inside. I pretend to be looking at some posters on the wall while I wait for him to enter. Then, with two quick paces, I move towards the exit and in true James Bond style, inconspicuously drop the prescription by the doorway. *Mission accomplished.*

'Excuse me, miss,' the elderly gentleman says. I push the door open and act like I haven't heard him. He grabs hold of my arm. 'You dropped this.'

Damn.

'Thanks very much,' I say as he hands me back my prescription.

It's a minor setback but, hey, I can always come back for therapy, right? God, that actually isn't funny. I dread to think what Martin would do if he found out my doctor was thinking of referring me for therapy. I shove the prescription into my handbag, along with the handful of leaflets about mental illness and coping with stress, and make my way towards the DLR.

—

All right, I admit it, after the initial shock had worn off I got curious and I did have a quick flick through the leaflets, purely out of intellectual interest. Dr Danes was right, CBT does sound useful. I actually ended up making a few notes.

I mean, obviously I'm coping fine but these 'strategies for tackling thinking errors' do make a lot of sense. Besides, I'm sure everyone makes them from time to time and these thinking errors do sound quite interesting. I really do like to be error-free in my work so it's only logical I would want to be error-free in my thinking. Not that I make errors in my thinking…

List #583: Summary of Cognitive Behavioural Therapy (for academic purposes only)

- Thinking error – catastrophising: When a stressful situation arises, write down the details. Go back to it the next day and look at whether your first judgement of the situation was accurate and whether there is anything you can do to help ease the situation.

    Example: Starbucks guy
    Situation: Martin made sure everyone knew it was me and a rumour spread
    Initial thought: End of my life
    Ease the situation: Get a new boyfriend who is older than me. Puzzle-man????

- Thinking error – mind-reading: Before you decide that someone is judging you, ask yourself if the person actually told you their opinion of you or if you are interpreting it and hence could be mistaking their meaning.

> *Example: Mr Samuel likes Martin more than me*
> *Reason: They play golf together*
> *Mind-reading? Maybe – he never said it out loud. Mr Samuel definitely loves money more than golf so if I make more money he'll like me more?*

- Research cognitive behavioural therapy (CBT) more thoroughly.

The next station is Royal Victoria. Please remember to take all your belongings with you.

I shove the leaflets in my bag, there is no need to tell Dan about it.

'Where did you sneak off to this morning?' Dan asks, looking up from his video game when I get in.

–

'I didn't sneak, you were being lazy and snoring.'

'So?'

'I went to the doctor's.'

'*Again?*'

'*Yes*. I wanted to see if he'd replied.'

'And?'

'He had,' I say and I can't help smiling as I walk into the kitchen in search of lunch. Dan follows me.

'Don't go quiet on me now, Princess. You kept me up all night with your pacing, the least you can do is tell me what happened.'

'Chill out, I was going to tell you,' I say, slumping down on the sofa with a packet of Quavers. (The fridge is still empty.)

'So?'

'Could you make me a cup of tea first?'

Dan just grunts and goes back to playing his game.

'All right,' I say. It was worth a try.

Dan presses pause and then turns to face me. The stubble on his chin is turning into a small beard I notice.

'He'd bought a *new* puzzle book and put it in the old jacket!'

'Tell me everything,' he says.

–

'Hmm, well it does sound like a guy,' he says, once I've filled him in. 'Probably gay though.'

'No,' I snap back.

'All the best ones are,' he says with a wink.

'Yes. Don't I know it,' I say and give him a dig in the ribs.

I sometimes wonder if Dan and I would have made a good couple. Then I remember if it wasn't guys I had to compete with it would be video games. I don't know what's worse.

'Do you really think he sounds gay?'

'The Dan gaydar never fails,' he says and resumes shooting aliens.

I'll have to ask Sofia what she thinks when I get to work on Monday. A shiver runs down my spine. I think about the torn-up pieces of birthday card, rotting in the kitchen bin. I'd almost forgotten what day it would be on Monday.

Eight

From: Sofia Jenkins
Sent: Mon 07:17
To: Cassidy Brookes; Martin Robertson
Subject: Sick

Hi Cassy, Martin,
I'm not feeling well and I don't think I can make it in today (food poisoning I think). Sally Lawson in the creative department will be covering for me if you two should need anything.
Hopefully see you tomorrow,
Sofia (Creative Designer)

My alarm clock buzzes and I bury my head in the pillow. It's Monday and today's the day. The very worst kind of day, when you know even before you open your eyes that it is going to be a really bad day.

For the past seven years I have done the exact same thing on this day. I've cooked a hot breakfast and brought it into the bedroom on a tray with a glass of orange juice and a croissant. Then I've sat at the end of the bed performing a foot massage while Seph opens a mountain of presents. But not this year. Today I just have to go to work as if it is any other normal day. I check my phone; no Sofia. Great. Could this day get any worse?

I find out the answer to my question an hour later as I'm walking across the seventh floor towards my office. The answer is yes.

'Oh, hi there!' squeaks someone I don't know. I turn around to see a young girl hurtling towards me. 'You must be Cassy. It is Cassy, isn't it?'

'Err ye—'

'Sofia said I'd recognise you,' the girl carries on, talking faster than the speed of light. 'She said you'd be the one in the most formal clothes and the first senior in the office.'

'Did she now?' I reply, trying not to look smug.

'Yes and I just knew it was you as soon as I saw your shoes.'

'Why? What's wrong with my shoes?'

'Do you know where Martin's office is?' she asks and ignores my question completely. 'I hear he's *really* cute,' she adds in a hushed voice.

'It's Sally, isn't it?' I ask, my patience already wearing thin.

'Oh yes, gosh, how silly of me not to even introduce myself.'

'Well, Sally, do you think you would be able to go over the design spec Sofia was working on for my 3 p.m. meeting?'

'I'll do it right away.'

I feel like I am in the aftermath of a talking hurricane when Sally finally gets the hell out of my office and wanders back to her own desk.

'Oh, Martin! Hi!' Sally's voice is higher than a chirping bird at 4 a.m. and somehow manages to bypass the glass windows of my office and penetrate my skull. Rubbing my palms on my forehead, my skin feels tight, I can feel a migraine forming already.

I witness her shamelessly waving to get Martin's attention. He has just casually strolled into the office. There is a solitary, fleeting look of surprise on his face and then he regains his perfect composure. I stand up and close the blinds, I don't think my stomach can handle such scenes this early in the morning. Back at my desk I pull out my to-do list. It looks like I'm going to have another long day in the office.

<u>To-do list</u>

- ~~Ask Sofia to~~ check design spec for today's meeting is done. *Do it myself*
- ~~Ask Sofia to~~ double-check client's RfP. *Do it myself*
- ~~Ask Sofia to~~ send out design ideas to new clients. *Do it myself*
- Call Sir Lockley's office (try begging this time).
- Go through latest results of MediaTech strategy.
- <u>*Prepare to pitch to partners for promotion.*</u>

'Good morning, Little Miss Bossy.' Martin's voice jolts me. I look up from my to-do list and glare at him as he invites himself to sit down in my office.

'I am not *bossy*.'

'Sally's words, not mine. Or maybe Sofia's?'

'Sofia does not think I am bossy!' I say and glare at him.

'Little Miss Grumpy then?'

I sigh loudly. 'What do you want, Martin?'

'I was just wondering if you fancied… me, no, ha, joke. I was just wondering if you fancied having a catch-up over coffee.'

'Is this your idea of a joke?'

'No. I think we need more of a team spirit.'

'Since when have you been a team player?' I ask, unable to keep a straight face.

'Look, I only wanted to build bridges but if you don't want to then—'

'No,' Oh God, what am I saying? 'Let's go.'

'Great. How about Starbucks?' A smile creeps on to Martin's face. I can feel my body temperature rising.

'You know, Martin, one day—'

My phone rings and saves me from saying something I might regret. I quickly recompose myself. 'Sorry, Martin, I'll have to take a rain check, but I'm sure there are plenty more people you need to build bridges with. See yourself out.'

I watch him go and then pick up the phone.

'Holywells, Cassidy Brookes, Account Director, speaking,' I say in my telephone voice.

'Hi, darling, how are you?'

'Mum? Everything OK?'

'Yes, darling, I was just calling for a quick chat.'

'Mum, I'm at work. Can we do this later please?'

'When exactly later, because you never answer your mobile and if by chance you do you say let's speak later. I'm beginning to worry this break-up is making you a recluse.'

'It's not.' I log on to my emails so that I can at least multitask for the rest of the call.

'So you're eating well?'

'Yes, Mum.'

'Lots of vegetables?'

'Yes, Mum.'

'Which ones?'

'Mum! I'm not doing this now. I'm at work and I need to go.'

'OK, Cassidy, but it wouldn't hurt for you to ring *me* every once in a while, or your grandmother for that matter.'

'Why? Is she OK?'

'Yes, just lonely. It wouldn't hurt you to stop by, you do work next door to her.'

'Mum, I really have to go. I'll speak to you later.'

Why do mothers know exactly how to make you feel terrible? She is right though, I should see Gran more. Mum and Gran have remained close since my dad died when I was little. We're the only family she has left. She doesn't actually live next door to my office but she is fairly close and I am her only grandchild excluding surrogate Dan. Right, that's it: I'm going to buy Gran a present in my lunch break. But first I need to figure out what to say to Sir Lockley's secretary.

'Lockley & Co., Sir Lockley's office, how may I help you?'

'Oh, hello, is that Lorella?'

'It is indeed, how may I help you?'

'My name is Cassidy Brookes? I work for Holywells? I sent you an email about arranging a meeting with Sir Lockley? About a new initiative we're launching?'

'I remember. Hello, Miss Brookes, what can I do for you today?'

'I was wondering if it would be possible to *squeeze* in a meeting in the next week or so. You see, Holywells is launching the project in early September and—'

'I'm afraid Sir Lockley has a very busy schedule so—'

'Does he keep a waiting list?'

'Miss Brookes, I have to be honest, in the fifteen years I've worked for Sir Lockley only one meeting has ever been cancelled and that was because the person he was meeting sadly died the day before.'

'I see,' I whisper.

'I'll let you know if anything becomes available,' she says, pity seeping down the phone line.

'Thank you, I—'

'You're welcome. Goodbye, Miss Brookes.'

–

The trouble with buying presents for Gran is, firstly, she hates presents and, secondly, she's impossible to buy for. Her house already looks like the interior of a Whittard store but crockery is my gran's one true love, so Whittard it is. I step onto the busy London street and pull my jacket tight around me, keeping my head down. Whittard isn't too far from the office, so I have plenty of time.

Whittard is one of those magical shops that makes you feel at home the moment you step inside. There's the friendly assistant offering you aromatic teas in small poly-styrene cups; an entire wall shelved with every different flavour of tea and coffee you can imagine; and a whole array of beautiful china mugs, plates and saucers. To top it off, there is *always* a sale. I run my hands over the table display of the latest tea and coffee accessories, then I see it. It's one of those teapots that fits snuggly on top of a matching tea cup, hand-painted, 1950s style, purple with white spots. Gran will love it. In fact, so do I. Two for £25, perfect.

Oops, I've already been gone forty minutes and I haven't even bought lunch yet, let alone eaten. I quickly pay and start to hurry back to the office, hoping that I make it before the few drops of rain turn into a downpour. I dodge through the slowly moving crowds, dart into the foyer and squeeze into the packed lift.

'Can you hold the lift, please?'

It's Mr Samuel; everyone in the lift is pretending they didn't hear him. *Don't they know how senior he is?* The doors are about to close. I elbow my way to the side of the lift and jam my finger on the 'open doors' button, to the dismay of the people around me.

'Ah, Cassidy, thank you,' Mr Samuel says as he does a little quick-step dance into the lift. 'Have you bought something nice?'

'Oh this? It's just a small gift for my gran.' My cheeks are burning but I have no idea why. I can't think of anything to say. God, this is the first thing you're taught in networking, always have a thirty-second elevator pitch ready.

Level Seven.

'Excuse me.'

Mr Samuel and I shuffle out of the lift into the seventh-floor corridor. *Come on, Cassy, think of something to say.*

'Mr Samuel, I'm glad I bumped into you. I have been meaning to ask whether you thought the partners and yourself would benefit from a more in-depth meeting on the project we're trialling for MediaTech. I know Martin took you through the basics but it would be great to demonstrate to you all the full potential of the programme.'

'I don't see why not. Why don't you set up a meeting?'

'Will do.'

Yes! I think I'd better pencil it in for first thing tomorrow. The last thing I need is Martin finding out about it and trying to bulldoze this meeting as well. If I nail this, I'll be right back on track for promotion. I'll have to put off going to see Gran. I need to get home and do some serious planning.

–

'Dan? Dan? Dan!'

'What? What's wrong?' Dan runs into my room.

'I can't decide what to wear. Blue suit dress or black shirt with cream blouse?'

'It's 4.30 a.m.'

'Hey, where are you going?'

'Back to bed.'

'But I need help.'

'Yes. On that front, Cassy, we most definitely agree.'

'So much for moving in to look after me,' I call out to him as he shuts my bedroom door behind him.

There are now more clothes on my bed than are left in my wardrobe and, although I seem to have clothes I don't remember buying, I can't find anything to wear. A few heavy sighs later, I give myself a mental slap. This isn't getting me anywhere. I need to make a decision. I think I will go for… the black suit with the silk green top that everyone says brings out the colour of my eyes. I have a nice pair of high, but not too high, Russell & Bromley shoes that will perfectly finish off the sophistic-ated businesswoman look. As long as no one cycles into me, everything will be fine.

–

'You're here early,' I say to Sofia, who is already busy tapping away on her keyboard when I arrive. She's still wearing her mauve coat. 'Feeling better?'

She grunts.

'You can't be having a bad day yet, it's only seven o'clock.'

'Martin rang me last night and told me he needed me in "super early, ill or not."'

'He did what? Sofia, he's not your boss.'

'It's fine. Besides, he actually looked pretty guilty this morning. He even made me a mug of herbal tea and gave me a packet of purple-coloured tissues, look.'

'That hardly justifies what he did. If you're not feeling well, you shouldn't be here.'

'No, I'm fine honestly. I was never really that sick, it was just a sniffle. I guess this is my punishment for pulling a sickie. Don't look at me like that, it's the only one I've ever taken. You'd have done the same thing in my situation. Don't fold your arms. It was Joey's birthday and I wanted to cook him breakfast in bed.'

A shiver takes hold of me.

'Anyway, I'd better get back to this. Martin wants these design slides ready for the meeting this morning.'

I gratefully start to walk away and then I digest what Sofia said. I turn.

'What meeting would that be?' I ask innocently.

'The one about the MediaTech project. You're on the invite list I'm sure.'

'I should bloody think so. It's my meeting!'

Sofia freezes. I don't think either of us have heard so much venom in my tone before.

'Maybe it's a different meeting?'

I don't even bother answering her. OK, I need to calm down, there is no need to panic. I can turn this to my advantage.

'Send me the slide pack once you're done so I can add a few things.'

'Sure. I just finished so I will ping it over now.'

'Oh, and if Martin asks for them, direct him to me.'

—

The slides are quite good, Martin has obviously been doing his homework, but they're not perfect. I add in a few slides from my original presentation which never got used and get them printed.

'Everything's going to be fine,' I say out loud to myself, to try to make it seem more believable.

I pick up my new teapot and head for the kitchen. The meeting is in thirty minutes so I have time to make a tea and have one final run-through of what I'm going to say. Once back at my desk, I start to flick through the slides when I hear a certain – unwelcome – someone approaching my office.

'I see you've made some suggestions to my slide pack,' Martin says in his usual condescending voice without a trace of anxiety or irritation. I wish I could do that. He's leaning on the door frame of my office as if he owns the place. 'Good to have you on board.'

'Good to have *you* on—'

Before I can finish he's walking away. I go to run after him but I clip the edge of the desk. I see the teapot falling in slow motion. I bend down to save it. I almost catch it but it slips through my hands. Tea sprays all over me.

Oh my God. The meeting is in ten minutes and my shirt looks like a five-year-old has shot me with a water pistol.

'Hey, I saw these by the printer so I thought I'd bring them ov— Oh my God, Cassy, what happened?' Sofia asks, holding the printed presentations in her arms.

'Martin happened,' I groan and wipe myself down. 'Please can you get those presentations to the boardroom? I'm going to have to change.'

Thankfully my organisational OCD is occasionally useful. I always keep a spare shirt in the office. Whichever one it is it will just have to do. I pull my jacket on and cover up as much of my shirt as possible. I rush over to the cupboard in the corridor and sift through the coats until I find my shirt. Amazingly it's green – the gods are finally on my side. I dash to the loos, hastily put it on and run to the boardroom.

Martin is already there, putting a copy of the present-ation on each seat. I curse Sofia but I know it's not really her fault, Martin has a knack for getting his own way.

'Listen, Martin,' I say in my don't-mess-with-me voice. 'This is my pitch and I'm going to take the lead all right?'

He looks up at me with an expression I can't read. Maybe it's the firm voice he likes? Whatever it is, he seems to be wrong-footed.

'I think you might want to do—'

'Not another word, Martin. This is my meeting and I'm going to do it my way, OK?'

Martin pretends to zip his mouth shut and then gives me a smile that I don't quite know how to interpret. To be honest I really don't care what mind games he's trying to play with me. I'm doing the pitch and that's all that matters. Oh God, here they all come. OK Cassy, take a deep breath and 'own-the-room'.

'Good morning, I think most of you know me, I'm Cassidy Brookes.'

I think everyone must love my outfit, they seem to do a double take when they see me. I guess I do look better when I actually make an effort with my hair and make-up. I should probably do it every day, especially with the promotion decision being on everyone's mind.

'The purpose of today's meeting is to go through the finer details of the marketing strategy for MediaTech's latest new platform venture. You'll see you have a slide pack in front of you that I will be referring to throughout the meeting.'

I can't believe how professional I sound. I have run a lot of meetings over the years, of course, but this is by far the most important. The partners look very pleased with the slide pack. They can't take their eyes off it!

–

'So that concludes the presentation. Are there any questions?'

None. I was half expecting Martin to try and show me up but he seems to have given me a break for once.

Usually I would say no questions at the end of a meeting means you've bored people silly and they just want to get the hell out of there, but this time I think they genuinely already have all the information they need. I was very thorough and clear (even if I do say so myself).

Plus they are all very senior and have to rush off quite quickly at the end to get to other meetings. It's a shame there wasn't any time for networking with them but I will send them a follow-up email when I get back to my desk. I'll show Martin I can play the game just as well as he can.

The guys on the floor all look up as I walk back to my office. Word must have already spread that I did an awesome pitch. Sofia comes running into my office, her heels clicking away.

'Cassy,' she whispers and closes my office door.

'Your shirt.'

'Nice colour, isn't it?' It's amazing how many people comment on my shirt if I wear green.

'Very but—'

'I only wore it because I spilt tea down the other one,' I say, laughing.

'I think you put it on a bit too quick.'

'What do you – ?'

'It's undone!'

Oh. My. God. No wonder the guys were staring at me! The top three buttons are open, revealing my red push-up bra. How long has it been like this?

'Did you tell her?' Martin has a huge grin on his face as he pops his head around my office door.

'How long?' I ask and turn my body away from him to re-button my shirt frantically.

He shrugs. 'Since you came into the meeting room.'

Noooooooooooooooo. The whole meeting? My knees feel weak. I sit down and let my head bang down hard on the wooden desk.

Wait.

'Are you telling me you knew *before* anyone else was in the meeting room and you didn't tell me?' I ask, getting to my feet.

'You wanted to do it *your* way, remember? "*Not another word, Martin*",' he says, imitating my voice.

'You complete and utter fu—'

'Cassy!' Sofia says.

'You might want to do your shirt up *properly* before you insult me,' Martin says and with a victorious smile walks off.

Oh bloody hell, it's come undone again! What a stupid, *stupid* top. I button it again and look at Sofia, tears in my eyes.

'Please tell me it's somehow not true?'

Sofia doesn't reply but her face says it all. 'Do you want to get lunch with me today?' she asks, gently.

'I can't face it,' I say, holding my head in my hands.

'It's not *that* bad,' she says.

'It is and you know it.'

Sofia doesn't say anything.

'Oh, distract me, please? Tell me about your wedding plans.'

'Oh, I don't know,' Sofia says, shifting her weight from one foot to the other.

'It's OK. I'm not going to break just because your relationship is great and I'm single.'

'I don't know about great,' she says and sits down opposite me.

'Why? What's happened?'

'It's just – Oh, don't worry about it, you've got enough on your mind.'

'No, tell me, I might be able to help.'

'Well, since we got engaged, it's like he's thought I am suddenly going to become a twentieth-century house-wife.'

I laugh.

'No really, he even said his mum's breakfast was better than mine the other day, after making me cook to a special recipe.'

'Well—'

'And… he gets snappy if I try to talk to him when the TV is on.'

'Oh,' I laugh. 'I think that's just a guy thing. Seph was the same.' I feel like the anchor of the *Titanic* just lodged itself inside my throat. Maybe I'm not ready to have girly conversations about boys yet.

'Anyway, I'd better get back to work,' Sofia says. 'Thanks for listening.'

'Anytime,' I stutter.

I push the thought of Seph out of my mind but all that replaces him are images of my unbuttoned green shirt. I replay the meeting over and over again in my head. Maybe I had my back to them most of the time? Maybe it wouldn't have been so noticeable when I was sitting down?

It's no use. I can't kid myself about it. I've massively screwed up. Who will take me seriously now? No wonder none of them stuck around to ask me any questions. They must have been too embarrassed. I should have known something was wrong when Martin was happy for me to take the lead in the meeting. He wanted me to mess up.

I force myself to send a follow-up email to the partners, although I make sure to draft it a few times so I can erase all the Martin-hating venting. I'm tempted to apologise about the shirt thing but I know it will only make matters worse. All I can do is a little damage control.

As for Martin, this means war.

Subject: MediaTech Project

Dear All,

It was a pleasure to see you all this morning and discuss the MediaTech project in more detail.

I would like to apologise for my wardrobe malfunction. Martin spilt tea on me and I had to change my shirt so that he didn't take all the credit for my work again.

If you have any further questions please do not hesitate to contact me.

Kind regards,

Cassidy Brookes (Account Director)

–

Drafts

Subject: MediaTech Project

Dear All,

It was a pleasure to see you all this morning and discuss the MediaTech project in more detail. If you have any further questions please do not hesitate to contact me (as the MediaTech project is wholly my idea and Martin is trying to take the credit to steal my promotion).

Kind regards,

Cassidy Brookes (Account Director)

–

From: Cassidy Brookes
Sent: Tues 13:01

To: +Digital_Partners; Martin Robertson
Subject: MediaTech Project

Dear All,

It was a pleasure to see you all this morning and discuss the MediaTech project in more detail.

If you have any further questions please do not hesitate to contact me.

Kind regards,

Cassidy Brookes (Account Director)

I finally pluck up the courage to leave my office mid-afternoon and go to my favourite place in the whole world: the stationery room. It doesn't matter how bad my day is, the stationery room always makes me smile. It's like my own personal Ryman. There are highlighters and pens galore. But today I want paper. I find a ring-bound A5 lined notebook that will do nicely. I also take a few white labels and a lovely new red fountain pen.

I don't even bother going back to my office. I sit in the corner of the stationery room and get to work. I stick a white label on the front and write in big red capital letters, 'MARTIN ACTION PLAN'. This little note-book is going to be used for the sole purpose of ruining Martin's career. I am going to be more fiendish, more devious and more ruthless than any other businessman that has ever made it to the top. Martin is going down.

Phase One: Embarrassment

- Get Dan to pretend to be a new client for Martin.

- Get Dan to make a complaint about Martin.

Nine

I genuinely don't know how I got here. I know I left around 6.30 p.m. to visit Gran on my way home and I remember walking down Cheapside towards Bank station. I was feeling all fired up and happy, congratulating myself on my new plan of attack on Martin, as I made my way down the bustling streets. I definitely remember reaching Bank station but then… Oh God, I really don't remember. My feet must have started working on automatic pilot and turned left at Bank rather than right. Now instead of walking down Cornhill towards my gran's house I'm standing inside, hovering by the reception desk.

'Good afternoon, can I help you?'

Yes. I think I do need help. I don't know what possessed me, I hadn't even been thinking about coming here, what with everything at work being so hectic.

'It's Miss Brookes, isn't it?'

Oh God, I can't turn and walk out now. I'll have to say something.

'Yes.'

Obviously I know I have to say more than just yes, but what? I haven't thought up a good excuse to come back to the doctor's yet. I can feel Janet's eyes staring at me, burning into my skull, probing for the reason, she's waiting to pounce.

'Sorry to trouble you,' I say and smile to buy myself a few more seconds.

Come on, Cassy, think!

'I seem to have misplaced the prescription I got from Dr Danes last week,' I say.

My eye twitches as I look at her, waiting to see if she believes me or thinks I'm a drug addict (or possibly a drug dealer).

'I see,' she says after what feels like ten minutes of examining my every facial flaw. 'Dr Danes is working the evening shift so she may be able to write you a new prescription today.'

Result!

'That would be great, thank you. I'll just wait over there, shall I?' I ask and take a couple of steps towards the waiting area and more importantly the unoccupied, weathered, green armchair.

'No, there's no need. I can do it while you're standing here.'

Damn. Why is there never a queue of patients when you don't mind waiting but always a queue when you're in a hurry?

Janet taps away on her computer screen. I lock my hands together in front of me to hide the fact they are shaking slightly but there's nothing I can do to make my eyelid stop fidgeting. I need to calm down, there's no need to feel nervous; a lost prescription is a legitimate reason to come back to the doctor's. It is really possible I could have misplaced my prescription (as opposed to what I actually did, which was forget all about it).

'Miss Brookes, would you kindly confirm your current address for me, please?'

'Sure,' I say and clear my throat. 'It's flat 5, Austen Court, London, E16.'

'Ah, OK,' Janet says and takes her hands away from the keyboard. 'I thought it was worth checking that we had the right address on file. Unfortunately, Miss Brookes, your address is out of our catchment area for general practitioner services.'

Busted. I thought Janet should have objected last time.

'You will need to register with a local doctor's surgery,' Janet continues.

'But you've treated me before,' I say innocently.

'We treated you for your foot injury because it was an emergency, in line with our policy. You have access to the walk-in clinics run by our nurses but I'm afraid you will need to register with your local doctor's surgery for GP services.'

Suddenly I can hear one of Dan's video games in my head saying, 'game over'.

'Here is a list of surgeries in London. It may be useful.'

'Thanks,' I say and take the leaflet from her. I shouldn't feel so down over this. So some weirdo replied to a few comments in a puzzle book, it's no big deal. I mean, what were the chances it would turn out to be the man of my dreams, my one true love, and losing contact with him now will mean we will never meet and I will end up being a depressed, wrinkly, old spinster?

Oh God. I *need* to find a way.

'There should be a couple in the E16 area on there,' she says and gives me a smile that says, 'you can leave now'.

Think fast, Cassy!

'Hang on, did I give you my E16 address?'

'Yes, that's right.'

'Oh, how stupid of me. That isn't actually my address.'

'Oh?'

Oh indeed. What the hell am I going to say? Think, think, *think*.

'No. You see… I used to live there… until very recently in fact, which is why you had it on file and why I said it just now. I'm still on autopilot, you see.'

'I see,' Janet says, like she's an inspector questioning a murder suspect. 'So where do you live?'

'I live around the corner.' Janet raises her eyebrow. 'With my grandmother.'

Janet continues to stare at me. Come on, Cassy, you can lie better than this.

'She's quite old and I've moved in so she doesn't have to be alone,' I say. Both my eyes are twitching now.

'Well, that's very kind of you. What's the address?'

'It's Rosemary House on Leadenhall Street, just around the corner from Leadenhall Market, EC3V.'

At least that isn't a lie. Gran really does live there and it's where I should be right now!

'And the phone number?'

'We are in the process of getting a new line.' I reply so quickly, I barely have time to register the question properly.

'Miss Brookes,' Janet says with a sigh and takes off her glasses. My palms are sweating.

'It's true,' I plead. 'I need to get the internet installed now I'm moving in so we need a new phone line.'

Where are these lies coming from?

'Well, for our records could we have the *old* number and then we can update your details when necessary.'

Crap. She's not falling for this. I'm not a fan of lying but if I give her Gran's number she's bound to ring and

131

check up on me. It's going to require a more devious mind than mine to help me out of this one.

'You can have her mobile.'

'That will be fine,' Janet says and smiles in a way that I know means she is going to check up on me because she doesn't believe a single word I'm saying.

I give her Dan's number; Gran doesn't even have a mobile. As she is typing in the digits, I inconspicuously pull out my phone from my handbag and lower my hand so she can't see my fingers frantically texting.

> **To: Dan Mobile Weds 18:23**
> Walk-in centre is on2 me. If they ring
> pretend to be my gran and say I live with u.
> Will explain lata. Cxx

'OK, Miss Brookes, I have updated your records. As for your prescription, I just need to see ID and have a quick chat with Dr Danes to see if she can write you a new one.'

'Sure,' I say and sift through my bag for my purse. The sifting turns into rummaging as panic begins to set in. I can't find it, please don't tell me I've left it in the office, or worse that it's been stolen! I furiously start shovelling things around in my bag, crumpled up bits of paper falling to the floor. God, I really need to shred all these stupid receipts and old lists.

'What is that?' Janet asks.

I follow her gaze; I feel sick. 'Oh my goodness,' I say in the best surprised voice I can find. 'Would you believe it, it's my prescription. It must have been in my bag the whole time.'

Janet opens her mouth but I'm already making for the door.

'Sorry to have wasted your time. Thanks for your help.'

I hurriedly close the door behind me before Janet can say anything else. I breathe a huge sigh of relief. That was way too close. I hope Dan reads my text before Janet rings him. I'll have to see Gran tomorrow, I need to get back to my real home and make sure Dan doesn't blow my cover.

–

Back at the flat, the lift still hasn't been fixed so I run up the stairs, taking them two at a time. I'm so out of breath when I reach the front door that I struggle to pull my keys out of my bag and after a good few seconds fumbling to get my key in the lock I pretty much fall into the flat.

'Dan? Are you in?' I call out, each word separated with a pant and deep intake of breath.

There's no reply but I can hear a plastic-sounding tapping which is only made by the fingers of a video-game addict on the controller. I slip my shoes off and lean on the wall for support. These shoes are far more beautiful than they are comfortable.

'So, you are in,' I say as I let my body drop onto the leather sofa and wipe away a bead of sweat from my forehead. I really need to start going to the gym.

Dan doesn't seem to notice any of this, his eyes are glued to the TV and the latest alien-killing spree. I can't bring myself to say anything more, my heart is thumping against the inside of my chest and my limbs feel weak.

Every now and then Dan takes a large bite out of a slice of Hawaiian pizza that smells delicious.

'Courtesy of Cassy's credit card again?' I ask eventually and make a slight nod at the pizza as I slowly pull off my jacket.

'Payment for playing your grandmother.'

'So Janet did call you?' I say, feeling alert again. 'I knew she would. Some people have got serious trust issues.'

'But you were lying,' he says, without taking his eyes off the screen.

'Yeah, but she didn't know that, did she? So did she believe you?'

'*Of course my pet*,' Dan says in a voice that does sound remarkably like my gran.

Awesome. Problem averted. For now at least.

I relax back onto the sofa and close my eyes, desperately trying to block out the annoying video game sound that is 'exploding alien'. I suddenly realise how alien my own life feels: running up staircases to make sure a receptionist thinks I live with my gran. It's crazy. Maybe if I sit here long enough things will fall back into place or, even better, transform into a life where Martin doesn't exist and I'm married to a successful doctor.

Congratulations, you've reached the bonus level.

'So when exactly are you planning on moving out?' Dan's voice slaps me back into reality.

'What are you talking about?'

'Aren't you going to live with your gran?'

'Very funny.'

'So… are you going to tell me then?'

'Tell you what?'

'About the mysterious Puzzle-man. What had he got to say for himself this time?'

'I didn't get a chance to look,' I say gloomily.

Dan falls about laughing like it's the best joke he's heard since he watched *Mock The Week*.

'It really isn't funny and, if you're going to be like this, I'm going to bed.'

'OK, OK,' he says and clears his throat, 'changing the subject, how did the meeting go?'

'Like a tsunami. I don't even want to talk about it.'

'Martin again?'

'How did you guess. Which reminds me, I need your help. Have you got plans this week?'

Ten

Dan's message beeps on to my phone as I sit hugging my morning coffee and staring blankly at the office floor. The department is quiet today. All the partners are in the weekly agenda meeting as I expected. I glance at my phone again. I'm not going to have any fingernails left at this rate. Dan will be getting his security pass from reception. I feel a bit sick. It's not like it's a big deal, though. Dan is just going to make Martin look bad in front of the graduates, they'll have a laugh and that will be that. It's just an April fool's joke... in August... before promotions...

It's. Not. A. Big. Deal.

Although I would feel a lot more comfortable if I'd been able to get Dan to tell me exactly what he was planning.

–

We laid the groundwork yesterday. It went like clockwork:

Sofia had sat down and logged on to her computer at 8 a.m. as usual. I'd practised what I was going to say over and over again. I was ready.

'Morning, Sofia, how are you?'

'Hey, I'm good. Glad it's Friday tomorrow.'

'Yeah, me too. I'm really looking forward to the bank holiday weekend.'

'What's wrong, you look down?'

'Oh, it's nothing. It's just I had a call about a new client yesterday who wants to come in asap, but I've got so much to do for the MediaTech project, I really don't think I've got time to fit him in this afternoon.'

'You could always ask Martin to do it,' Sofia said, sarcastically.

'Actually that's not a bad idea. Do you think he would?'

'Are you kidding? He's told me to make scouting out new clients for him my top priority!'

I bit my tongue at that point and forced myself to remain focused. That is *not* part of Sofia's job description.

'Great. Would you mind asking him if he could do it for me? He might think I'm taking the piss if I ask.'

'OK. Do you have the client's details?'

'Oh, they're all on here,' I said and handed her over a post-it note I'd written earlier. I felt a twinge of guilt for keeping Sofia out of the loop, but Dan had convinced me that no one else could know. I sent a text to Dan the second I sat down at my desk.

> **To: Dan Mobile Thu 08:17**
> Step 1 – completed!

Two hours later (and after checking my phone so many times I'd had to put it on charge) the next part of the plan had fallen into place.

I tried to concentrate but I ended up spending most of the morning staring at the digital clock in the bottom corner of my computer screen. Eventually I heard him – well, I heard the middle-class, slightly snobbish suburban accent that Dan and I had decided would be convincing.

'I'm here to see Mr Robertson?' he said, looking very sharp in a suit. (I didn't even know he owned a suit.)

'Ah, Mr Douglas? Nice to meet you,' Martin said, appearing from his office and shaking Dan's hand. 'Please, come through.'

Martin gestured for Dan to follow him into his office.

Dan gave me a quick wink before disappearing.

Step 3 is a go, I thought, unable to keep a huge smile from my face.

It was in the last fifteen minutes of their meeting that doubts started to creep in. I'd paced around my office and gone through all the possible outcomes. What if Dan forgot his accent or accidentally let it slip that he knew me? What if Martin realised it was a set-up? I was close to hyperventilating when I spotted them coming out of Martin's office.

'Have a safe journey home,' Martin said as he walked Dan to the lift. Martin saw me looking at him and took it as an invitation to come over.

'Interesting guy,' he said.

'Who?' I asked, nonchalantly.

'The guy you set me up with.'

For one second we looked each other in the eye and I thought he'd figured it all out, but he hadn't.

'It wasn't a blind date! Do you think he'll do business with the firm?'

'Too early to tell. He seemed a bit dim.'

I had to dig my nails into my hand to stop myself from reacting to that – Dan is not dim!

'So how did you come across him?' Martin asked.

'Friend of a friend asked me to do him a favour.'

'So you got me to do the favour instead?'

'I thought you'd relish the chance to get an extra client.'

'Quite right, I was just…' Martin looked up to the ceiling as if searching for the right words, 'surprised by your kindness,' he decided upon. 'I guess I should say… thank you.'

'You're welcome,' I replied and swallowed hard as a churning feeling rotated in my stomach.

–

I have the same churning feeling now as I re-read Dan's message.

> **From: Dan Mobile Fri 09:03**
> I'm here. Time for some serious ACTION!!!

What does he mean, *serious action*? It's only supposed to be a prank… Maybe I should call it off. I mean, this whole thing was planned while I was pissed off with Martin over the shirt incident, which I guess wasn't entirely his fault. It's really not like me to be so vengeful. I'm honest and hardworking and earn my respect.

Oh God, I think this is a mistake.

'I want to speak to the manager this instant!'

Oh God, Dan's here and quite clearly he didn't get my text in time. Everyone has stopped working and they're all staring at him. Luckily the blinds are pulled in my office and I can peer secretly through the slats to see what's going on.

'Mr Douglas? I didn't expect to see you back here so soon. How can I help you?' Martin says and smiles at him.

'You can't. I want to see your manager.'

Martin raises an eyebrow and shoots a look in my direction.

'Is there a problem? I'm afraid my manager isn't available. But if you'd like to step into my office we can discuss any issues.'

'Who is your manager?'

'Mr Samuel, but I am afraid he's in a meeting. Can I help?'

Dan shoots a look in my direction. Oh God, he obviously thought Martin was going to say his manager was me!

'My problem is you,' Dan says, his voice a little higher pitched than normal. Oh my God, I think he is improvising.

'Oh?'

'You were totally unprofessional yesterday and I want to make a formal complaint.'

Oh my God. He's just said that in front of everyone, including the partner's secretaries.

'I'm sorry you feel that way, but I can assure you—'

140

'It's because I'm gay, isn't it?'

Bloody hell, this is out of control. I need to do something.

'What is going on here?' Mr Samuel arrives at the scene, closely followed by his secretary – she must have pulled him out of the meeting. This was not supposed to happen. I never meant for the partners to find out.

'Mr Douglas wants to make a formal complaint against Mr Robertson for being unprofessional and homophobic,' Sofia says from behind her desk, her cheeks flushed.

Martin, for the first time ever, looks speechless.

'Martin?' Mr Samuel says to him, looking a little speechless himself.

'It's a misunderstanding, Tom.'

'Why don't the three of us discuss this in your office?' Mr Samuel suggests.

'Actually I think it would be better to discuss it in Cassy's office,' Martin says.

My whole body has gone cold.

Mr Samuel, lost for words, walks determinedly over to my office followed by Martin and Dan, who is beginning to look rather sheepish.

'Well, Martin,' Mr Samuel says and closes my office door, 'could you talk us through what happened here?'

'Perhaps Cassy would like to,' Martin says.

I think I'm going to pass out. I'm standing up but I can't feel my legs. I look from Martin to Dan to Mr Samuel.

'Well,' I say and swallow hard, 'Daniel is a… friend… of a friend… I asked Martin to have a meeting… with him… yesterday, because—'

'What Cassy is *trying* to say, is that this whole situation is a set-up.'

Oh my God, he's going to rat me out. This is going to be the end of my career.

'I noticed,' Martin continues, 'that most of the graduates commented in their mid-year appraisals that they don't know how to interact with clients effectively so I've been working on a few ways to tackle this. One idea was a role-play. I thought that it would be good for Cassy and myself to demonstrate to the graduates how to handle difficult situations that may arise with clients.'

What?

'I asked Cassy if she knew any actors who would be willing to work with us to run us through a few role-plays.'

Dan's gesticulating at me to close my mouth which is hanging open in shock. How on earth has Martin come up with that on the spot?

'I wanted it to be authentic,' Martin continues, 'so I asked Cassy not to tell me who the actor would be or when they would be used. We scheduled it for a Friday so that there would be minimal disruption. Sorry, Tom, I thought Cassy would have warned you.'

Mr Samuel gives me a stern look of disappointment.

'I am so sorry, Mr Samuel. It got a little out of hand.'

'Yes well, I'm all for you using initiative, but please keep me informed in the future.'

I'm struggling to think of something to say when Sofia knocks on the door.

'Sorry to disturb you all. Cassy, your grandmother has been trying to get through to you. She's on line one and she sounds very distraught.'

'You'd better take that, Cassy. I'll see Daniel out,' Martin says and smiles, victory his again. I watch the three of them leave my office. I don't know whether to be happy or devastated. How has he managed to turn a discrimination complaint into an accredited initiative scheme? At least Martin didn't rat me out, although he still made me look stupid and he came out looking brilliant. But, on balance, I guess I deserved it.

'Hello? Gran?'

'Cassy, is that you?' Gran sounds so scared my heart skips a beat as I imagine the worst.

'Yes it's me, Gran. What's wrong? Are you OK?'

'Yes, pet, but the doctor rang. She was ever so worried about you.'

'About me?' My heart is thumping so fiercely in my chest that I'm concerned for my rib cage. 'It's OK, Gran. Don't worry. I'll come around and explain everything.'

Janet must have looked up Gran's number in the phone book. I eventually hang up the phone after assuring Gran that I am well enough to come around and visit her. I pick up my jacket and the Whittard bag with Gran's teapot and shut my office door behind me.

'Hey, Sofia, I've got to go and see my gran quickly. She's only around the corner so I shouldn't be too long. Do you mind covering for me?'

'No problem. I hope she's OK?'

'Thanks.'

'Cassy, wait. What happened in there?'

'Oh, it was just… a misunderstanding.'

Sofia looks less than satisfied with that answer but no doubt Martin will fill everyone in on his latest award-winning graduate development scheme. I'm still running over Martin's ingenious lying capabilities when I reach the foyer and see Dan waiting for me.

'Hey, got a bit out of control up there, eh?'

'One way of putting it,' I say as we head through the revolving doors. 'One thing I don't understand is how Martin knew you didn't really want to put in a discrimination complaint?'

'I think I can answer that one. He gave me this on my way out.'

Dan hands over a Hugo Boss carrier bag. I can feel that there is some sort of picture frame inside and as I pull it out my heart sinks a little. It's a photo of Dan and me kissing under the mistletoe at last year's New Year's Eve party. Seph had wanted to go out with his mates so Dan had been my plus one. Martin must have known all along that I was setting him up.

'See you at home,' Dan says, sounding very sorry for me.

'Yeah, see you later.'

'Is your gran OK by the way?'

'Yeah, just Janet the busybody from the walk-in centre checking up on me.'

'Ah, thought it might be,' he says and laughs.

'What?'

'Nothing. It's just, I always thought I was the devious one, but you've got more lies and schemes going on at the moment than I ever have.'

Dan waves and walks to the station leaving me standing on the street outside Holywells contemplating what he said. I have gone a little nuts lately, but this promotion stuff is just so stressful. The digital strategy conference is in ten days and I'm still no closer to securing the promotion or getting any major new clients. I guess I really am crap at 'playing the game'. I should just stick to the good old-fashioned, 'credit where credit's due' theory. As for my antics at the Threadneedle NHS Walk-in Centre, that's a little nuts, but that's a matter of the heart. Everyone is allowed to be a little crazy in their search for true love, right?

–

I only have to press the bell once before Gran lets me in. Usually I have to wait outside for a good ten minutes, even after a painful conversation on the phone trying to explain to her I'm using a mobile and currently standing right outside her house.

'Oh, Cassy, pet, thank goodness. The doctor said some horrible things. Horrible,' Gran says. She sounds breathless and guilt vibrates through me. I never meant to get her involved in all this nonsense.

'I'm sure she didn't mean to frighten you,' I say as we both sit down in the living room. It's spotless as usual. I don't think Gran has gone a day in her life without doing some kind of cleaning. She was a maid at one of London's top hotels for over fifty years and even now she still manages to keep her home immaculate.

'She said that you needed to come and live here with me,' Gran continues, 'because you need to go to the doctor's but you live too far away to get to the doctor's, but I told her you're not sick!'

I don't think that is quite what Janet said, but poor Gran looks so worried and it's all my fault.

'I think the doctor must have been confused, Gran.'

'You would tell me if something was wrong, wouldn't you?'

'Of course, but I'm fine, Gran, honestly.'

'Because you can stay in the spare room.'

'I'm OK, Gran, really, don't worry. Why don't I make us both a nice cup of tea?'

'That would be lovely. I better call your mum again.'

'Oh?'

'Yes, I left her one of those machine calls earlier.'

My heart sinks. I don't think Mum is going to fall for the doctor-must-have-been-confused argument. I'm thinking about how I'm going to explain myself to Mum as I boil the kettle. Hot steam starts spreading condensation over the small kitchen window and over the sound of the bubbling water I can hear Gran leaving a new message on Mum's answerphone.

'Everything is all right now. Cassy is not sick and she has insisted that she is fine to stay in her own flat.'

I use the new teapot for Gran and almost have as much choice of china for my cup as I would have if I were standing in a Whittard store.

'What's that, pet?' Gran asks as soon as I walk into the room with the tray of tea and biscuits.

'I bought it for you. It's one of those new all-in-one teapots. Do you like it?'

'Oh it's lovely, pet. Thank you.'

'The cup fits under—'

'Shh, shh, dear. *Catchphrase* is about to start.'

I smile to myself, it appears Gran is satisfied that there is nothing wrong with me.

'Well I'd better be getting back to work,' I say a little reluctantly when the credits for *Catchphrase* roll down the screen. I really don't spend enough time with Gran.

'OK, pet,' she says, before letting out a gigantic sneeze.

'You're not getting sick are you, Gran?'

'Oh no, pet, it's just a little dust. Although, I haven't been to get my flu jab yet.'

Flu jab. Why does that mean something to me? Of course! The walk-in centre had a poster up for over-65s to come in and see the nurse on weekday mornings to get a flu jab ahead of winter! I'm already reaching for my phone and dialling Sofia's number.

'Holywells, how may I help you?'

'Hi, it's Cassy.'

'Hey, how's your gran?'

'Not great, I'm going to take her to the doctor's and I probably won't bother coming back to the office by the time that's done. I'll just work from home.'

'OK,' Sofia says. 'And don't worry, I'll look after your calls. It's been totally dead while you've been out the office anyway. Hope it goes all right and see you on Tuesday.'

I do feel a tad guilty as I hang up the phone, I've lost count of how many white lies I've told today but I couldn't tell her it was just to get a flu jab, could I? I don't think anyone would approve of using your gran to write in a puzzle book to a mystery man, not even Sofia.

—

This was such a good idea, I think as Gran and I walk arm-in-arm to the Threadneedle Walk-in Centre. Not only do I get to avoid Martin until after the bank holiday, I can convince Janet I live with my gran and I will be able to check the puzzle book while I'm there! Obviously getting Gran the flu jab is the most important part, but it does seem to be working out well for me too.

Gran is quite a good walker for her age. She's used to the crowded London streets but I am glad I can act as a bodyguard against tourists who aren't looking where they're going. Is there anything more annoying than a tourist stepping out right in front of you to take a picture of a pigeon? I'm still trying to think of something more irritating when we reach the walk-in centre twenty minutes later.

The only tricky part of the plan is making sure Gran doesn't give the game away when we see Janet…

'Good afternoon, how may I hel – Miss Brookes, how are you?'

'Hello, Janet, I've brought my gran for the flu jab.'

Janet's eyes widen as she studies the elderly lady behind me. I can see her mouth salivate as she ponders all the questions she can ask my gran to try to catch me out.

'Was that another person for the flu jab?' says an unmistakeable, light, high voice from around the corner. Sure enough the young nurse I met when I twisted my ankle comes bouncing into view. She's wearing four-inch heels and has Barbie-pink nail varnish. In fact, she reminds me of Elle Woods, the bubbly sorority girl played by Reese Witherspoon in *Legally Blonde*. And before you think it, I'm not being stereotypical about blondes or nurses, for the record, Elle Woods aces a law degree at Harvard.

'I'm Nurse Clarkson, but you can call me Lucy,' the Elle Woods look-a-like is saying, more to my gran than to me.

'I'll just wait out here,' I say.

Lucy nods and then disappears around the corner again with my gran. I can't help a little smile creeping on to my face as I see the look of disappointment mixed with annoyance on Janet's face. I go over to the old armchair.

Crap. A woman with a huge twin buggy has beaten me to it. I sit down a couple of seats away.

'Excuse me, do you mind if I get a magazine?'

'Sure,' she says and awkwardly wheels the buggy out of the way.

I fumble through the magazines, trying to look casual. My heart skips a beat every time it's not the puzzle book, fearing that it will be gone. But it's still here. I do my best not to look ecstatic. One of the babies cries and steals the mother's attention and I quickly swipe out the puzzle book. I settle down in my less than comfortable plastic chair and search for a message from Puzzle-man. I can't wait to see what he has written this time.

The bottom right-hand corner of one of the pages is folded over. It's the cryptic crossword page and he has left me another message. It says:

> *Check this "answer" out when you need to relax, you'll love it!*

I look down at the puzzle more carefully. He has shaded in several of the squares in the answer grid. They must spell out the name of the place he wants me to visit!

Bloody hell, he must have done the whole puzzle in his head to work this out.

'Mrs Truby?' Dr Danes calls.

I smile at the lady with the buggy as she makes her way over to the consulting room, the twins are very cute. As soon as she is gone I dive into the green armchair, so that I am out of Janet's sight. I haven't got time to do the whole puzzle now so I take a few pictures of it on my phone. I can feel myself getting excited. Just then I hear the distant voice of Nurse Clarkson, aka Lucy, becoming not so distant.

'It was lovely to meet you, Mrs Brookes,' she says, holding my gran's hands in hers as they reach reception. 'You take care now,' she says and waves goodbye.

I can see Janet putting down the phone and getting ready to pounce. I quickly hide the puzzle book back in the pile of magazines.

'You're very lucky to have such a lovely granddaughter,' Janet says to Gran.

'Indeed I—'

'Well, we'd better be off,' I cut in and shimmy Gran towards the door.

—

I solved the clues within an hour of getting home – much to Dan's annoyance, as I jumped up and down every time I worked out a new letter. Together the letters spelled, 'ST PAULS TEA CAFE'. I'm starting to think Puzzle-man must be my soulmate. Is there anything more amazing than suggesting going to a tea café to relax, through a cryptic puzzle? I looked it up on Google straight away. Tea is at 1 Paternoster Square. That's near St Paul's Cathedral, about a fifteen-minute walk from my work. I can't believe I haven't heard of it. I'm going to go tomorrow. It's going to be the best bank holiday weekend ever!

Eleven

What an ungrateful arse, I think as I walk along Cheapside. I keep my head down and walk even faster than usual, muttering and cursing Dan under my breath. I had been thinking of seeing whether he wanted to come to Tea with me, but I didn't even finish saying 'good morning' before he jumped down my throat. This was not the start to the bank holiday weekend I had imagined.

All I had done was try to be helpful. I'd had a nice lie-in until midday and I thought I would go downstairs and check my post. I'd seen Dan's keys lying on the kitchen table and I thought while I was checking my post, I'd check his, too. To be helpful!

'You had no right to go snooping through my stuff,' was the only thank-you I got. Dan snatched the post out of my hands the moment I called out to tell him that I had collected his post for him.

'I wasn't going to read it. I was trying to do you a favour. The amount of post you have it looks like you haven't collected any since you moved in here.'

'So what if I haven't? It's got nothing to do with you,' he snarled.

'I was just trying to be helpful.'

'Well, don't. I don't need your help.'

'Oh whatever. I'm going out.'

I stomped around the flat getting my stuff and slammed the door behind me. I've replayed the conversation over and over again but I still can't see what I did wrong. Dan just overreacted.

I reach the crossroads by St Paul's station. Tea should be just down the alleyway which leads to the cathedral. I can feel the morning's irritations flying out of me with every step I take. I wonder if Puzzle-man comes to Tea a lot. Maybe he'll be there when I arrive. Ten more paces and I can see the sign. The café looks idyllic.

Inside it's charming. The tables are made of old oak, some round, some square, others rectangular, each unique. There are a few people sitting down, some enjoying afternoon tea, others casually reading a book while their tea brews. I look up at the large blackboard listing teas. There are so many: traditional, herbal, scented, decaffeinated, you name it. It's like I've walked into the brewer's heaven.

I like the sound of the Superteas that are apparently designed to combat the modern day issues of not getting enough sleep, happiness and energy. Sounds like I could do with one. Shall I go for Felicitea (the happiness tea)? Or maybe Serenitea (the calming tea)?

'G'day, what can I get ya?' the waitress asks in a heavy New Zealand accent.

'Could I have a pot of Daintea please?'

'Sure can, would ya like any cake to go with it?'

I gaze longingly at the beautiful homemade cakes on display. I shouldn't. But then again, the description says that Daintea contains a special South American herb that is supposed to aid weight loss so, maybe a slice of cake won't hurt.

'Could I get a slice of the carrot cake, please?'

'Sure thing. Take a seat and I'll bring it over.'

'Is it OK if I sit outside?'

'Good idea, today's a beaut.'

I sit down at one of the small garden tables and close my eyes as the late August sunshine streams down and warms my bare arms. I'm wearing one of my favourite light green, casual dresses with black leggings and slightly more make-up than usual (in case I happen to bump into Puzzle-man). I feel like I could be anywhere as I sit here with my eyes closed. The London streets sound so different without the usual drumming of work shoes on the pavement. Today the streets are full of happy, excited voices.

'*Peut-on voir* Big Ben, *maman*?' calls a sweet child's voice. I find myself feeling excited about the prospect of seeing Big Ben myself. I don't know when the last time I truly looked at it was. As I open my eyes, I see the little boy drop his teddy bear in his haste to get a better view of St Paul's Cathedral. I dash over and pick it up.

'Oh, excuse me. Err, *pardon*?'

'Ah, *merci*, thank you,' his mother says as I hand the bear back.

I return to my table and my thoughts.

A few moments later, I can hear a pair of footsteps approaching and I watch as a couple wander past the café very slowly, hand-in-hand.

'The show starts at seven so we've got a few hours to see the sights and get dinner,' says the man, who is maybe late thirties. 'How about we walk along the river?'

I can almost taste their attraction, it might be a third or fourth date.

'Here's ya cuppa and cake.'

The lovely Kiwi waitress is looking down at me as she places the tray on my table.

'Thank you,' I say as she walks back inside.

I know I should leave it to brew but I'm desperate to know what it smells like. Bringing the open teapot to my nose, the steam fills my lungs and I breathe deeper than ever before. It smells like fresh figs and pears. My whole body sinks into the chair as my muscles relax and my mind clears. I feel so calm and peaceful as I watch enthusiastic tourists take countless pictures of the seventeenth-century architecture and sit back to admire St Paul's Cathedral myself. Maybe she made me Serenitea by mistake? Whatever tea this is, Puzzle-man was right, this is an experience that everyone should have. I pour myself a cup of tea and cut a first mouthful of carrot cake with my fork as my phone starts to vibrate.

> **From: Dan Mobile Sat 14:07**
> Sorry I lost it. You should know better than to wake me up on a Saturday morning xxx

> **To: Dan Mobile Sat 14:10**
> Sorry too. You can come and meet me at Tea if you like, it's amazing! xx

> **From: Dan Mobile Sat 14:12**
> Haha. I'm still not dressed. C u at home later xx

What on earth does he mean by that? I soon lose interest in trying to work Dan out and turn my thoughts back to Puzzle-man. It's so surreal to think the only reason I'm sitting here is because someone told me to visit in a puzzle book. I pull out my notebook and flick back to my list about who Puzzle-man might be. I come across my *How to Stop Martin getting Promoted* list and strike a line through it. No more games. I'm going to get my promotion fairly or not at all.

<u>List #578 v2: Who is Puzzle-man? (Cont'd)</u>

- He is a man (Sofia and Dan agree)
- He goes to the doctor's at least once or twice a week
- ~~Doctor~~ they are all female
- Janet?
- Must be a patient
- Gay? Unlikely
- Married? Maybe but unlikely
- *He likes tea and is good at puzzles... Man of my dreams — 99% certain!*

It's not much more to go on than when I did the first list, the only new clue is Tea. Maybe he works here? All the doctors are female and so are the nurses (at least all the ones I know about — I wonder if I could get a list of employees?). Dan's wrong about him being gay, I just know it. He could be married though… Maybe he is one of the staff's husbands? No. He must be single. He's nice. He wouldn't lead me on. OK. This isn't helping. I need a plan of action.

'Would you like another cuppa?' the waitress asks as she collects my finished plate.

'Erm, yes please. Could I have the same again? Just the tea not the cake.'

'Sure, do ya mind coming to the till to pay?'

I follow her back into the café. Pulling out my purse from my bag, I bump straight into a man trying to leave.

'Sorry.'

'No problem,' he says to me as our eyes meet. Oh my God. I think it's him. He's tall, late-twenties and has the kindest smile I think I've ever seen.

'Have we met before?' he asks me as I continue to gaze at him.

'I'm not sure, you don't go to the Threadneedle NHS Walk-in Centre do you?'

'No.'

'Oh right,' I say with an awkward laugh. *What the hell was I thinking?*

'Sorry,' I say, 'you just reminded me of one of the doctors there.'

'John, are you ready?'

'Yes, babe,' he says to the lady walking behind him.

'Excuse me,' he says to me.

I move out of the way and watch as the married – *married* – couple leave the café and drop the money for my tea onto the counter with my head bowed in shame.

I feel like a total idiot as I sit back down. Grey clouds have filled the sky and there's a chilly breeze. I pull my cardigan tight around me. As stupid as I feel, I can't shake the thought of meeting Puzzle-man for real. I *have* to know who he is. I wonder if he does come here often. Not that I'm planning to be a stalker or anything. Although... potentially... I could come here for a tea break during the day. I mean it's so close to the office and I'm not planning to go back to Starbucks anytime soon. I start to scribble out a new to-do list.

It's not long, but it should be effective. Firstly, I need to make an effort (which shouldn't be too taxing) to come here on weekdays for tea. And secondly, I need to somehow get a list of employees at Threadneedle Walk-in Centre. I wonder if they list the employees on the NHS website. I reach for my phone at the exact moment it starts to ring. Great.

'Hi, Mum, how are you?'

'What's all this about you having to live with your grandmother?'

'I'm fine, too, thanks for asking.'

'Well?'

I still haven't thought about what I'm going to say. Mum will know if I lie but if I tell her the truth... Oh God.

'It's a long story,' I say and sigh, hoping she will decide to drop the subject.

Mum waits patiently for me to fill the silence.

'Basically,' I take a deep breath so I can rattle it all off in one sentence. 'I want to go to Threadneedle Walk-in Centre's doctor's surgery and I'm not in the catchment area but Gran is, so I told the centre I have to live with Gran to look after her. They called Gran to confirm and she misunderstood what they said. Happy now?'

'Well, it's not the smartest thing you've ever done. Why do you want to go to Threadneedle anyway? Dr Sheryl has always been your doctor.'

'It's more convenient.'

'Right, well, I won't condone it but you do work very long hours so I can understand why you want a convenient doctor's surgery. But you really did worry your grand-mother something chronic.'

'I know. I'm really sorry, I didn't mean to.'

'So how are you?'

Oh great, here we go.

'Fine.'

'Are you eating well?'

'Yes, Mum, but I really have to go. Can we speak later?'

'Yes, darling, in great detail. I'll expect you and Dan around two.'

'What are you talking about?'

'Afternoon tea tomorrow. Dan said you could both make it.' So that's what Dan meant. 'It's not a problem, is it?' Mum sounds so anxious there's no way I can let her down.

'It's fine, Mum. I'm looking forward to it.'

'Excellent! I have a surprise for you.' Oh God, not another one of her surprises. 'See you tomorrow, darling. Love you.'

'Love you too.'

I hang up and pull on my jacket. It's really turned quite cold and I think it's time I got home. I go inside to use the bathroom and try to restrain myself from buying all the teas to take home. If I'm going to be coming here every day there's no point.

The next station is Royal Victoria.

Ouch! The door collides into my elbow as I almost miss my stop. That will teach me for daydreaming. The two lists I made at Tea somehow turned into six separate action plans on the train ride home. I'm going to go straight on to the Threadneedle website when I get in.

The walk from the station is only two minutes but it's enough to get me drenched. I don't have a strong view on global warming but all this volatile weather is really starting to piss me off.

'Catch any cats?' Dan asks, watching with glee as I step inside looking like a bedraggled animal.

'No, just a cold, probably.'

I wring my hair out over the bathroom sink and wipe off what's left of my make-up. I leave all my soggy clothes in a heap and pull on my nice cotton pyjamas and head for the kitchen to make a warm cup of hot chocolate. Three minutes later I am curled up on the sofa next to Dan, logging on to my laptop. I can't believe I haven't thought to look up the walk-in centre's staff on the website before now. I click through on to the 'Meet the Team' page, there's Janet, the longest employee of the Threadneedle Walk-in Centre. I scroll down past Dr Danes and the other two doctors, both female. There is only the one nurse I've already met, Lucy. So no help there.

'What are you sighing about?'

'It's driving me mad. I need to find out who he is.'

'Ha. Let's hear it then.'

'What?'

'Your latest plan of action. Don't give me that look, you were at that café for over three hours. You've definitely made a list by now, if not several.'

I shrug my shoulders. 'I thought I might go to the café during the day, you know, in case it's his local, too.'

Dan snorts so loud he almost chokes. 'I can see the headlines now, "Cassy Brookes, Social Media Expert Turned Stalker".'

'Getting a cup of tea hardly makes me a stalker, Daniel.'

'But going out of your way to get tea in the same shop as someone you want to find is by definition the action of a stalker.'

'It's the local café to my office!'

'You don't drink herbal tea.'

'I do now. Here, I bought you some,' I say, walking over to my bag that I had left in the hallway. I pass him a little paper bag from Tea. Dan pulls out the metal cylinder and reads the label.

'Eternitea, the anti-ageing tea, ha-de-ha-ha-ha, you're so funny. You need it more than me, Cassy. Have you noticed you've got crow's feet?'

'I most certainly do not!' I retort, rushing over to the hall mirror to check. I mean, there is no way you'd say I have crow's feet. 'OK, so I may have a small line but it's not a wrinkle. It's just the lights in here are so bright it's no wonder I need to squint a little,' I say.

'Whatever, Princess. You're probably just losing your sight. Another sign of premature aging.'

'Well, at least I don't have to dye my hair its natural colour to cover up grey hairs.'

That gets Dan's attention.

'Oh yes. I know you do that,' I say and cross my arms in triumph.

'I do not! I only use dye because it has been scientifically proven that using natural hair dye nourishes your hair.'

'Dan, that's not why you use it and it's also a load of crap. Companies say that to make idiots like you buy it.'

Dan pokes his tongue out at me, a classic sign of Cassy-victory. I sit down next to him and twiddle the business card I picked up on the way home. I stopped off at Bea, my favourite bakers – which happens to be quite close to Tea – to get a card to give to Puzzle-man. If Tea is the master of specialist teas, Bea is the master of cakes. It's like walking into a sponge-heaven. The cupcakes are incredible just to look at let alone eat. So what shall I write on the card?

My thank-you gift to you.

Now I just have to come up with an excuse to go back to the walk-in centre. It needs to be believable. Janet might have fallen for the grandmother trick but she's still got her doubts about me.

'What do you reckon, Dan?'

'About?'

'What excuse can I give to go back?'

He thinks for a minute and shrugs. I lean over and shake his shoulders.

'Come on, Dan, you're the mastermind in our friend-ship.'

I start to tickle his side.

'All right. All right. Let me think. Why not just get a flu jab yourself?'

Brilliant. So simple. Why didn't I think of that?

'Anyway, I'm off out.'

'Out where?'

'Who are you, my mother?'

'Is it a date?'

'Something like that.' He pulls a funny face and goes off to get ready. It's about time Dan got back out there.

'I'll be expecting all the gossip tomorrow!' I call out as he waves goodbye. Perhaps Sunday afternoon tea is going to be more entertaining than I thought.

Twelve

I get the taxi to pick up Gran on the way to Mum's house in Buckhurst Hill. The weather is perfect. There are a couple of small fluffy clouds in the sky and a very gentle breeze. Mum has already set the table in the garden when Gran and I arrive. I help Gran onto a sunlounger and pour us both a cup of tea.

'So, darling, how are you?'

I smile to myself and sift through my mental notebook for the list of all the vegetables I've eaten this week.

Mum looks a little disappointed when she has to pass around the cucumber sandwiches before Dan arrives. It's usually me that's late, not him. I hope he's OK. She leaps out of the garden chair when she hears the doorbell. (As would anyone who hadn't heard it before, it's three times as loud as necessary and chimes the song, 'Oh what a beautiful morning'.)

'Oh my goodness!' Mum's voice sends a chill down my spine. I run into the house.

'Mum? Dan?'

They're standing in the hallway.

'Bloody hell, what happened to you?'

Dan's face looks like a bruised pear. His left eye looks like a prune and his nose is most definitely swollen.

'It's nothing. Hi, Ann,' Dan kisses Mum on the cheek and I see him wince as her skin touches his. 'Have you ever noticed that door handles move when you're drunk?'

Mum laughs awkwardly and sends me a surreptitious find-out-what's-going-on stare before hurrying back into the garden, no doubt to give Gran a heads-up. Dan and I walk behind her.

'Seriously?' I lower my voice. 'Are you seriously going to try to blame *that* on a door handle?'

Dan doesn't even look at me.

'Hi, Peggy, excuse the face, make-ups not made like it used to be and I had a bit of a disagreement with a door last night.'

Gran looks at Mum and then at me but she doesn't say anything. Dan soon finishes off the sandwiches. I watch him; he's actually wincing with each mouthful. Horrible images start to race through my mind. What if he was attacked last night and doesn't want to admit it? When Gran goes to the toilet I make my move.

'Do you want some more tea, Mum? Oh, it's gone cold.'

'Don't worry, I'll make a fresh pot.'

I wait until she is out of earshot and then pounce.

'What do you want me to say?' Dan asks after five minutes of evading the question.

'The truth.'

'Fine,' Dan sighs. 'I got into a fight. Happy now?'

'I only wanted to make sure you were OK.'

'Well, I'm fine,' he says, 'great, actually.'

'Great.'

'Great.'

'Super.'

'Super.'

'Excellent.'

'Ex—'

'Here we are.' Mum returns with more tea and I gladly accept.

'Have you told her yet?' Gran asks when she gets back.

'Told me what?'

'I was waiting for Dan to arrive.' Mum's face has lit up. My stomach starts to twist. 'I was talking to Rose from church last week, about how sad you've been since you were dumped.'

'Gee, thanks, Mum.'

'Now, now, Rose has been extremely helpful.'

'What's that supposed to mean?' I look over at Dan. He's doing his best to keep a straight face.

'Rose knows a very nice gentleman who has agreed to go on a date with you.'

For a moment the words don't quite make sense. Or maybe I just don't want them to be true.

'You've set me up on a *blind date*.'

'Yes, dear,' Mum says, beaming.

'No way.' I cross my arms like I did as a child in a full-blown tantrum. Mum and Dan's words breeze over my head, *it will be fun, it's all arranged, you just need to get back out there.*

'I'm not wasting good money on a man I've never met.'

'He's paying,' Mum says.

'I bet he's old.'

'Late twenties.'

'Ugly then.'

'Apparently he is quite the looker *and* fantastic with kids. Rose said he is always helping out with the youth group and the community soup kitchens.'

'Oh, it doesn't matter what I say, you have an answer.'

'Honestly, Cassy, he sounds all right,' Dan pipes in.

'I don't care. I'm not going.'

'Oh, that's a shame,' Dan says. 'Still, I can understand why you feel insecure. I mean, you haven't been on a date in so long you'd probably mess it up.'

'Reverse psychology, really?'

'No, I mean it. From what I've heard he does sound a little out of your league.'

'Is that right.'

'Well, any guy who would take someone to Le Papillon for a first date must be pretty minted and very well connected.'

'Did you say Le Papillon?'

'Oh didn't we mention that earlier?' Dan smirks.

I sit up straight. 'So when exactly am I supposed to be meeting this man?'

'Tonight.'

'*Tonight!* I don't have anything you could wear to Le Papillon!'

'Well, it doesn't matter, you don't want to go anyway.'

'No, but… I can't cancel on such short notice. It would be rude.'

Dan smiles. 'I thought you'd say that.'

–

'How about this?' Dan holds up an old prom dress from my university days. 'All right, maybe not. Seriously, Cassy, your wardrobe options are shocking. Have you been shopping this century?'

'You know,' I say, sitting on the bed in my underwear, 'this is actually fun. I've missed all this.'

'Found it. This sexy number will do nicely. I assume you're going to do a quick manicure before you go?'

'Are you offering?' I smile at Dan.

An hour later I glance at myself in the mirror, unrecognisable from my old self. So this is Cassy Brookes without Seph's shadow. I think I like it. Until a little while ago, mentioning Seph's name had been so painful but standing here now, I feel like a completely different person. I just wish I could have had more closure. Seven years is a long time to share your life with someone. OK, I'm decided. I'm going to send him one final email.

Hi Seph,

Please read this.

I'm not trying to get back with you, or blame you, I just want us both to have some closure. We were together for so long and we had so many good times I feel I learnt who I was while I was with you. It is weird not waking up with you every day, but at the same time I think you were right to leave when you did. If we stopped making each other happy then it was the right thing to do.

At first I blamed you but now, having had time to reflect, I have realised that it was my fault, at least in part. I neglected you and put work first. Which was stupid because you were always more important to me than work. I hope you find happiness.

In some ways I will always love you.

Cassy x

I put my phone back in my bag and step into the fresh air. I'm actually quite excited: Le Papillon here I come!

—

The man's got taste, I'll give him that much. I've only dared dream of dining at Le Papillon. I would quite happily spend an evening just walking past the entrance, the four white pillars and red carpet. Just being shoulder-to-shoulder with its diners feels like a night out. The cheapest meal would cost me a week's rent. Not to mention the best part of all this: Le Papillon is one of the many strings to Sir Lockley's bow and it's often quoted in the press that he dines here regularly, maybe serendipity is on my side tonight.

'Good evening, Mademoiselle, do you have a reservation?'

'Erm, well it's a bit embarrassing really, I'm on a,' I lean in and lower my voice, 'blind date.'

'Ah, please follow me.' He holds out his hand and takes my coat. I follow him down the five steps to the restaurant. The walls are a soft red and adorned with delicate gold-coated candle sconces. I look up. The room is two storeys tall and a glass dome roof lets in natural light.

'Here we are, Mademoiselle.' I lower my gaze.

'Martin!' I shriek. People at surrounding tables momentarily look up. Seconds later a tall, thin man in a penguin suit is beside me.

'Good evening. My name is Pierre and I will be your waiter tonight. May I get you something to drink?'

'Water,' I say eventually.

'And a double vodka with lemonade,' Martin adds. Usually a man making decisions for me would annoy me but I think he is right. Alcohol is definitely required.

'This is a surprise,' Martin says when I sit down. 'I only did this as a favour to Rose. What's your excuse?'

How typical of Martin to steal the best reason.

'To keep my mother happy,' I say which is mainly true. 'How the hell do you know Rose Fairlop?'

'I volunteer as a mentor to her youth group as part of Holywells charity programme. Look, we can call it a night if you want.'

'No, we're here now.' I may as well make the most of what is likely to be my one and only meal at Le Papillon, even if it is with Martin. 'We may as well eat.'

Martin leans back in his chair with an amused look on his face like he can see right through me.

'Listen, about the whole, fake meeting thing, I—'

'Don't worry about it,' he says. 'I know you've been harbouring a resentment ever since I beat you in the pub quiz.'

'I'd hardly say you beat *me*.'

'What would you call it then?'

Pierre returns with my drink and the menu, giving me the perfect excuse to ignore the question. I look down the right-hand column, I'm definitely going to be ordering the most expensive thing on this menu.

'I'll have the lobster, please.'

'The roast duck for me, please.'

Martin didn't bat an eyelid at my order. I'm beginning to wonder if we're on the same pay.

When the food arrives it smells delicious, at least Martin's does. I don't really like lobster. Once we had it at a marketing conference in Brussels and I was violently sick the next day. I don't know why I ordered it.

'Actually, the lobster is for me,' Martin says. Pierre looks at little puzzled but quickly switches the plates. 'I remember Brussels too,' Martin adds when Pierre is out of earshot.

He looks so different sitting here in front of me. I think for the first time I'm seeing the real Martin. The bravado of Martin Robertson has fallen away.

'You know,' he says. 'I've always nearly admired you.'

'Wow, well I think that is the best *nearly* compliment I've ever had.'

'It's true,' he says, shrugging his shoulders. 'I sort of like your... *approach* to the job.'

I feel myself relax and a small smile of pride form on my face.

'If you weren't so naive you'd be a superstar.'

And the smile vanishes.

'I am *not* naive!'

'OK, sorry.'

'I'm not!'

'Look, Cassy,' Martin says with a sigh. He studies me as if questioning whether I can handle what he is about to say. I give him a look that says, 'I'm all ears'.

'You have two choices here. Either you carry on thinking that the world is fair and that if you work hard you will get promoted or you start living in the real world and do what the rest of us do... *play the game.*'

'But—'

'*But it's not right,*' Martin says, imitating my voice. '*I want to succeed on merit.*'

I glare at him.

'The world just isn't that black and white, Cassy.'

For the first time I catch a glimmer of insight into the rationale of why all the women in the office have kissed Martin (and some a lot more than kissed). He really does have a sexy glow about him when he gets animated about reaching the top. I'm not sure that's a good quality in a boyfriend though. I'm about to reply when something catches my eye.

'Oh my God, I think that's Sir Martin Lockley over there. Look!'

Martin continues to eat his lobster.

'That's so typical of you, acting like it's not a big deal. He's a legend, a pioneer of the retail industry.'

Martin looks at me, thoughtfully. I can't tell if it's amusement or sadness.

'Oh my giddy aunt. He's walking over to us.'

'*Giddy aunt?*' Martin's mouth slides into a grin. I stand up as Sir Lockley reaches our table.

'It's a pleasure to meet you, Sir Lockley.' I say and put out my hand, quite why I'm not sure.

'The pleasure is mine, miss?'

'Cassidy Brookes.'

Sir Lockley takes my hand and kisses it gently. He smiles at me and a shiver runs down my spine. It's as if I've seen that smile somewhere before.

'Pierre tells me you work with my son at Holywells.'

'Really? I—'

'Hello, Father.' Martin sighs without getting up. I find myself back in my seat; I think I just partially fainted. 'I didn't realise you were in town.'

'Is that all you have to say? You haven't returned a single one of my phone calls in the past six months.'

'Well, you are sort of crashing my date.'

'Ah, well, don't let me stop you.' Sir Lockley smiles at me again and I try to smile back but my entire body is paralysed. I watch as he makes his way to the door and Pierre helps him into his coat. I turn my gaze back to Martin who has returned to his lobster. He puts down his knife and fork and looks straight at me.

'I'd appreciate it if you didn't mention this to anyone.'

'That we've been on a date or that your father is a multi-billionaire?'

Martin smiles at me and suddenly the resemblance is obvious.

'I thought we weren't on a date?'

'That's what you told your father, *Sir Martin Lockley*.'

'I only said that to make him leave.'

'Of course,' I say. If I wasn't in a state of shock, I may have found that embarrassing.

'So, Martin Lockley Junior... I don't understand why you have kept it a secret.' My mind is going into overload. How could I have not known this? Is this how he got his place at Holywells? 'Your surname?'

'Robertson is my mother's maiden name. Lockley is too obvious.'

'But—'

'The reason I don't tell people is because of the way you're looking at me right now.' Martin leans in closer. 'I worked hard to get to where I am today. I earned my place at Harvard and I—' Martin pauses. 'I'm sorry.'

'Would you like to order any desserts?' Pierre interrupts.

'May I have the chocolate fondant, please?'

'Make that two,' Martin says.

Martin and I make small talk while we wait for the desserts but it doesn't feel as comfortable as before. The desserts arrive. They look amazing but I can barely taste mine. Curiosity has completely got the better of me.

'I'm sorry. I have to ask. Why don't you want to speak to your father?'

'It's complicated.'

'That's just life. Listen, my dad died when I was ten and I would do *anything* to be able to speak to him one more time.'

Martin lets out a small sigh and lowers his spoon. He looks at me with such intensity I look away.

He talks quietly. 'I have two brothers, Rob and Jason, one older and one younger. All the memories I have of my father from my childhood involve him, in some way or another, telling us – no, demanding us – to follow in his footsteps, to honour the family name, to be exceptional.'

A frown ripples across Martin's forehead and for a moment he seems caught up in his own thoughts.

'His expectations were so high. Impossibly high. Too high for Rob, my older brother, to bear. When he was about fourteen, Rob began to hang out with the wrong crowd. He got into a few fights. My father was so disappointed in him that he practically disowned him. He wouldn't speak to him; he wouldn't even look at him. He made Rob feel like a stranger in his own home. So one night Rob just left. Ran away. That was fifteen years ago and none of us have heard from him since. We don't know if he's dead or alive.'

'I'm so sorry.'

'Everything changed after Rob left,' Martin continues. 'Suddenly my father wanted to be Dad of the Year. He spent so much time with Jason and me but he couldn't fix what he'd broken. He was still the same man, with his high expectations. And he couldn't bring Rob back, though he spent millions trying to find him.'

'But there's always hope. Hope that he might get in contact one day.' The words sound silly as I say them but I can't bear to see Martin look so upset.

'That's what I tell myself. That's why I help out at soup kitchens all over London and it's why I volunteer with Rose's youth group. No child should ever feel alone or trapped. No one should ever be told what career they have to do or be dictated to by pushy parents. Maybe Rob will reach out one day or maybe he never will, but at least I can help some teenagers so they don't have to end up on the streets.'

I reach out and take Martin's hand in mine. 'That's a lovely, positive way to handle a horrible situation.'

Martin sighs. 'OK, no more talk about my father, agreed?'

'Agreed.'

Martin gives me one of his infectious smiles and the intensity lifts.

'So, Miss Brookes, I do believe that I know your Achilles heel.'

—

'I take it you forfeit,' I say in the back of the taxi.

'What?'

'The clue, clearly it was too hard for you.' He's spent the past ten minutes with a pained look on his face, trying to work out my latest cryptic clue.

Martin smiles. 'Churchill,' he says.

Damn. I really thought I'd got him with that one. Martin insisted on escorting me home, which, given it's East London and gone 2 a.m., is probably sensible. All the same, sensibleness had nothing to do with why I agreed.

'OK, Little Miss Cryptic, your turn.'

He pulls me towards him and whispers a clue in my ear. The sudden closeness catches me off guard and my mind goes blank. The taxi pulls up outside my apartment block.

'I think that means *I'm* the champion,' Martin says.

'No way, you are not winning this game. Come on.' I pull Martin out of the taxi and he quickly throws some notes at the taxi driver who happily takes the huge tip. I rack my brains as we make our way up the stairs but I can't solve it. I put the key in the lock.

'Cassy, I should probably go.'

'Ah, I've got it. Love!'

Our eyes lock and suddenly it feels like all the oxygen in the world has disappeared. My chest feels heavy and hot. I can't bring my eyes away from his. He's looking at me so intensely it's like we're talking.

'Your turn for a clue,' I whisper. I turn the key in the lock. 'Cassy, I—'

The door opens so suddenly I fall forwards. Arms hold me up but it's not Martin.

'Seph.'

Thirteen

'What the hell are you doing here?'

'Me? What's *he* doing here?' The way Seph says the word 'he' makes me feel nervous and leaves no space for doubt that this really is happening. There is no way this is a dream.

'You remember Martin from work,' I say, trying to regain control of the situation.

'*Try* to pay attention. That was *not* the answer to the question I *asked*.'

'We had client drinks,' I lie. 'Martin was just walking me home as it was so late.'

'Well, she's home now,' Seph says, glaring at Martin.

'Are you sure you're OK?' Martin asks me, completely ignoring Seph.

I nod. Martin looks like he wants to say something but instead just turns towards the stairs. Seph and I watch Martin leave but I imagine the thoughts running through our heads are quite different.

'I thought you'd look happier to see me,' Seph says as I close the door. Suddenly all the alcohol I've drunk seems to have taken over my bloodstream.

'I'm just a little stunned. In a good way. Where have you been? Are you here to stay?'

'Oh, stop the inquisition, will you? *Mock the Week* is about to start.'

I sit beside him on the sofa and prepare myself to watch a *Mock the Week* rerun on Dave that no doubt we've both seen before. Judging from the state of the living room I'd say he's been here all evening. I don't need to know where he's spent the last few months, in fact I don't want to know. I can tell by the way he's sat back down on the sofa like he owns it that he's come back for good. He isn't going anywhere. I move closer and he puts his arm around me. My head won't stop spinning. Is this really happening? Are we back together?

We have a quick chat during the advert breaks of *Mock the Week* while I drink two litres of water and three cups of coffee. He says my email really meant something to him and he's realised I'm the one he wants to be with for the rest of his life and that he thinks we should try again. Talk about irony. There was me, sending the email to move on, and now he's decided to come back.

I go to the bathroom and splash some water on my face. It's been such an emotional day it's no wonder I'm not feeling more excited. I had just got myself pumped up to be a single, independent woman but ultimately being back with Seph is the right thing. We were together for seven years and it's worth us giving it another go. I just need to make an effort.

I can hear him putting his stuff back in the bedroom as I clean myself up in the en suite and slip on some new underwear. He's in bed when I come out.

'Hey,' I say, leaning against the door frame. He doesn't reply.

I go over to him and pull back the duvet slightly. I laugh. Is he really going to play this game now? We're supposed to be mature adults.

Oh give me a break! I think he is actually asleep. I pull off the Ann Summers underwear and climb into bed next to him. I shuffle up close to him but he pushes me away in his sleep. I chuckle to myself. I should have known. Nothing about today has gone the way I planned, why did I think it would end any differently?

–

For a few seconds when I wake up I think it is Martin snoring lightly beside me. I close my eyes and try to digest everything that happened yesterday. Then I turn to look at Seph, the man I should be ecstatic to see sleeping next to me. Except I'm not. Not even close.

Maybe we don't need to have the big relationship reunion like you see in the movies. He doesn't have to hold me in his arms and whisper in my ear how he will never let me go again. Perhaps he doesn't even have to kiss me goodnight. We were together so long that maybe it does make more sense to slip straight back into our old lives.

'Seph and I are back together!' I whisper in the darkness and do my impression of an excited child at Christmas. Even my acting sucks. I close my eyes and try to picture my future with Seph the way I used to. I can see our wedding, our first house in the country, our first baby (a boy) and our second (a girl). I can see us holding hands in Oxford's Sheldonian at their graduations (he did Physics, she did English). Mum and Dan are there too but they both look sad. They smile at me sympathetically. I look down at my hand, the ring is gone. I look up. Seph is standing at the graduation with another woman.

I throw back the covers and get out of bed. This is all happening too fast. Putting on my dressing gown and slippers I go into the bathroom to brush my teeth.

'Cassy?' Seph calls out.

'Sorry, did I wake you?'

'Yes.'

'Sorry.'

'What's for breakfast?'

I make my way into the kitchen in search of ingredients for breakfast. All I find is some porridge, out of date white bread that has a little mould forming on the crust and a dribble of orange juice. I sort of broke up with breakfast when Seph broke up with me, favouring a croissant and a coffee on the train. As for Dan, his idea of breakfast is leftover takeaway pizza from the night before (or even the night before that). Dan still hasn't texted me back to tell me where he stayed last night. I dread to think what he is going to say when he finds out. The only thing more concerning is what Seph is going to say when he finds out Dan's moved in. Maybe Dan will go back to his flat? I feel more than just a twinge of sadness as I go back into the bedroom. I put on some clothes and take out my special notebook from my bedside drawer. This one is just for Seph and has his all-important breakfast list.

'I'm just going to pop out for some breakfast stuff.'

Seph grunts.

Switching the slippers for my old trainers I grab my handbag and gently close the front door behind me. A naive little part of me is hoping that if I make a good enough breakfast and pretend everything is back to normal then it will start to feel less like a nightmare.

List #30: Seph's Perfect Breakfast

- Orange juice.

- Eggs.

- Bacon (extra fatty).

- Beans (must be Heinz).

- White bread (fresh and uncut).

- Sausage (not Cumberland).

- Hash browns (n.b. most important item, if not in Tesco go to Sainsbury's).

When I get back, Seph is up. I say up, what I mean is, he has changed from lying in bed to lying on the sofa. It's funny how when it's someone you love, even the sight of them scratching their balls and then putting their hand in a family-sized packet of Doritos is not enough to make you raise your voice. Today, however, after I've just gone out in the pouring rain to get food, watching Seph eat Doritos is infuriating.

'Morning,' I say.

Seph looks up at me and nods before going back to watching a repeat of *Have I Got News for You*. I put the food on the counter slowly, trying not to rustle the Tesco carrier bags (a pet hate sound of Seph's). Then I start to play Jenga – for the first time in almost seven months – with the pots and pans, gently coaxing them out, making as little noise as possible. The disadvantage of an open-plan flat is that when your boyfriend is trying to watch TV and you are cooking his breakfast the sound of the clanging is worse than going hungry (or so Seph tells me).

'About bloody time,' Seph says when I pass him his breakfast tray. He gives me a wink so I know he meant it in a playful, loving kind of way.

'Not bad,' he says when he's licked the plate clean.

'Really?'

'Yeah, apart from the bacon wasn't crispy enough and my mum's eggs are still better.'

Damn it. I never cook the bacon right. I might actually have to ask my mum for some advice.

'So I was thinking we could go out somewhere today, make the most of the bank holiday?' I venture as I place the plates in the dishwasher.

'Nah, I'm beat.'

'OK, a lazy day would be nice. How about we go out for dinner tonight? Celebrate getting back together.'

Seph thinks about this and then says, 'To be honest I'm trying to watch my finances. Why don't we stay in and cook instead?'

'You mean why don't I cook?' I notice the irritation in my tone too late to do anything about it. 'Tell you what, let's get a takeaway. My treat,' I add hastily, before Seph can complain. He loves takeaways.

–

'What the hell is your problem? You've been moping all day,' Seph says that night when he is tucking into his dinner. 'Is it because I ordered Indian?'

'No,' I say and sigh lightly. Although, picking the one takeaway I don't eat was a little inconsiderate.

'Well, what then? I'm not a bloody mind-reader.'

'It's just… Dan said he'd be home by—'

'Who are you his mother?' Seph's comment makes me wince. He hadn't taken the news that Dan had moved in very well.

'It's not just that,' I say in an attempt to change the subject. 'I'm worried Martin is going to get promoted instead of me.'

'Who's Martin?' Seph puffs out his chest.

'The guy you saw last night. We went for client drinks, remember?'

'Well, you knew something like this would happen sooner or later.'

'What would?'

'You couldn't expect to keep up with a man's career forever.'

'Why the hell not?'

'Because you're a woman,' Seph says, bluntly. He looks at me with pity in his eyes, as if to say 'it's not just because I'm a woman, but because I am a simple woman'.

'What era are you living in?' I say, the feminist in me taking over.

'Don't start, Cassy. This is exactly what I'm talking about.'

'I'm not starting. I'm asking.'

'You're getting all hormonal. Which, incidentally, is exactly why women don't get promoted above men.'

Sod him. I storm out of the room into the bedroom. It wasn't supposed to be like this. I was getting on with my life. I was happy being on my own. I sit on the edge of the bed, my arms folded, taking deep breaths, trying to calm down.

Half an hour later I feel a bit stupid. There were bound to be teething problems. We went to bed so late last night I'm just in a bad mood. I overreacted didn't I? I mean, he is right. I do plan to stop working, or at least do flexi-time, when Seph and I have kids. Maybe women aren't supposed to have the high-powered careers?

'Seph...' I call out as I walk down the hallway to the living room, 'I'm sorry, you're totally right... What? Where are you going?'

'Out. The guys are having some beers.'

'I thought you were too *beat* to go out tonight,' I say and try to hide that I feel hurt.

'I've changed my mind.'

'OK, well I'll come with you,' I say and pick up my bag.

'No. Frankly, I need some space and given I've only been back for a day what does that say about you?'

–

Two hours later I've decided it says a lot about me but even more about him. There is no getting around it. The truth is I was much happier (even if I was a little crazier) being on my own, being able to spend more time with Dan and my mum rather than having to cook, clean and nurture a grown man. I didn't have to worry about getting home at a certain time just to avoid an argument or make sure I didn't breathe too loudly when the television was on.

There was a time when none of that stuff bothered me. When I wanted to get home early to see Seph, when I wanted to spend every waking minute with him. But now, I want to put myself first. I want to stay up late eating pizza with Dan and be swept off my feet by a mysterious Puzzle-man. I want to put my career first and play the game for real, like Martin said.

Straight after the break-up, I was able to put words into the mouth of the imaginary Seph in my head. I was able to make him understanding, loving and funny. The real

Seph has undermined me, told me I won't succeed in my job, that all I'm good for is making him food and I don't even excel at that. When I really think about it, maybe the truth is that my life was better without him. I hear the key turn in the lock. I stand up, my heart pounding. I know what I have to do.

'Seph, we need to – Dan!'

'Did you say Seph?'

'Where have you been?'

'Never mind that, why the hell did you think I was Seph?'

'He's moved back in but—'

'Are you *mad*?'

'You don't understand, I've decided to—'

'You can't seriously be considering giving it another go. You're finally getting yourself sorted.'

'I know that's why—'

'I bet you've been making lists.'

'Well, of course, I always make lists but that has nothing to do with what I'm trying to tell you. I've decided to—'

'It has everything to do with it! You like to think you make lists because you love being organised and efficient, but that's not true. You make lists because you feel helpless, controlled by—'

We both jump as we hear the sound of fumbling keys scraping the door.

'—that moron,' Dan says and points viciously at the door.

'Look, I'm going to dump him OK? For good this time. Just, quick, wait in the spare room, I want to do this myself.'

Dan raises an eyebrow but does as he's told. I take a deep breath. The door opens.

'Seph, we need to talk.' He looks at me, his eyes are glassy and I can smell the alcohol on his breath. He walks straight past me towards the bedroom.

'Night,' he calls back. I run around him and put my arm against the wall, blocking his escape.

'I said we need to talk. Now.'

He grabs my arm. 'Listen—'

'No, you listen!' I pull away from him. 'This isn't working anymore. It's over.'

Seph bursts into laughter. 'You're breaking up with me?'

'Yes and you need to leave. Now.'

Seph laughs louder.

'I mean it. You need to get the hell out of here.' I push him and suddenly the laughter stops. His nostrils flare. I take a step backwards.

'Who the *fuck* do you think you're talking to?' he bellows.

'A drunken idiot.'

Seph clenches his fist. 'You f—'

'Fabulous woman is the phrase you're looking for,' Dan says, stepping in between Seph and me. He grabs hold of Seph's raised fist and pushes him backwards. Seph, looking bewildered, loses his footing and half falls onto the sofa.

'What's he doing here?' Seph spits, jumping back on to his feet.

'I happen to live here. Unlike you.'

'Look here, you—'

'Go and wait in the spare room, Cassy,' Dan says, calmly. I want to but my legs won't move. I've never seen Seph this angry before. Dan begins walking around the room, picking up Seph's things and stuffing them into a carrier bag.

'Don't you dare touch my stuff, you gay prick.'

In a split second, Dan grabs Seph by the arm, twists it behind his back and pushes Seph onto the sofa. Seph looks up at me, shell-shocked. He doesn't even try to say anything to me when Dan goes into the bedroom. He just looks at me, like a petrified five-year-old. When Dan comes back he is holding Seph's rucksack. He stuffs the carrier bag inside and then flings it at Seph.

'So what? You're going to let Dan throw me out, are you? Not that it matters. I'll just stay round one of my other whores' flats.'

'What did you say?' My voice is barely audible.

'You didn't think I was only screwing you?'

Dan walks up to him and grabs him by the shirt. I think he means for his voice to be low so I can't hear but although he talks through gritted teeth I catch everything. 'Another word and it will be your last.'

Dan looks over at me. 'Go in the bedroom, Cassy.' This time I do as Dan says. I want to scream at Seph, but my dignity saves me from talking to him anymore. I close the bedroom door, lie on the bed and hold the pillow over my head to block out the raised voices. I still make out the sound of a punch and then what I think is a rucksack falling down three flights of stairs.

'You dumb homo. She's not good enough for me anyway!' I hear Seph shout, his voice echoing up the stairwell.

The front door slams shut and seconds later, Dan comes into the room. He doesn't say anything. He just lies next to me and holds me. As he puts his arm around me I see the graze marks on his right-hand knuckles. I don't like violence but I can't deny that inside I'm happy Dan hit him. It's finally over and I'm glad.

Fourteen

No Tuesday has ever felt so good. Freedom flows through my veins. It's funny, I don't feel the same way I did when Seph left the first time. I know now that breaking up with him is the best thing I have ever done and it's not my fault the 'relationship' fell apart. I may not be perfect but he was a cheat, a controlling moron and certainly not the father of my future children. I've treated myself to an extra-long shower, put on my best suit and carefully applied my make-up. I feel more alive than I have in weeks, months, maybe even years.

'Hey, Sofia,' I beam. 'Sofia?'

She doesn't look up.

'Are you all right?' I ask, backtracking past her desk again.

'I'm fine,' she says, her voice wavering.

'You're clearly not fine. What is it? What's wrong?'

'It's nothing, honestly,' she says and forces a smile.

Her eyes tell a different story. They are red raw with deep, dark rings around them and for the first time since I have known her she is not wearing purple. Instead, she is wearing a worn, shapeless, beige dress. I glance at her hand. There's no ring.

'Oh, Sofia, I—'

'Cassy,' Martin says, making me jump out of my skin, 'can I see you in your office for a moment, please?'

'Right now?' My stomach tenses.

'There's no time like the present,' he says with his Colgate smile and holds open my office door, inviting me in.

Reluctantly, I leave Sofia and follow Martin inside, closing the door behind me. He casually walks around the room, looking at the pictures I have hanging on the wall. He stops at a photograph of our Holywells graduate class taken just after we got through our first year. I cringe, I deliberately bought too small a frame and cut Martin out of the photo.

'Martin, about Sunday—'

'Did you get back with him?'

'So what if I did?' I ask, a little stunned by his directness. He stares at me, hard, like he can't believe Seph would take me back.

'There's no need to look so surprised,' I say.

'Sorry,' he says, composing himself and running his fingers through his hair. 'It's just that I thought you had more sense.'

'Excuse me?' Seph might be a dick but something in Martin's tone makes me defensive.

'You know, Cass,' he says and puts his hands in his trouser pockets, 'feeling alone is no reason to take back your ex.'

'I beg your pardon?'

'You're better off without him.'

'We have one meal together and suddenly you think you know me?'

'He's an arsehole, Cassidy.'

'Well, it takes one to know one,' I snap back and fold my arms.

'Yeah. It does,' he says quietly.

I'm too stunned to move.

He steps closer to me and my chest feels heavy and hot just like it did when we stood outside my flat.

'Five years we've worked together,' he says. 'Five Christmas parties. Five summer parties. Five charity events. He's come to two.'

'So what,' I say and take a step backwards, trying to gather my thoughts. 'You're keeping tabs on my relationship now?'

'No, but he does. He threatened me at both.'

What?

'He tries to control you, Cassy. Anyone can see that. He's threatened by your intelligence, although, most of us are.'

I open my mouth but I don't know what to say. Martin heads towards the door. He looks back at me.

'You know, if there is one flaw in your armoury, it's him. Maybe you should think about that.'

He shuts the door behind him and leaves me motionless with the hairs on my arms standing on end.

What the hell just happened?

—

There's a knock on my door. The clock says 10.30 a.m. I don't think I've moved a muscle since Martin left. Why didn't I just tell him Seph and I are over? Why does he care?

'Cassy?' Sofia's timid voice creeps into the room.

'Just to let you know, our eleven o'clock cancelled.'

'OK, thanks. Oh, Sofia,' I try to shake the thought of Martin, 'before you go…' I stand up and close my office door. 'Do you want to talk about it?'

She bursts into tears. 'I'm sorry. I'm sorry. This is so unprofessional, I know.'

'It's OK, here, sit down, and tell me what happened.'

'Joey… we had a fight on Sunday and – and he just walked out.'

'Have you heard from him since?'

'He came back but…'

'But what?'

'Oh, Cassy, we'd been arguing because I thought he was seeing someone else. Then he stormed out and didn't come back until the next day. I think he must have been with her. I just don't know what to do.'

I don't know what to say. I put my arms around her.

She takes a deep breath.

'I'm sorry, Cassy. I should get back to work.'

Sofia puts on a fake smile and makes her way back to her desk. The rest of the morning goes very slowly. I can see through the window that Sofia is running to the bathroom every half hour, poor girl. I wish I could do or say something to make her feel better. Seph and I weren't engaged but I do know at least a little of what she must be going through. As the minutes tick by my mind keeps running over what Martin said. Was he playing some sort of a game? I think I know he wasn't. He was… sincere.

I want to speak to him again but it will have to wait. I've got an informal-feedback lunch with Mr Samuel in an hour and I need to focus.

–

I sit down opposite Mr Samuel in the cafeteria and psych myself up for this chat. I look forward to these quarterly catch-ups. I may not be the best at networking but one piece of advice I did listen to on that introductory week of training at Holywells was, *make sure you get regular feedback*. This is my nineteenth lunch date with Mr Samuel and probably the most important as it will be the last time I get to ask his advice before I pitch for the promotion.

'So, Cassidy, what's on your mind?' he asks, after I've given him a quick update on my current projects.

'Well, I—'

'Sorry to disturb,' Martin says, placing a hand on Mr Samuel's right shoulder. 'Tom, I just wanted to check you were still OK for the cricket this afternoon? We'll need to leave in about half an hour.'

'Oh yes, I'd completely forgotten. In fact, Cassy, do you mind if we cut our lunch short?'

'No, not at all.'

I watch as Martin and Mr Samuel walk side by side to the lift, laughing away like old school friends. I chuckle to myself: what an idiot I am. For one ridiculous moment I'd wondered if Martin cared about me. I thought that maybe I'd started to see the real him – but it was all an act. All he cares about is getting promoted. *Learn to play the game*, that's what he said to me and that's exactly what I'm going to do. The digital strategy conference is in six days. That means I have one hundred and forty-four hours to secure the biggest client Holywells has ever had and I'm going to do whatever it takes to nail it.

From: Lorella Beaumount (on behalf of Sir Lockley)
Sent: Tues 2.15pm
To: Cassidy Brookes
Subject: Re: Meeting with Sir Lockley

Dear Miss Brookes,

I'm afraid there have not been any cancellations in Sir Lockley's diary. I appreciate you have a fantastic business opportunity for Lockley & Co. and I will pass on your message when Mr Lockley returns from his travels.

Regards,

Lorella Beaumount (Executive Personal Assistant)

—

From: Lorella Beaumount (on behalf of Sir Lockley)
Sent: Tues 4.23pm
To: Cassidy Brookes
Subject: Re: Re: Meeting with Sir Lockley

Dear Miss Brookes,

Thank you for the flowers. I'm afraid it will not be possible to arrange a video call with Sir Lockley.

Regards,

Lorella Beaumount (Executive Personal Assistant)

—

From: Lorella Beaumount (on behalf of Sir Lockley)
Sent: Weds 7.30am
To: cass3000@hotmail.com
Subject: Sir Lockley

Dear cass3000@hotmail.com

For security reasons I cannot disclose Sir Lockley's itinerary.

If this is Cassidy Brookes, please be assured my previous emails were accurate and correct.

'Are you sure about this?'

'Absolutely,' I say to Sofia, standing by the Holywells lift. She's looking at me with a mixture of concern and amusement.

'OK, well good luck. Rather you than me. I hear the needles are pretty big.'

'All good things in life require a little pain,' I say more to myself than Sofia.

I am temporarily putting my Lockley & Co. campaign to one side because the time has finally arrived for me to get a flu jab. Sofia said I should leave it a while, so that it didn't look too suspicious.

'Where are you off to?' asks a familiar voice, but unfortunately not one I want to hear.

'Lunch,' I say breezily.

'Me too. I'll walk with you.'

Oh crap.

'Actually, I've got to pop into the doctor's on the way.'

'The doctor's again, eh? Where are you really sneaking off to?'

'It's the truth,' I say. A nervous tension runs through me. What if Mr Samuel has also noticed my trips to the doctor's? – I have taken quite a few long lunches and come in late a couple of times.

'All right, Cass, I'll cover for you,' he says, deliberately trying to wind me up.

'There's no need to cover for me, I won't be long. I was just running through a few things with Sofia,' I say and nod in her direction. 'So if you don't mind...'

'Actually, Sofia, I've been meaning to bump into you.' The lift dings.

'Oh well, you'd better get the next lift then,' I say and jam my finger on the 'close door' button. 'See you later.'

I run my fingers over the embossed Bea business card in my pocket as the lift descends. I have a final glance at my hair in the semi-reflective lift door before making my way out of the building.

–

The queue at Threadneedle is longer than usual. Janet spots me almost instantly. She quickly looks away and pretends not to notice me but I catch the little sigh and a flick of her head that says 'what is it this time?'. I don't feel guilty. This is genuine. It's important to get a flu jab.

'Good afternoon, Janet, I just popped in on my lunch break hoping I could squeeze in a flu jab,' I say chirpily when I reach the front of the queue.

'We only give flu jabs if you're over sixty-five or pregnant.' Janet looks at my stomach for a few seconds too long and makes me wish that I hadn't eaten a huge bar of chocolate last night.

'Well, I am *definitely not* pregnant.'

'I see,' she says, her eyes making the final judgement.

'However, when I was reading the flu jab leaflet the nurse gave my gran last week,' I say, ignoring her tone. 'It said that if you're the main carer for an elderly person you should get a jab too.'

Ha, I have done my homework!

'Hmm, that is true in cases where, if the carer got sick, the elderly or disabled person's welfare may be at risk.'

'Yes, exactly. Since I have just recently moved in with my gran, I don't want to risk getting ill and leaving her uncared for.'

I smile, appealing to her sympathetic side. Janet doesn't look amused but clearly her protocols leave her unable to argue with me.

'I'm happy to wait if there is a queue,' I add, already heading towards the old chair, with the Bea business card hidden in my jacket pocket.

'No need. Nurse Clarkson was just about to go for lunch but I'm sure she can squeeze one more in,' Janet says. She looks at me sternly to make sure I am aware that I will be making the nurse work five minutes of overtime. As if by magic Reese Witherspoon's younger sister appears.

'Is that someone else for the flu jab? Oh hello, didn't you bring your grandmother to get a jab last week?' she asks, not in the slightest put out at having to 'squeeze one more in'.

'Yes, that's right. Good memory,' I say, smiling.

'People are forever telling me I have a good memory,' she says with a proud smile. 'I'm Lucy, by the way.' She beckons me to follow her. 'I never forget a patient,' she carries on, more to herself than to me. 'I've been here two years now and not one patient escapes my memory.'

How ridiculously far-fetched is that statement? Not to mention entirely impossibly to prove. I give one last, longing look at the green armchair as Lucy opens the door to her examination room. How am I going to manage to get the Bea business card in the puzzle book now? There's no way I'm getting a jab for nothing. I hate needles. If there is one thing I dread more than rush hour on the Underground, it's needles.

'I was the only one who could remember she had put it in the jewellery box for safe keeping.' Lucy is *still* talking about how good her memory is. 'Funny place to leave the garden shed key I suppose, but it all worked out in the end.'

What the hell is she going on about?

'So what do you do?'

'I work at a digital marketing agency.'

'Ooh, like *Mad Men*?'

'Sort of, but a bit less wining and dining.'

'Oh, OK.' Lucy winks at me as if she knows exactly what life at Holywells is like. 'Gosh, I'm quite jealous, all those sexy men in suits. We get a lot of them coming in here. It's one of the perks.' She winks at me again. 'So are you like, an assistant?'

'No,' I grit my teeth and remind myself she is the one holding the needle. 'I'm an account director.'

'Oh, no good to me then,' she says. 'My boyfriend is my *account director* or at least his credit card is.'

Lucy laughs at her own joke. I smile. There's no right response to that.

'He treats me to everything.'

I'm not sure if it's the size of the needle or Lucy that is making me feel nauseous.

'Simon's family is *loaded*. But it hasn't changed him if you know what I mean? He's so down-to-earth. He bought me this for my twenty-first birthday last year.'

Lucy extends out her hand. She has a beautiful Swarovski ring on her index finger. Its purple gem is surrounded by small diamonds and sparkles so brightly I'm not sure how I didn't notice it sooner. Swarovski is my one true love and apparently Lucy's too.

'Lovely nail varnish,' I say, unable to resist winding her up.

'Oh no, not the polish, the ring.' She smiles at me like I'm a simpleton. 'I chose it, of course.'

Of course.

'So what does he do?' I ask as I try to distract myself from the sharp scratch of the needle being stuck into my left arm.

'Oh, he doesn't need to work. His dad sometimes asks him to play a round of golf with him.'

I see. 'Loaded' compared even to those considered by most as well-off then.

'Simon says that his only job is looking after me. He's so sweet. He picks me up from work every day. Even if I'm running late he waits and never gets cross.'

Lucky Lucy.

'Actually, that sounds like him now,' she says and looks longingly out of the window. 'He's taking me to lunch.'

We hear it before we see it.

'It's a limited edition Aventador LP 700 with V12 engine.'

'A what?' I say, taken aback.

'A Lamborghini.' She smiles. 'Lovely isn't it,' she says when the car is in sight. (Its bright orange bodywork is quite hard to miss!) 'I bought it for him for Christmas.'

'*You* bought it for him?'

'Well, I used his credit card, but it was still a nice surprise for him.'

Nice? How does that conversation even go? 'Hi honey, I bought you an orange car for two hundred thousand pounds of your own money, surprise!' *Why would anyone date this girl?*

'Can you believe it?' she is saying. 'He actually wanted to pick me up from work in a Mini! Not a new one either, one of those rusty old ones that are like ancient.'

Lucy has such a look of disgust on her face I decide not to mention that I would much rather be picked up by my boyfriend in a vintage Mini than a playboy's orange monstrosity. For some reason I find myself wondering what car Martin drives.

'OK, all done. If you feel light-headed or nauseous don't worry, just rest, it should pass.'

'Thanks,' I say, jumping to my feet, ready to make a quick exit before Lucy can tell me anymore of her boyfriend's amazing qualities. Even through all her super-ficial talk, it's clear how much she loves him.

When I reach the reception area, Janet is on the phone. She doesn't notice me and that's the chance I need. I dart over to the waiting-room chairs, rifle through the magazines and then slip the Bea business card inside the puzzle book.

'Miss Brookes?'

I jump about two feet. Janet is standing behind me. She could try out for the grim reaper, especially with the facial expression she has at the moment.

'Oh hello, I was just having a quick sit-down, feeling a little dizzy after the jab.'

'I see. Shall I fetch Nurse Clarkson?'

'No, no. I feel much better now thanks. I'd better get back to work.'

Janet's stare follows me across the room as I make my way to the door; the suspicion on her face is so intense it's as if she expects me to try to hide in the store cupboard.

Back in the fresh air, I forget all about protocol-loving Janet and stroll happily towards the office feeling pleased with a job well done plus the added bonus that I won't get sick all winter – although it does mean I'll have no excuse to go to the doctor's when it gets colder. Still, I might not be doing this then. I mean, how long can this really go on for? I stop in my tracks. I hadn't thought about that before. What is going to happen? Will we ever meet? Will the messages just stop one day?

The thought continues to play on my mind when I'm back at my desk. I think I should ask him to meet. It's no stranger or more dangerous than internet dating, is it? I suppose there is a chance he is a psychopath going to collect his anti-psychotic medication every day and that he'll forget to take it and murder me. But the probability is low. No. I've made up my mind. I'm going to ask him to meet. Now I need another excuse to go back and it will have to be good.

–

'How about this,' Sofia says as I sit with my head resting on my palm, exhausted by my Google search of 'reasons to visit a doctor'. She proudly drops a sheet of pale blue paper on my desk. (I think my obsession has been a good distraction from the Joey situation.) I glance down at the leaflet. Oh my God, this is better than I could have imagined.

'It came in the post on Saturday and I thought it was the same place you'd been going to. I meant to give it to you this morning.'

'This is perfect! But... I mean... I don't need to be *tested*.'

Sofia looks at the ground and I pretend to have received an important email.

'What about Dan?' she asks, breaking the awkward silence.

Dan! Of course! Why didn't I think of that? 'Sofia, you are a legend. We'll probably go before work tomorrow.'

'Shouldn't you check with him first?'

'He'll be cool about it,' I say.

Sofia nods but doesn't look convinced. I'm sure he'll do it with a little persuasion…

DON'T RISK IT, TEST IT
Are you practising safe sex?
Even if the answer is yes you may still be at risk of STDs.
Come along to our open clinic for a free test.
Every Thursday morning at the walk-in centre.
THREADNEEDLE NHS WALK-IN CENTRE
Threadneedle Street London

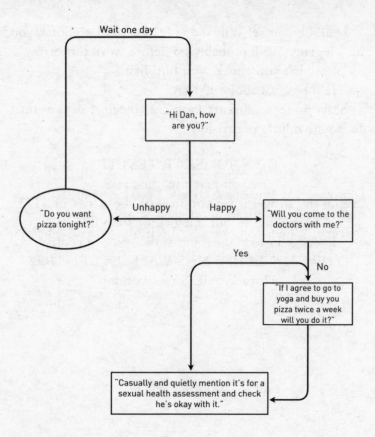

Fifteen

I know what I'm going to say. I've perfected it (having made small modifications at each station I passed on the journey home). I check that the leaflet Sofia gave me is safely tucked into the inside pocket of my bag and open the front door.

'Hi, Dan, how are you?'

Dan pauses his game and sits back on the sofa.

'What do you want?'

How does he always know?

'Nothing. I was just asking how your day was. Do you fancy pizza tonight? It's on me.'

'No.'

'You don't want pizza?'

'No, I'll have the pizza but whatever you really want to ask me, the answer to that is "no".'

'Why do you assume I have an ulterior motive whenever I want to do something nice?' I ask, putting down my bag and coat and nonchalantly making my way to the kitchen to prepare my fifth cup of tea for the day.

'Past experience. I suggest you try the grovelling approach instead,' he says.

'Changing the subject,' I say as the kettle clicks to say the water is boiled, 'Sofia came up with an ingenious plan of how I can get another chance to write to Puzzle-man.'

'Did she now?' I can't see his face from here but I can tell he has a wry smile on it.

'Yeah,' I carry on regardless. 'She found out the walk-in centre is running a… clinic tomorrow.'

'Clinic for what?'

'General health check and stuff.' I rub my eyelid.

'How interesting,' he says, mockingly.

'Yeah. Sounds good, doesn't it?'

'Sounds perfect for you.'

'Hey, Dan, you're probably overdue a health check. When was the last time you went to the doctor's?'

'I'm not sick.'

'Neither am I, but—'

'Depends on who's assessing you.'

'No, seriously, Dan, I bet you could do with a check-up.'

'No thanks.'

'But—'

'Cassy, this is the time to start grovelling.'

'The thing is, Dan,' I say in my sweet, I-only-need-a-very-small-and-tiny-favour voice, 'the receptionist is starting to get a bit suspicious. But if I was just there as your moral support—'

'Who takes someone to the doctor's for moral support?' Dan asks, half sniggering.

'Lots of people,' I say, a little indignant. I always used to go with Seph when he wasn't feeling well. 'Come on, it will be fun.'

Dan raises an eyebrow at me.

'I'll buy you two pizzas a week *and* go to yoga again.' Dan gives a little defeatist-sounding sigh. 'If I must,' he says. 'But just for the pizza, you cramp my style at yoga.'

'Great. We can go first thing, before work.'

He raises his eyebrow again. Maybe asking him to get up at 6 a.m. is stretching the favour a little far.

'OK, I'll let work know I'm going to be a little late in tomorrow.'

I lean over and give him a big hug which he tries to shrug off as his attention turns back to his video game, a different one I notice. He is now shooting zombies rather than aliens.

'That can't be the pizza already,' I say as I put down my half-finished cup of tea to answer the intercom.

'Should be. I ordered it before you got in.'

From: Cassidy Brookes
Sent: Weds 20:00
To: Thomas Samuel
Subject: Doctor's Appointment

Dear Mr Samuel,
I'm afraid I have to go to the doctor's tomorrow morning.
Apologies for any inconvenience, I will make the time up in the evening.
Kind regards,
Cassidy (Account Director)

From: Thomas Samuel
Sent: Weds 20:30
To: Cassidy Brookes
Subject: Re: Doctor's Appointment

That's fine but please do hurry back as Martin is out tomorrow morning as well.
TS

I am determined to make the most of my rare weekday morning lie-in. I take an extra-long shower. I let the warm water soak into my skin, the pounding spray massaging my shoulders. When I finally decide to get out, I put on my dressing gown and go into the kitchen to make a bowl of Kellogg's Special K. I have convinced myself that I should try the two-week diet. It's not that I've put on weight (all right maybe half a stone since the break-up), but it would be nice to look good in the new suits I'm going to buy as a reward for getting promoted. That's if I ever manage to get this meeting at Lockley & Co. Of course Martin would have no problem getting a meeting. In fact, I'm surprised he hasn't. Then again, he did seem determined to make his way without using his father's name. I have to admit I do respect him for that.

Enough about Martin, I say to myself, and start combing my hair. I think I will put a bit of make-up on today. I should really start making more of an effort now I'm single, if I plan on meeting someone new that is. A large, choking lump forms at the back of my throat just thinking about it. I don't have a group of single girlfriends anymore. I haven't gone on The Pull since I was nineteen and frankly it's not something I ever want to do again.

I block out the thought and finish my cereal watching the breakfast television. I'm tempted to go back to bed for twenty minutes but with Martin out of the office as well I don't want to be too late. Martin hasn't counter-attacked since I got Dan to pretend to be a client so I need to stay on top of my game.

'Dan, time to wake up!'

Dan snores on my shoulder throughout the train journey as I work my way through the newspaper cross-word. The shudder of the train as we arrive at Bank jerks Dan into life. He shuffles off the DLR after me, his shoulders hunched like he is eighty-five. He's wearing the tracksuit he's worn all week and sticks out in the crowd of commuters like a sore thumb as we make our way to the walk-in centre. Funnily enough, though, he fits right in when we get inside. In fact, it's probably about time I told him what today's clinic is going to be testing him for.

'Please sign-in at the reception desk,' says Lucy, soon to be dubbed, Nurse Chatterbox.

'I'm just here as moral support,' I say, hoping she won't give me an update on the latest events in her personal soap-style love life. She nods and hands Dan what looks like a questionnaire.

'Erm, Dan, I meant to tell you—'

'Sorry, I think you've given me the wrong form?'

Damn, I should have told him sooner.

'No, that's right. Just fill it in and give it to the doctor when you're called,' she says to Dan.

'But why on earth do you need a list of my previous sexual partners?' Dan asks, loud enough to attract the attention of everyone in the waiting-room.

'Well,' Lucy blushes a little, 'if the tests come back positive, it's important we can contact anyone else who may be infected.'

'Why the hell would it matter? It's just *general* checks, like blood pressure?'

Lucy looks from Dan to me, completely perplexed.

'This is a clinic for a general health check, right?'

'No. This is a sexual health clinic. We are testing for chlamydia, syphilis and HIV.'

Dan looks from her to me. Double damn.

'Ben Dover?' A wave of sniggering washes through the waiting-room. A boy, maybe sixteen or seventeen, casually stands up and high fives his surrounding friends. He looks so pleased with himself for using a clever pseudonym as he does the Rude Boy swagger over to the doctor. A male, handsome doctor!

'Are you having a laugh?' Dan yells, his face suddenly blood red. The whole waiting-room is looking at us again, as all five-foot eleven inches of Dan explodes into a rage, mainly directed at me I think, but addressed to everyone. 'I don't have a bloody STD. And there's no way you're sticking anything up there. Bloody hell, Cassy, you're the one who wanted to come!'

'Me?'

Oh God. He's going to blow my cover.

'Yeah,' Dan says, his expression has changed from outrage to devilish. I don't need to be a genius to know what's coming next. 'I mean, Cassy, I know I said I would help you out, but trying to make out I have an STD when you're the one with the rash. Well, that's just taking liberties.'

'I don't have a rash!'

Everyone's eyes are on me. With every second I can feel myself shrinking until I feel the height of a matchstick. I'm rooted to the spot. Lucy holds out the form for me. What can I say? No, I don't need it? Run out of the centre? I don't think my legs will allow it. So many eyes are burning into me. I reach out and take the form. Anything to get this moment relegated to history so I can start to erase it from my memory.

'Right well, now that's sorted, I'll leave you promiscuous people to it,' Dan says.

By the time I turn around Dan has already disappeared out of the centre.

'Miss Brookes,' Janet says and gives a little, almost disapproving nod.

This day could not get any worse.

I drag myself over to the armchair on autopilot and keep my eyes fixed on the stack of magazines to avoid seeing all the smirks that I'm sure are currently being directed at me. The armchair doesn't seem as comfortable as usual and I don't feel the rush of adrenalin as I fumble to find the puzzle book. My heart isn't banging in my chest as I flick through the pages looking for a message but I keep searching. I'm sure reading another cryptic clue from Puzzle-man will cheer me up.

-

There's nothing. I've gone through the book seven times: front to back, back to front, randomly. I've even checked a couple of the other magazines in the stack. Nothing. But the Bea business card is gone.

'Justin Time?' A second roar of teenage sniggering fills the room. I bang my feet together and click my heels. *There's no place like home. There's no place like home.* A few of the kids are texting and I have a vision of this morning's events appearing on YouTube: 'Cassy Brookes Hides a Rash'. The idea of my mum seeing it makes my stomach churn. I can't do this. I stand up and head for the exit.

'Cassy?' I turn around and my head starts to feel light.

'Rose? How lovely to see you,' I say as casually as possible. 'What are you doing here? Nothing serious, I hope?'

'Oh no, we've booked some of the youth group in for a follow-up careers advice session.'

'Oh, right. By "we", do you mean—' A lump in my throat makes each word a little harder to pronounce.

'Martin, yes, dear, I do,' her eyes sparkle. 'He said he had a lovely time on your date. Are you OK, dear? You look awfully pale.'

'Quite well, I've already seen the doctor. In fact I was just leaving.'

'Oh, that's a shame. You'll miss Martin.'

'That's a pain but I am running really late. Lovely to see you,' I start walking backwards towards the door. 'Bye, Rose.'

I catch sight of Lucy talking to Janet and trip over the skirting by the entrance.

'Wow, steady.' Strong, firm hands catch me. I turn and my eyes lock with Martin's.

'Cassy Brookes?' The doctor's voice snaps me back into the moment.

'Sorry, you must have made a mistake. I only needed a prescription,' I say. 'Must run.' I pull myself out of Martin's embrace and dive through the door before anyone can say anything else.

As soon as I'm outside I start running and I don't stop until I'm safely in the Underground. There's no way I'm going to work now. I'm going straight home and killing that so-called best friend of mine.

From: Cassidy Brookes
Sent: Thurs 11:00
To: Thomas Samuel
Subject: Fw: Doctor's Appointment

Dear Mr Samuel,
I'm very sorry but I have been to the doctor's and I am not feeling very well at all. I think it is best if stay home today. I will remote in and do some work from home.

Kind regards,
Cassidy (Account Director)

–

From: Thomas Samuel
Sent: Thurs 11:07
To: Cassidy Brookes
Subject: Fw: Re: Doctor's Appointment

Hi Cassidy,
Don't worry, Martin called to tell me he bumped into you. He said he is more than happy to cover your meetings and work on the MediaTech project.
I hope you feel better soon. Best wishes,
Thomas Samuel (Partner)

Sixteen

I'm sorry but the person you have called is not available. Please leave your message after the tone.

I'm sorry but the person you have called is not available. Please leave your message after the tone.

'Pick up Dan.'

I'm sorry but the person you have called is not available. Please leave your message after the tone.

'You won't be able to avoid me for ever.'

I'm sorry but the person—

I'm going to kill him.

'Literally kill him.' I dig my nails into my hands. The woman opposite me ushers her little boy to move a few rows down the carriage away from me and gives me a concerned stare, like I'm some kind of nutter.

I seriously am going to kill him as soon as I get off this bloody train. A rash! What if one of the kids tells Rose? What if Martin tells Mr Samuel? I don't know what's worse – my mum finding out or Mr Samuel. Oh why did Dan have to say that? He could have just said we'd made a mistake with the clinic, anything other than that. Not to mention, the trip was completely and utterly pointless: there was no message in the puzzle book and the new most likely suspect for Puzzle-man, Dr Handsome, thinks I have unprotected sex!

This is Royal Victoria. Please remember to take all your belongings with you.

I power walk to my flat and start cursing Dan from the moment I enter the lift (which has finally been fixed).

Third floor.

'Dan, you are a total—'

'Excuse me, love.'

I almost walk into a levitating sofa as I step out of the lift. Seconds later I realise it is being carried out of a flat by the two hunkiest-looking men I have ever seen. I take a step backwards and feel the cool metal of the lift door on my back as I suck my stomach in and scrunch up my toes to avoid getting squashed.

The fleeting thought of being splattered to death momentarily disorientates me but now a knot is forming tight in my chest. This is Dan's sofa, being pulled out of Dan's flat. Looking over the top of the sofa, I can just about make out the top of Dan's head.

'Dan?'

I squeeze around the back of the bulky guys as they decide to take the stairs. Dan is slumped against the wall by my front door, looking at the ground.

'What the hell is going on?' I ask.

He doesn't answer. I reach out and put my hand on his shoulder but he shrugs me away.

'What does it look like?' The venom in his voice thrusts me back a few paces.

'Like you're letting these guys burgle your flat, that's what,' I say, my nervous-humour kicking in. He doesn't even blink. He turns his back on me and walks into my flat.

'You could go to jail for faking an insurance claim,' I say and follow him inside, desperately trying to find some sign that this isn't as serious as it looks.

Dan goes into the kitchen and reaches for the corner cupboard where we keep the booze. He doesn't go for the red wine, he takes out the whisky that used to be Seph's. Dan doesn't drink whisky. He hates it.

'Dan, don't—'

He pours it into a half-pint glass and starts gulping.

'Wow, wow, wow, that's enough!'

'Says who?'

'Me, your friend. I know we were fighting but you don't have to drown all your sorrows in one go.'

'Are you simple or something?' he shouts, his face scarlet.

'I'm sorry, you know I don't cope well in situations like this.'

'Oh well, if *you're* not coping.'

'That's not what I meant. Oh, this is coming out all wrong. I just meant—'

'You're not the only one with problems! Christ, you don't even have problems. You just create them to make your life less meaningless!'

Dan throws the glass in the sink. Whisky splatters over the worktop.

'Take it easy.'

'Nothing about this is easy!'

He bursts into tears. I reach out to him but he pushes me away. He storms into the living room and starts throwing his controllers into a cardboard box.

'Dan, just tell me what happened.'

He picks up his PS2, stares at it for a second and then slams it into the box too. The sound of the plastic shattering on plastic is the only thing that defies the stark silence. He slumps down to the floor, leaning on the wall. I sit down beside him. I don't know how long we sit there; every second feels like an hour. I've never seen him like this. I can hear the two men coming back up the stairs. They're laughing but I can't tell what they're saying. Then there is more shuffling and the clicking of metal. I think they must have un-mounted his flat screen TV. I want to go over there, tell them to stop, to put everything back and piss off, but something is stopping me. Dan starts to whimper a little, his shoulders arched forward with his head in his hands.

'Dan, what's going on?' I ask, softly, and help Dan onto the sofa.

'They're repossessing my stuff.'

Well, I'd gathered that much. That must have been why that man came looking for him and why he got so defensive over his post. The signs were there and I missed them. But, I mean, it would be the last thing I'd look for, he inherited a ton of money when his dad died. I mean…

'You're loaded.'

Crap, I didn't mean to say that out loud.

'Was. Past tense,' he says and wipes his nose on his sleeve.

'You can't go from wealth to bailiffs that quickly. It's not like you put money in stupid investments, it's all in ISAs and bonds,' I say with a nervous laugh. 'Right?'

Dan's face says no.

The leather squeaks as I move a little closer to him on the sofa. I slowly extend my arm like a child reaching out to stroke a horse, a little scared they might get bitten. Dan doesn't bite, he lets me hold him and he cries in my arms.

'It's OK, Dan,' I say and gently kiss his cheek. I can taste his tears on my lips. 'We can work this out. Just tell me how this happened?'

He starts to speak but he can't get his words out. Tears fall down my cheeks. I wish I could stop him hurting but his cries keep getting louder.

'Was it fraud?'

'No,' he murmurs and shakes his head. He wipes his eyes and takes a deep breath.

'A con man?'

'In a way,' he says and a kind of laugh escapes him. 'It was Luke.'

'*Luke?* But how?'

'He said he had some connections in the stock market. He told me the trade was a sure thing. It was and we doubled up. But then he heard of another, even better trade. He wanted more money. That time it didn't work out.'

We fall silent again as I try to digest this new information. Luke, the really cute personal trainer Dan dated for eight months, is also a broker.

Actually... I can sort of believe it. He certainly had the gift-of-the-gab and Dan is so trusting. I'm not surprised Luke persuaded him to invest some money. *Some* money, that is. But surely not *all* of Dan's money.

'*Everything* I had,' Dan says, reading my mind.

Oh my God. Why didn't he come to me? (I think I already know the answer to that.) I pull Dan into another

216

large hug as a thick layer of guilt envelops me. I should have noticed. I should have been paying attention.

'The black eye?'

'That was one of Ralph's men.'

'And all the dates you've been going on?'

'I've been camping outside Luke's house. I wanted to confront him but I must have had the wrong address.'

Dan breaks down. I hold him tighter.

'It's going to be OK. We can fix this, together.'

Is it? Can we? Dan's eyes tell me he's asking the same questions as I am.

'We *will*,' I reassure him. 'I can help with this.'

'Thanks,' he says, quietly.

'OK,' I say, pumping myself up to turn this situation around. 'First, we need some music to drown out those fat gits and then we need—'

'A list?'

'You read my mind,' I say and breathe a sigh of relief as I see Dan smile for the first time today.

'Have you got all your accounts and stuff?'

Dan scuttles off to the bedroom and comes back with a crate of paperwork. It is not the best account keeping I have ever seen but certainly not the worst. I'm about a tenth of the way through sorting everything into piles when my mobile rings and ABBA begins to sing 'Dancing Queen'.

'Ignore it,' I tell Dan.

'You seriously need to change that ring tone.'

'Yeah, yeah.'

While sorting paperwork, I make a mental note of everyone I know who might be of use: bankers, accountants, anyone who owes me a favour.

ABBA fills the room again. I turn my phone off without even checking who's calling. This is more important right now.

'I'll order a pizza. My treat,' Dan says. His face seems to have had a weight lifted from it. Have I really missed all the signs that he was going through a crisis? Have I really become so self-involved?

I'm surrounded by paperwork when the pizza arrives.

'I'll get it,' I say, but it's too late, Dan has pressed the intercom and is already heading for the door. The sound of Dan's life being towed away magnifies a hundred times when he opens the door.

'Here's your pizza… Dude? Your pizza?'

'Oh, yeah, cheers.'

Dan walks back into the lounge in a daze. 'It's all right, Dan, we'll sort this out.' He nods and kneels down next me.

'Bloody hell, Cassy. I think we're going to need another pizza before we've got through all of this lot.'

–

By 6 p.m. I am starting to think Dan is right about needing a second pizza. The paperwork is sorted and we're just going through the emails Dan and Luke exchanged about the 'investment portfolio'. The more I know, the less it seems like a trade and the more like a scam. It really is a mess and I'm not sure whether anything we have here would stand up in a court of law. I'm totally out of my depth.

'So, what do you reckon? Can we get my money back?'

I'm saved from answering that question by the landline ringing.

'Probably a cold caller,' I say. 'Do you want another drink?'

Cassy? Cassy? Are you home yet? It's Mum. I've been ringing your mobile but it keeps going to voicemail. Where are you?

'She probably just wants us to go to yoga again. I'll call her back later,' I say to Dan.

The 'We Will Rock You' instrumental plays as a voice sings: *I will, I will, call you back…*

'How about I change my ringtone when you change yours?'

'It's your mum, again.'

'Just leave it. I'll call her later.'

'It might be serious,' Dan says and accepts the call.

'No, it—'

'Ann? Hi, how are you?… I'm fine… Yes she's here…'

Nice one, Dan. I give him a stern glare and point at how much filing I have left to do as he hands me over the phone with a cheeky grin and a shrug.

'Cassy?' Mum's voice sounds awful, full of worry, the tone she used whenever I had a temperature as a kid and she worried about whether I had meningitis or tuberculosis (even though I'd had the vaccines).

'Hi, Mum, are you OK?'

'Yes. It's you I'm worried about.'

'Me? I'm fine.'

'Well, that's not what Rose told me.'

Oh God, how much has Rose said? How much does she know?

'What's Rose got to do with anything?' I stall for time. I try to get Dan's attention but he is busy ordering a second pizza on the laptop. (All we seem to eat these days is pizza. No wonder I've put on weight.)

'She said she saw you at the Threadneedle Walk-in Centre today.'

'Yeah, I was picking up a prescription for some sleeping pills.'

'That's not what Rose said. She said you had gone to an... *STD* clinic.'

Keep calm. Keep calm.

'What? You must have misheard her,' I say, trying to keep my tone as uninterested and un-rattled as possible but Dan can see my expression. He starts making large hand gestures at me to tell him what's going on. He sits up close to me and presses his ear on the other side of the phone.

'She said you have a rash!'

Dan snorts and I slap him hard as he runs off to the kitchen to continue laughing.

'Cassy? What is going on?'

'That was all a misunderstanding.'

Mum goes quiet and waits. She waits because she knows that there is a little high-pitched voice inside my head saying, *if you don't tell her she won't let it go, she'll find out, it will look worse, you'll never be able to look her in the eye again, your life will be over...*

I hold my breath. I. Won't. Give. In. To. The. Voice. Finally I say, 'Well if that's everything Mum, I'd better get—'

'Cassidy Ann Brookes.'

'It's not what it looked like, Mum,' I say, so quickly it reeks of guilt.

'Well, then tell me what it didn't look like, Cassidy.'

'Dan was playing a practical joke.'

Silence. Again.

'Ask him if you don't believe me.'

'Sweetheart,' Mum says, her voice no longer stern but that gross, lovey-dovey voice mothers can put on. 'I was young too, once. We've all had moments, done things that we aren't proud of. Why do you think we had that little chat about rebounds?'

'Yes but—'

'What kind of rash is it? Is it *down there*?'

'Mum!' I can't handle this.

'I've had several—'

'Mum, stop talking or I will hang up! I do not have a rash and I certainly don't want to know if you were stupid enough to get one.'

Mum goes quiet again.

'I'm sorry, that's not what I—'

'I think you should come to confession.'

'*Confession!*' I say, just as Dan walks over to me. He goes straight back to the kitchen for a second spout of uncontrollable laughter.

'Yes. The church is running the sacrament of reconciliation tonight and I think you should come.'

'Firstly, I haven't been to church in over seven years and—'

'Even more reason why you should come to confession tonight. It starts in an hour so you'd better leave now. Give my love to Dan.'

With that she hangs up before I have any chance to protest. God, this is a nightmare. I really want to get to grips with all this Dan-Luke stuff tonight but I'll never hear the end of this if I don't go to church now. Dan finally stops laughing, tears in his eyes, but these ones are from sheer delight.

'Dan. I'm really sor—'

'Forget it,' he says and ruffles up my hair. 'I wouldn't want to keep you from confessing your *many* sins. Besides, you'll never hear the end of it if you don't go.'

I smile at him. He always understands. He's always there for me when I need him. It's just me that's the bad friend.

'Listen. Come to my office in the morning around eleven. Bring this stuff. I'll free my diary. I'm sure some of my ex-clients will be able to help us sort this out.'

'You sure?'

'One hundred per cent, we're going to wipe the floor with him. OK, I'd better get going, I don't want to have to confess to being late for confession.'

'It might put you in a better light than if you tell the priest your real confessions.'

'Ha ha. I think you're getting the two of us mixed up. Right. Keys. Bag. Shoes. OK, I'm ready, see you later.'

'See you. Oh and Cassy?'

'Yep?' I say, poking my head back around the door.

'Love you.'

'Love you too,' I say and blow him a kiss.

List #604: Confessions

- I'm sorry for all the sins I committed 12–84 months ago.
- I'm sorry I haven't been a good friend to Dan.
- I'm sorry I've lied to the Threadneedle Walk-in Centre about:
- Losing my ear-ring.
- Needing sleeping pills (and losing the prescription).

- Living with Gran.
- Wanting a flu jab.
- Dan having chlamydia.
- ~~I'm sorry I tried to sabotage Martin's promotion~~ I am sorry for the way I went about sabotaging Martin's promotion.

Seventeen

God, what a nightmare. And by nightmare, I mean a literal nightmare, not the tangled cobweb my life is turning into.

Last night I dreamt that I was walking up the hill to my old secondary school. I climbed over the metal railings and jogged over to the sports field behind the playground. I could see there was someone waiting for me. It looked like a shadow at first, or maybe a ghost. But as I got closer the outline became more solid. It was a woman. She had a slightly hunched back and was holding a book.

Who was it?

Rose Busybody Fairlop.

She was just standing there, in the middle of the grounds and as I got to within a few paces of her she gave me a motherly smile and held out her arms. Then all of a sudden I teleported (as you do in dreams) to Epping Forest, not too far from where I grew up. Rose was with me and we walked over to a group of people I didn't recognise. They were building something out of books. I can't really remember what happened next but I know how it ended. They locked me in a ten-foot-square prison made out of puzzle books with only one small barred window made out of fountain pens. Then Rose started shouting, 'This is your penance. This is your penance.'

Rose was at the service yesterday evening.

'Oh Ann, it's so lovely to see you,' she had said and taken my mum's hand in hers.

She had insisted we look at her display board of the youth group. It was full of photographs from various excursions. Martin was in nearly every picture.

'Oh, Cassy, it's so lovely to see you *here*. Do you know, I think the last time I saw you *here* was when you were about to start university?'

She kept emphasising that the last time she saw me *here*, at church, was years ago. Just to make sure we were all aware that she had seen me recently, just not *here* at church. The organ had begun before I could reply.

'Oh! We'd better take our seats,' she'd said. When she was about to walk away and leave us in peace she turned and gave me a motherly smile, just like in my dream.

She sat in the adjacent aisle and glanced back over to us, waved, and gave my mother a sympathetic smile that said 'there is still hope'. I closed my eyes to avoid sending daggers at her. What a snitch. Hasn't anyone ever told her gossiping is a sin, too?

Besides that, the service wasn't too painful and moved fairly quickly to the part where we all had to queue for our turn to go into the small box rooms hidden in the walls of the church in which we were to confess our deepest and darkest sins. I'd made a list of what I wanted to confess on the train. It turned out to be longer than I thought so I decided it was better to focus on the past year.

'Bless me, Father, for I have sinned. My last confession was seven years ago,' I had said, before I began to rattle through my list.

In the end I only got around to telling Father Roger about neglecting Dan and how I've been so preoccupied with my love life and work I'd failed to be there for him when he needed me. When I started thinking about it, there were so many evenings that I had got home and just ranted about Martin or hunched over my notebook, making a list of how to get promoted, oblivious to everything else going on around me. I'd asked Dan to be a fake client when I should have been asking what was going on in his life. I was selfish and I prioritised my promotion over the person I care about most in the world.

Father Roger told me I needed to spend some time reflecting on the severity of each event and say ten Hail Marys which I duly did. But all it did was make me realise what an underachiever I am, not just as a friend but also as an employee. Being a successful account director is all about building strong relationships and if I can't even be a good friend to someone I love, no wonder Martin is doing better than me. Dan says I shouldn't be feeling guilty, that he shut me out because he was ashamed. He said I should fight for the promotion but I wonder if it's too late, the digital strategy conference is in three days and I still have no new super-duper client.

> *The next train approaching platform one is for Bank.*

Stupid bloody nightmare. I'm so tired and I'm running super late for work. Thank God it's Friday and the partners will be in their weekly agenda meeting.

'*Martin, please save me!*' That's what I shouted from my prison of puzzle books. Remembering it is making me feel cold and empty, the same way I felt when I woke up at 2 a.m., 3 a.m. and 4 a.m. Maybe it was some sort of sign? It must have meant *something* at least. The puzzle-book stuff is obviously because I searched in the book and found nothing, but also identified the potential Puzzle-man, aka Dr Handsome. But calling out for Martin is the worrying part. I have to prepare myself in case he really does get promoted over me.

The DLR is absolutely packed with no chance of getting a seat. I slot in between two men in dark suits, both engrossed in their morning papers, both of whom are pretending they can't see the other ten people trying to squeeze on and that they can't hear the request for them to 'move down the carriage'.

The more I think about it, the more I think that dream was a warning. I need to pre-empt Martin's gloating, but how?

There's no space to get out my notebook so I will have to make do with a virtual list. I hear quite a few tuts and huffing and puffing as I accidentally knock a few people off balance while trying to locate my phone in my Mary Poppins-style handbag. Wrapping one arm around an aqua-coloured pole, I put my newspaper under the other arm and hold my coffee in my left hand so I can carefully use my right hand for typing.

> *The next station is Bank, where this train termin-ates. All change please.*

'Argh!'

The train jerks forward more than I'm expecting as we enter Bank station. I lose my grip on the pole, my body lurches forward, as does my coffee, all over one of the commuters.

'Oh my God, I am so sorry!' I say.

He does not look happy. I had deliberately loosened the plastic lid on my takeaway coffee to cool it down and currently I'm not sure if that was a good or a bad thing. It means that most of my coffee just landed on the back on some guy's suit that looks like it might have been from Gucci. But, on the plus side, it wasn't as hot. Obviously that is a very small positive and one that the man – who I'm hoping is kind – doesn't seem to be too bothered about right now.

He doesn't even speak to me. He sighs loudly, pulls off his jacket and wipes it down with his hand, causing droplets of coffee to fall onto the platform floor.

'I really am so sorry. Here, take my card. I'll pay for the dry cleaning.'

I rummage in my bag for a business card but I can't find one.

'Take mine.' He holds out his card without looking at me, still focused on his jacket. I take it and continue standing there like a little timid schoolgirl as I watch him walk off, leaving me on the platform holding a half-empty coffee cup and a wet newspaper. I step past the small puddle of coffee and throw my paper into the see through bin along with the cup. I glance down at his business card.

Edmund Carter, Managing Director
Lockley & Co.
King William Street, London.

It's funny how fate intervenes at the most unexpected moments. Another train arrives on the platform, with a second crowd of London commuters packed in like sardines. I turn to get a head start on the Underground Army assault course before they all disembark. I walk past my usual exit at Bank station and head for King William Street instead.

Comparing the offices of Lockley & Co. to Holywells is like comparing Buckingham Palace with McDonald's (and Holywells has a nice office). The entire Lockley & Co. building is made out of glass and steel. Looking in from the street you can see the famous fish-tank wall at the rear of the foyer which extends some ten storeys. I accidently revolve around the doors twice, distracted by the size of the crystal chandeliers that make Tiffany look like a pawn shop. My footsteps echo across the foyer as I make my way over to the reception desk, each receptionist more glamorous than the last.

'Good morning and welcome to Lockley & Co. How can I help you?' The young receptionist looks at me with such care and attention I feel like royalty.

'Oh hello,' I say eventually, after staring at her for far too long, 'I have an appointment with Mr Edmund Carter?'

I hadn't considered what I would say when I got here so that seems as good a statement as any.

'What's your name please?'

'Cassidy Brookes.'

'You don't seem to be on his list. Let me check with his personal assistant.'

'Actually, I'm probably not on there.' Her eyes narrow and suddenly I feel like the servant found eating the canapés. 'You see, I'm a friend of Sir Lockley's son.' She looks over at security. 'And by friend,' my eyelids go into overdrive, 'I of course mean girlfriend. Sir Lockley and I know each other well. Why only the other day I was saying how helpful all his staff were, particularly the receptionists.'

'Oh, I'm sorry to have kept you waiting, Miss Brookes,' she says and for a nanosecond looks flustered. 'Sir Lockley is in the office today. I'll let him know you're here.'

--

Oh crap. Oh crap. Oh crap.

With every second the glass lift takes me closer and closer to the seventeenth floor where Sir Lockley is expecting to see Martin's girlfriend. One blind date hardly qualifies me. Oh God, this is a whole new level of *winging it*! The door slides open and I step out to another enormous foyer devoted solely to Sir Lockley.

I force my feet to step out of the lift and anxiously walk over to the reception desk. A beautiful Spanish lady with long auburn curls is sitting behind the desk. I brace myself. I don't need to read her name tag to know she is Lorella Beaumount. I'm about five paces away from her when a huge tinted-glass door opens on my right and I am face-to-face with Sir Lockley for the second time in my life.

'Miss Brookes, what a lovely surprise. Lorella tells me you are here for a meeting with Edmund?'

I had been pondering this moment while I made my way up to his office and I only see one option. I'm going to have to tell the truth.

'Actually, Sir Lockley, I spilt my coffee down him on the DLR this morning and owe him the money for dry cleaning. I really came to see you.'

I watch as Sir Lockley does his best to hide his amusement and out of the corner of my eye I can see Lorella shaking her head.

'Please,' he says, 'come into my office.'

I follow him inside what can only be described as a double penthouse apartment. We walk about one hundred metres over cream carpet that is so soft I want to curl up and fall asleep on it. The space is flooded with natural light and I find myself staring out at a spectacular view of London. He gestures for me to sit on one of two leather sofas.

'So, Cassidy, may I call you Cassidy?' I nod.

'I'm so glad to meet you again. Martin never introduces his girlfriends to the family.'

'Oh, I'm not really his girlfriend,' I say at lightning speed.

'Oh, sorry, it's just the way he was looking at you in Le Papillon, I assumed... Never mind, my mistake.' He smiles. 'So tell me, Cassidy, to what do I owe this pleasure?' His tone suggests Lorella has filled him in on my multiple phone calls and emails. I put the thought out of my mind. I simply can't miss an opportunity this good.

'I have a proposal that I hope you will consider.'

My five-minute pitch is better than all the practice runs I've done in the mirror and after half an hour of questioning he's totally bought into the idea.

'I just have one final question,' he says.

'Fire away.'

'Does Martin know about this?' I pause for a moment.

'Absolutely.'

'Well, in that case, Cassidy, send over the contracts and I'll see you at the digital strategy conference for the big unveil.'

–

As I follow Mr Samuel's assistant to Holywells' seventh-floor boardroom my hands are shaking with adrenalin. She gives three light taps on the door and pokes her head around it. 'Excuse me, Mr Samuel, Cassidy Brookes is asking to see you urgently.'

'Send her in.'

'Good morning, all,' I say, stepping into the partners' agenda meeting. I'll be a regular here one day. 'Mr Samuel, please could you sign off on this new client. I wouldn't bother you with something mundane like this but Finance won't approve it without your consent.'

'Why on Earth not?'

'Because it's for fifty million pounds.'

The expression, 'you could hear a pin drop' doesn't come close; you could hear an atom move in this room. Mr Samuel takes the paper from me.

'You got Lockley & Co. on board for your new Medi-aTech project?' Mr Samuel passes the paper around the room, all the partners looking from the paper to me.

'I met with him this morning and he's one hundred per cent on board. The only condition he has is that he is the lead sponsor of the programme and he launches it personally at the digital strategy conference.'

'Absolutely. We can agree to that. Err, gentlemen, in light of this, shall we reconvene early next week. Cassy and I should discuss this in more depth immediately.'

There is a general rumble of agreement and I get several handshakes and pats on the back as they leave. Mr Samuel has a genuine skip in his step as we walk back to his office together.

'Can I ask how you even got him to have a meeting with you?'

'Serendipity and perseverance,' I say and offer no further explanation.

'Well, whatever you did it worked. This will be a huge boost to the department and Holywells in general. And he is definitely available for the digital strategy conference? Because we could always rearrange for a different day?'

'He's free,' I say, unable to mask my glee. 'I thought that after an initial introduction by yourself, I might take the clients through the MediaTech project and then pass over to Sir Lockley?'

'Excellent plan.'

'I know I'm supposed to be pitching for the promotion tomorrow but given this new workload I'm not sure—'

'Oh, I think it's safe to say the promotion is yours. Off the record, of course. It won't be official until the conference.'

'Thank you, Mr Samuel.'

'Thank you, Cassy. I'd better call Finance, unless there is anything else we need to discuss?'

'Actually, there is one other thing. I was wondering, do you think we could keep this just between us until the conference. I think it would make such an impression to announce this at the event. If you tell someone here it's like Twitter.'

'A fantastic idea. I'll email the partners now.'

I breathe a heavy, internal sigh of relief. That takes care of Martin. He told me he hasn't spoken to his father in months so by the time he finds out it will be too late. Now to tell Sofia!

'Right, come on, get your coat. We're going for a celebratory drink,' Sofia says, jumping up and down.

'But it's 2 p.m.,' I say to her, very tempted to start jumping up and down myself.

'I hardly think Mr Samuel is going to care if you leave early on a Friday and I'll get Sally to cover me. Besides it's a double celebration.'

'Why's that?'

'The wedding is back on!'

'Oh my God, congrats. When did this all happen?'

'Yesterday. Joey and I had a long talk. He stayed at a mate's house that night. I can't believe I ever doubted him.'

'Oh, I'm so happy for you.'

'Well, get your stuff then.'

'Oh all right,' I grin, 'let's go.'

–

Sitting on the roof terrace with a Mojito, watching clouds flutter along in the sky, I can't imagine how life could get any better. A few hours later the terrace begins to get busy as people finish work.

'I'd better get home,' Sofia says. 'I just got a text from Joey asking where I am. He sounds so worried, bless him. I completely forgot I promised to cook him a special dinner tonight.'

'Ha, I remember those days, slaving away in the kitchen,' I say, thinking of Seph.

'Do you miss them?'

I smile. 'Not one bit,' I say and follow Sofia out, slightly less soberly than I would have liked. How many cocktails did we have? We sway together towards the station.

'We're still on for shopping tomorrow, right?' she asks, planting a kiss on my cheek. 'We need to get you a killer outfit!'

'Definitely,' I say and wave goodbye as we walk to our respective Underground lines. This has been such a great day. Nothing is going to spoil my mood. I can't wait to tell Dan.

—

'Nothing ever changes with you, does it,' Dan says, once I've finally got my key to open the door. He's sitting on the sofa next to his large rucksack that he bought when he decided to go travelling in Thailand (although he never actually went). His arms are folded and his eyes seem to be doing their best to burn a hole straight through my head. His muscles look rigid, his whole body stiff, like he's been turned to stone from sitting there waiting for me for so long.

'Does it,' he yells.

'What? Oh crap, I left my shoes on the train.'

'Are you *drunk*?'

'No,' I say and take a wobbly step backwards from the shock of Dan's furious tone.

'You are, aren't you? It's seven o'clock!'

'I've had a good day.'

'Well, I haven't.'

'Why, what happened? Oh crap!' I completely forgot I'd told Dan to come to the office today. 'Dan, I'm so sorry but something miraculous happened,' I say, taking a few steps towards him. But he instantly gets to his feet and evades my feeble attempt at a hug.

'This better be good.' Dan says, like he's talking to a convicted terrorist who is pleading for immunity.

'Well, I was on the DLR thinking about a dream I had about being trapped inside a prison made out of puzzle books and—'

'You mean to tell me that you couldn't spare an hour of your day to help me because you were too busy with your disturbing obsession with a puzzle book?' Dan explodes. He picks up his rucksack and starts flinging his remaining video games inside. All the time he carries on fuming and cursing, drowning out my attempts to explain. He stops and looks at me as if searching for clarity.

'Was it too much to expect you to care more about me than some weirdo Puzzle-man you've never even met?'

'It wasn't about that. It was the only chance I had to—'

'Jesus Christ, Cassy, you're even lying to yourself.'

'I'm not. Honest.'

I can feel tears forming.

'Forget it, you selfish bitch. I'm out of here.'

Dan opens the door and I grab hold of his shoulder.

'No, don't go. I'll help you. Let's do it now.'

'Oh I see,' Dan says, shrugging me off of him, 'you're so much better than the rest of us you can work even when you're completely wasted. Well, thanks but no thanks, I don't need your help.'

'Dan, please,' I say, putting my hand on the door frame to stop him leaving, 'it's not what you think. I—'

'I, I, I. It's all about you. You. You. You. You…' Dan pushes my hand out the way and I fall backwards into the room. He looks right at me. 'YOU!' he screams and with that he slams the door shut.

He's gone.

Eighteen

To: Dan Mobile Sat 00:12
Please pick up the phone. I'm so sorry,
please let me explain xx

To: Dan Mobile Sat 09:33
Hey, hope you're OK. Where did you stay
last night? Please talk to me. I know I
messed up and I'm truly sorry. Please let
me know you're OK xx

From: Sofia Mobile Sat 10:19
Hey, where shall I meet you? I was thinking
Oxford Circus station at 12noon? xx

To: Sofia Mobile Sat 10:21
Hey, do you mind if I take a rain check?
Dan and I had a fight last night and I want
to stay in, in case he comes back xx

'I thought you weren't going to show up,' Sofia says, giving me a kiss on the cheek and a hug when I arrive at Oxford Circus.

'Sorry, I wanted to wait to see if Dan would come home. I have no idea where he stayed last night.'

'Ah, don't worry. Dan seems like the kind of guy who can take care of himself.'

Until this business with Luke I would have believed her. Sofia links arms with me and gives me a determined tug.

'So, where shall we go first? I vote Karen Millen.'

We spend the next few hours trying on expensive clothes and shoes and finally decide on a light grey trouser suit with three inch, grey suede shoes.

'You look amazing,' Sofia says as I look at myself in the full-length changing-room mirror. 'All you need to do now is smile.'

'Sorry, I just can't stop thinking about Dan.'

'Still no text?'

I shake my head.

'He'll come around. What are you going to do about the conference?'

'What do you mean?'

'Weren't you planning on bringing Dan?'

'God no, I couldn't risk it after the whole fake-client incident.'

'So who are you bringing?'

'Myself.' I look at Sofia in the mirror. Her arms are folded.

'You can't go alone.'

'I've just got out of a seven-year relationship. I don't have a book of potential dates to ring up.' Sofia's face lights up. 'And don't even mention the words male and escort.'

'I wasn't going to,' she says, looking very smug.

'Puzzle-man,' she says. 'You should invite Puzzle-man.'

'Ha, you're kidding. He could be a pyscho.'

'What happened to, "he's my soul-mate"? Come on, Cassy, it's better than no date and you're dying to meet him. This is the perfect excuse.'

'But the seating plan is done.'

'I can pull some strings and get it changed easily.'

'Even so, it's too late. I don't have time to invite him.'

'It's only three. We could go to the walk-in centre now and slip an invitation in the puzzle book.'

'You really are serious, aren't you?'

'Deadly. Now come on, take that off and let's pay.'

Forty-five minutes later we're half way up Thread-needle Street, the walk-in centre is just out of sight.

'Are you sure you can pull this off?'

'Trust me,' Sofia says. 'I used to do this all the time to get out of history lessons in school. Just make sure you catch me.'

'When?'

'Now.'

Sofia falls backwards and I throw my arms out just in time.

'Help! Please!' I call out to a passing couple. 'My friend, she's fainted.'

'Here let me help you.' In one strong, muscular movement the man sweeps Sofia up into his arms.

'There's an NHS walk-in centre not too far down this road,' I stammer, my cheeks red.

–

'Oh my, what's happened here?' Janet asks when we arrive, quickly taking control of the situation. 'I'll call the doctor.'

When Dr Danes arrives Sofia has magically come to but Dr Danes insists on an examination.

'I'll wait out here for you,' I call after Sofia and Dr Danes. 'Thank you so much,' I say to the couple, acutely aware I'm under the Janet microscope. I catch her eye; she looks at me hard but doesn't say anything. I make my way over to the chair and quickly sift through the pile for the puzzle book. I slip in the card we bought on the way. I just have to hope he sees it before Monday afternoon.

> *If you're free, I'd be delighted if you'd be my date to my work conference this Monday (short notice I know). It starts at 5pm at the Elderflower Hotel. Hope to see you there.*

'I so could have made it in Hollywood,' Sofia says, linking arms with me as we walk back to Bank station. 'Just think, this time on Monday the four of us will all be standing around having a drink laughing about this.'

'So I'm finally going to meet Joey?'

'Yes, he didn't want to come. Apparently he dated some girl at Holywells and he didn't want to risk bumping into her, but I forced him to come anyway.'

'Oh, sounds serious?'

'Nah, he said it was just a fling. Besides I wouldn't mind meeting his ex. Show off my ring,' she says and parades her ring in front of me.

'Sofia, that's evil,' I laugh.

'Ha, yeah. I was only joking. I doubt she'll be there anyway. Joey said it was years ago.'

'Well, I'm glad you persuaded him. I can't wait to finally meet him.'

'You'll love him.'

'I'm sure. See you at the conference.'

Nineteen

Promotion day is finally here. I still haven't heard from Dan but I have promised myself (and Sofia) not to think about him until after the conference. It's due to start in an hour. I'm glammed-up and reading over my speech in the back of the taxi.

The driver pulls up in front of the marble steps that lead to the Elderflower Hotel. Its late-Edwardian architecture transports me into the world of *Downton Abbey*. The lobby is the size of my flat and has beautiful red velvet chaise-longues on either side. The reception desk looks like it is made of Swarovski crystals held in place by a platinum framework. A silver board with an ivory paper sign points the way to the Digital Strategy Conference. MediaTech has booked the entire right wing of the Elderflower Hotel. It's separated into three areas: a bar lounge with dance floor, an auditorium for the daytime sessions that are just for the staff, and a dining hall where I will be doing my presentation this evening. I take a sneaky look.

There are twenty round tables, each seating ten. It's like a wedding reception. They have white cloths with beautiful red-rose table features in crystal glasses. Each chair has a velvet red cushion on it. I walk through to table three where my team will be sitting. Our names are embossed in gold on the place settings. I walk around the table. John, Charles, Paul and Sally will have their backs to the stage, then Mr Samuel and Veronica, then me and my blank name tag (I didn't know what to call Puzzle-man) and then Sofia with – my knees almost give way beneath me.

How could this happen? Is it a joke? Is Martin finally getting me back for the fake meeting? Maybe the assistants used an old guest list from a Christmas party and picked the wrong plus one? I don't know. Both seem unlikely. I stare at the place setting, fighting the urge to rip it up. Seeing Seph's name, here, on my big day… I grab the card and fold it back on itself. Joey will just have to have a blank one like Puzzle-man. It's almost 10 a.m. and I make my way into the auditorium.

'Cassy! I saved you a seat.' Sofia beams at me.

'Thanks.'

'You OK?'

'Not really. The place settings…'

'What about them?'

'They messed up Joey's.'

'Oh my God, are you kidding? Joey *hates* things like that. He'll feel like he's not being included. I'll have to speak to the Events Manager.'

Sofia stands up but it's too late, it's started and I didn't even get to tell her the full story.

'Good morning, everyone,' Mr Samuel says. 'I'm so delighted to welcome you all here today and let me be the first to tell you that we have a *big* surprise in store for you later.'

-

Mr Samuel's talk is so inspirational that I soon put Seph to the back of my mind. I don't care if it was a mistake or

Martin; this is my big day and nothing is going to spoil it. The moment the session ends Sofia darts out of the room. I'd been hoping she'd come with me to meet Puzzle-man – in case he is a real creep and one of us needs to get security. But I can understand her concern about the place setting. She wants it to be perfect for Joey. I know how that feels. I make my way to the bar lounge, my heart beating faster with each footstep. In mere moments I could be meeting Puzzle-man for the very first time.

Stepping into the bar lounge is like walking into a Playboy mansion. A pathway of blue and white neon lights leads to a large, circular, black marble bar in the centre of the room that is surrounded by black velvet stools. Along each wall are American-style booths, already full of clients, deep in animated conversation.

I perch on a stool, making sure I can see the entrance. The bartender smiles at me.

'Can I get you something?'

'I shouldn't. I'm giving a presentation later.'

The bartender turns to see if anyone is watching and then pours me a shot of vodka.

'You look like you need it.'

'Thanks,' I say hesitantly. Maybe some Dutch-courage will do me good.

'You look nervous. Waiting for someone?' Martin sits down beside me.

'My date, if you must know.'

'I'm hurt. I thought our date went so well.'

I look up at him and wait for a wry smile to form but it doesn't.

'Did you put Seph on the guest list?'

'No.'

I look right into his eyes.

'Cassy, honestly, I didn't.'

'For once I believe you.'

'Having said that, I do have a different confession to make,' he says.

'Me too.' I sigh. My stomach knots. I know I have to tell him about his dad.

'It's about all the secret correspondence—'

'Oh, thank God you already know.' I breathe a sigh of relief.

'I was so worried to tell you,' he says.

'*You* were worried. How do you think I felt? So you're really not angry?'

'Why would I be?' He laughs and I finally relax.

'I think deep down I knew you'd guessed. I should have told you sooner and not gone to all the trouble of these secret communications.'

'But if you knew I knew, why didn't you just tell me?'

'Well, you were so sure you didn't want your dad assisting your career. I thought—'

'What's my father got to do with anything?'

'Because he's the one I've been emailing in secret, my new client. I thought you knew. Why, what were you talking about?'

Martin stares at me and finally says, 'It's not important.'

'OK,' I say slowly. 'So, no hard feelings then?'

'None at all.' Martin straightens his jacket. 'You did what you needed to do.'

'I knew you'd understand.'

'Of course, and congratulations.'

'On what?'

'On becoming an opportunistic snake.' He smiles at me the way he does at clients and suddenly I feel as though we are standing miles apart.

'Martin, I—'

'Hey, Cassy.' Sofia puts her hands on my shoulders.

'Excuse me,' Martin says.

'Any sign of him?'

'Who?' I ask as I watch Martin walk away. I think I might have really upset him.

'Puzzle-man,' she whispers.

'Oh no, not yet. Did the place setting get changed OK?'

'Yeah, it was nothing. You really had me worried for a minute,' she says and slaps my arm.

'What do you mean?'

'Some idiot had just folded it backwards.'

My throat clamps shut. *It's not possible.*

'Has anyone seen Cassidy?'

'Cassy, Thomas is looking for you.'

There's no way.

Sofia waves her arm. 'We're over here, Thomas.'

There's a hand on my shoulder. Mr Samuel. 'There you are. Can I have a moment?'

'I need to ask Sofia something.' I gulp. It hurts.

'OK… Well, go on then.'

Go on then.

'Cassy, are you all right? You're shaking. Are you sure you're going to be OK to do this presentation?'

'I'm fine.'

I think I might be sick.

'Well, we'd better get moving… So… Are you going to ask Sofia whatever it is?'

Yes.

No.

I don't want to.

'Cassy?'

Maybe I'm wrong. But my gut says I'm right. What if I'm right? Sofia needs to know. I need know.

'Cassy, we really need to—'

'What's Joey's surname?' I blurt.

'Y'what? Is that it?' Sofia says and both she and Mr Samuel start laughing.

I try to laugh but it's more of a hiccup.

'So – so what is it?'

I watch the shaping of Sofia's mouth and a piece of me dies before she even finishes saying it.

'O'Carroll.'

How the hell did this happen?

–

'There's really no need to be nervous,' Mr Samuel says.

Mr Samuel had dragged me away from the bar and onto the stage before I knew what was happening. I hadn't said anything to Sofia. I didn't know how, or what, or if I even should, or could. I feel as though I'm in a trance and no one realises. I can reply but I can't hear my responses. It's like I'm living in two worlds at once.

'I'll introduce you and then you can do the presentation and introduce Sir Lockley.'

How can this be true? Joey is Seph? How could I not have known?

I nod along with Mr Samuel as I re-run the past few weeks in my head. Sofia pulled a sickie for Joey's birthday. *It was the same day as Seph's.*

'Cassy? Are you listening?'

Joey went missing for a night. *It was the same night Seph came back to me.* He was planning to leave her for me. He was playing us both. My disbelief morphs into rage. Sofia needs to know.

'Cassy!'

'What? Yes. Intro. Presentation. Sir Lockley. Got it. Thanks, Mr Samuel. I'd better go and re-apply my make-up.'

I have to find Sofia.

'OK, but make it quick,' Mr Samuel calls after me.

–

I 'excuse me' and 'pardon me' through the groups of clients and Holywells staff. Sofia is already sitting at table three. Alone.

'I need to talk to you,' I say, sitting down next to her and trying to work out exactly how to tell her this news. 'Where's Seph? Joey, I mean Joey. Where is he?'

'In the bathroom. Cassy, are you OK?'

'This isn't about me. It's about you. You have to break up with him.' My eyes are stinging. It's like I'm going through the stages of grief in fast forward: from denial to shock to rage and finally to the full, catastrophic realisation of this bloody mess.

'Oh, Cassy, please don't cry,' she says and takes my hand. 'I know you must be upset that Puzzle-man stood you up but—'

'No, no, no. You don't understand,' I say, barely able to keep my voice from breaking. 'Sofia, you have to trust me. Joey isn't who you think he is.'

'What do you mean?'

'He's Seph. Joey is Seph.' Sofia pulls her hand away from me.

'What are you talking about? This is nonsense?'

'It's not nonsense.' I wipe a tear away. I will not cry. 'He came back Monday night, right? With only a rucksack?'

'So what?' Sofia stares at me.

The lights dim and everyone is told to take their seats. I look around. Seph is nowhere to be seen. Maybe he saw the seating plan and decided he was better off out of it. I lower my voice as Mr Samuel steps on stage.

'He came from mine, Sofia. He slept in my bed on bank holiday Sunday night. He told me he had been cheating and I kicked him out.'

'You're lying.'

'I can prove it. Your ring, it has the letters M J R inscribed on the inside.'

Sofia gasps and puts her hand on her chest.

'I'm so sorry to have to tell—'

'And now, let me hand over to Cassidy Brookes.' The lights are suddenly on us. I stand to a round of applause. I find myself walking to the stage thinking only of Sofia's broken heart.

'Thank you, ladies and gentlemen.' I look up at the hundreds of faces. At the back of the room I see a silhouette that I would recognise anywhere. It's Seph. He's walking towards Sofia. I dig my nails into my palm. There is no way I'm going to let Seph ruin this moment for me.

'I am delighted to announce the launch of Holywells' co-venture with MediaTech.' My voice is working but my eyes are locked on Sofia as Seph sits beside her and takes her hand. She pulls away and pours herself a glass of white wine, looking up at me, her eyes full of hate. I let automatic pilot take over and my rehearsed presentation-speech begins.

I've barely been talking for twenty minutes when Sofia reaches for the red wine, having finished the white. Martin has sat in the seat where Puzzle-man should be sitting and is looking at Seph with an expression I can't read. I contemplate shortening the demonstration.

'Rather than show you the full power of—'

'Oh, I think we all want to see it. Don't we, ladies and gents?' Mr Samuel riles up the audience. He seems oblivious to Sofia.

'Well, if you insist,' I say and reluctantly activate the demo. This isn't going to end well.

–

It's the final slide. There's a large round of applause but I can't enjoy the moment. Sofia is swaying on her chair. I glare at Seph. He had the nerve to stay for the whole presentation. Was he hoping I'd crumble? I'd never give him the satisfaction.

'And so, with no more ado,' I take a deep breath. 'May I present the ambassador of the scheme and project's lead business associate, Sir Martin Lockley!'

The room claps in appreciation. Sofia gets to her feet and cheers like it's a football match.

'Woo, great speech, Cassy. Is there no end to your talents?'

Mr Samuel leans over Seph and whispers for her to sit down.

'Don't forget to thank all your friends for supporting you to glory.'

I stop half way down the steps from the stage, watching my career ending before my eyes.

'Or maybe you thank your friends by sleeping with their fiancés.'

Everyone looks at me.

'Sof—'

'Shut up, Joey. Or should I call you SEPH!' Sofia throws the rest of her glass of wine over him, some of it landing on Mr Samuel. I rush over as if there is something I can do to help but Martin is already there.

'Come on, Sofia.' Martin takes her by the arm.

'There you are, ladies and gentleman,' Sir Lockley says. 'You can always count on my son to save the day.'

A collective gasp swirls around the room as people look from Sir Lockley to Martin. No one looks more astonished than Mr Samuel.

'Why don't we have a short toilet break and reconvene in five minutes?' Sir Lockley says as a rumbling of chatter spreads across the room.

I reach table three. 'Mr Samuel, I can explain.'

'Not now. Martin, get them out of here, please?' Martin nods and escorts Sofia, who is now sobbing uncontrollably, out of the room. Seph starts to make his way out. I follow him.

'Don't think you're getting away that easily,' I say when we reach the lobby.

'Don't *you* think you've done your career enough damage for one day?' Seph smirks before walking calmly out of the building. I hold back the tears and watch as Martin guides Sofia towards a taxi. He whispers something in her ear and gives her a hug. I stand at the entrance of the dining hall. Sir Lockley has already started his speech. I go to walk forward but Martin steps in front of me.

'Probably best not to create another scene.'

'I'm so sorry, Martin. I should never have gone behind your back.'

'All's fair in love and war.' His voice is so cold. 'It's quite ironic really.'

'How exactly?'

'Losing Seph, getting into bed with my father, all of this,' he points at the room, 'was for a promotion and, if you'd just trusted that you were good enough, you would have got it anyway.'

The audience clap as Sir Lockley finishes his speech. Martin goes into the room and is instantly swarmed by clients. I walk back into the lobby and sit down. How did I get everything so wrong?

Twenty

It's the morning after and the lift dings.

You can do this, I tell myself.

The doors slide open and I'm engulfed by a loaded silence. I can feel everyone's eyes on me, and hear their unspoken judgements. The walk from the lift to my office feels like an eternity. When I reach Sofia's desk she isn't there. Inside my office I rest against the closed door.

I can get through this. I can.

I sit down and start to sift through my emails.

> From: Charles Milligan
> Sent: Tues 09:44
> To: Cassidy Brookes
> Subject: Catch-up?
>
> Hi Cassy,
> I hope you are well. I know this is coming slightly out
> of the blue but I was wondering if you would have time
> for a catch-up, maybe over coffee?
> Best Wishes,
> Charles (Graduate)

--

> From: John Regents

Sent: Tues 09:50
To: Cassidy Brookes
Subject: Coffee?

Hi Cassidy,
I hope you are feeling well.
I was wondering if we could meet up for coffee/ lunch
sometime. I would greatly appreciate some feedback
from you on my performance.
Kindest regards,
John (Graduate)

–

From: Paul Blume
Sent: Tues 09:56
To: Cassidy Brookes
Subject: Catch-up?

Hi Cassy,
Would you have time for a quick catch-up, maybe a
coffee or drink after work?
I would appreciate the chance to get to know you
better and hear about your experience of being a
graduate at Holywells.
Thanks,
Paul (Graduate)

Three invitations for coffee before 10 a.m. would be
enough to tell me something was wrong even without all
the sheepish looks I keep getting from people as they walk
past my office. It's like sitting in a goldfish bowl except
my memory doesn't reset every four seconds. I should
have stayed in bed and called in sick. I can't seem to get

comfortable in my chair as I try to focus on all the admin I have to do. My mind keeps wandering and I keep re-reading the emails. They may have sent them out of pity but it feels like more than that. Do they know something I don't?

Sofia would know. I can't erase her sobs from my mind. I don't think she'll ever forgive me. How self-absorbed do you have to be not to realise your colleague is dating your ex-boyfriend?

I need a cup of tea.

On my way to the kitchen, I see Martin, who spots me at the same moment. I take a step towards him when I hear a familiar voice.

'Oh, Martin?' Sally puts her hand on his waist, a little too low for a colleague. 'Mr Samuel asked if you can meet him in his office.' Martin disappears so quickly it could be mistaken for a magic trick.

Sally catches me watching him. 'He's looking fresh today, isn't he?' she says.

'If you say so,' I reply and head back to my office. I don't feel thirsty anymore.

–

My office is like a prison and the warden has come to torment me.

'Hey, hun, how are you doing?'

If it wasn't for the genuine concern on Sally's face I would have given her a speech as to why I am not her 'hun'.

'I'm fine, thank you.'

'If you ever need to talk, I am a great listener.'

'I'll keep that in mind, thank you.'

'My mother always says you just need a friend and then all your problems are halved. Although she says it a bit better. I think it's something like, "a problem cut in two is a problem shared". No, that's not it. "A problem shared is—'

'Sally, is there a point to this?'

'Well, I did hear a rumour and then I got the email.'

'What email? Who from?'

'Martin sent an email to some of us.'

'Show me,' I say, and follow Sally over to her desk. I feel sick.

'He said… Well, I think it's better if you read it.' She passes me a print out. I let out a shriek. I read it again and again and again. This just can't be right.

From: Martin Robertson
Sent: Tues 09:32
To: Charles Milligan; John Regents; Paul Blume; Sofia Jenkins; Sally Lawson
Subject: Well done everyone

Dear Team,

Firstly I would like to say thank you for doing an excellent job over the past few months, it has not gone unnoticed by me or senior management.

Secondly, and on a slightly more serious but delicate note, many of you are aware that Cassidy Brookes has been going through a very difficult time in her personal life and I would ask all of you to do your utmost to be supportive and respectful to such a valued member of our team.

Kind regards,

Martin (Head of Accounts)

'I, I don't,' my throat tightens. 'Please tell me this isn't true?'

'I think it happened this morning,' Sally says, looking at her feet and shifting her body weight from one leg to the other. 'Cassy, I—'

I don't wait to hear another word. I ignore all the eyes that follow me down the corridor to Martin's office. How dare he talk about me in an email like that? A tear slips down my face. Mr Samuel promised me that promotion. I know I messed up but I can fix it. I just need time to talk to him. Mr Samuel and the other partners are crowding around Martin's office. They're shaking his hand and patting him on the back, laughing the way you do at meaningless jokes. I want to join them, to ask what's so funny, but my legs have gone cold.

I'm the joke.

Surely it's not what it looks like. *But of course it is.*

The corridor seems to darken around me. It's like I'm looking through a magic telescope and all I can see in the small circle of light at the end of the tunnel is Martin, smiling. That's what I should be doing right now. I should be shaking everyone's hands and saying, 'thank you for this wonderful opportunity'. Instead I am lip-reading Martin saying those words.

'Can I have everyone's attention, please?' Mr Samuel's voice rings in my ears, his words vibrate through my skull. People are gathering around me.

'Hey, Cassy, is this what I think it is?' one of the graduates whispers in my ear. I can't answer.

'I am pleased to announce that Martin will be taking over the role of Head of Accounts, effective immediately. I hope you will all join me in wishing him the very best in his new role.'

The office comes alive with cheers, whistling and clapping, but it all sounds far away from me, like I'm in an alternate world that only just overlaps with this one. I hear the distant ding of the lift and slowly turn my head to see staff from the cafeteria walking towards us holding trays of champagne.

Soon I have a glass of champagne in my hand but I don't think I said thank you to whoever gave it to me. I don't think my mouth is working. I don't remember how to talk.

'To Martin.'

'To Martin!' everyone says in unison and raise their champagne glasses.

I bring the glass to my lips but the bubbles burn them. I try to swallow a mouthful but my throat is so dry the drink stings and goes down the wrong way. Someone puts their hand on my back. Sally.

'Are you OK, Cassy? Cassy?'

Lots of people are patting Martin on the back. Congratulating him. Shaking his hand. He's mobbed as if he is some sort of celebrity. I guess he is a celebrity. He's the son of Sir Lockley. He soon will be a celebrity in his own right. He'll appear in the company's magazine as the high-flyer turning around the business with his team's new media platform. Maybe my name will be put in the small print somewhere.

–

The phone rings. I'm back at my desk, although I have no recollection of how I got here or how long I've been staring at my keyboard. There are water droplets on my notebook. I lick my lips. They taste of tears. I wipe my eyes and pick up the phone.

'Holywells, Cassidy Brookes, Account Director, speaking.'

'Cassy, pet, is that you?'

'Yes, Gran, it's me. What's wrong? Are you sick?'

'No, no pet, I'm just a little…' Gran's voice sounds so frail. My heart feels like it is beating in my mouth.

'How do you feel?' I ask, already getting my stuff together so I can race over to her house.

'I felt a little dizzy but I think I'm fine now. I shouldn't have rung.'

'No, no, you should. I'm on my way to see you now.'

I conference-connect my mobile, grab my bag and run out of the office. All this crap with Martin has become irrelevant.

'I'm leaving the office as we speak,' I say to Gran. I can barely hear her on the other end of the line as she tries to reassure me that there is no need for me to come over. I feel like I am in a scary movie. I wish this was just a movie. I count to ten through the revolving doors, trying to keep calm and not set off the safety-stop by walking too close to the glass.

'Gran, are you still on the line?'

'Yes, pet.'

'Good, I'll be there soon.'

Maybe I should call an ambulance? But if I do, I'll have to hang up the phone.

I sprint all the way through Leadenhall Market.

'Pet? I think someone is at the door.'

'Yes, it's me, Gran,' I say, panting. 'Will you let me in?'

'But you're on the phone?'

'Yes, I'm on my mobile but I'm outside too. Will you let me in?'

259

Finally I hear shuffling from inside and the locks slowly being undone.

'Gran, how are you feeling?'

It was a silly question. She looks like a grandmother when she opens the door. I mean, she's always been my grandmother, but she's never really looked like an elderly person. Today her wrinkles seem deeper, her blue eyes less sparkly and her beautifully soft hands look frail as she tries to re-lock the door behind me.

'Don't worry about that, Gran. We're going straight to the doctor's.'

'Oh no, please no. Would you make me a cup of tea first?'

'Are you still feeling dizzy?'

'No, just a little tired,' she says, her voice very weak.

'OK, well let's sit you down in the living room and I'll make you a nice cup of tea.'

Steam from the kettle rises up over the cupboard doors as I pace around the kitchen. I'm toying with the idea of calling Mum out of work to come and meet us at the doctor's. Gran doesn't seem to be dizzy anymore, but she must have felt very ill to ring me in the first place.

Gran is sitting on the armchair by the window when I bring in her cup of tea, strong with extra milk, no sugar. I've never quite managed to make her the perfect cup of tea but she says I'm getting better.

After twenty minutes she is still only halfway through the cup of tea but she seems to have perked up and some colour has returned to her cheeks. I decide I don't need to bother Mum.

'OK, do you want to finish that up and we'll go to the doctor's?'

'Oh, I feel much better now.'

'I think we should go just to be on the safe side,' I say and hold out her coat.

Once she's wrapped herself up warm and put on her slip-on comfort shoes, I go out to hail a black taxi.

'Threadneedle Walk-in Centre, please,' I say sixty seconds later. I help Gran into the back seat and do up her seat belt.

—

The walk-in centre is busier than usual. There are a few people waiting to speak to Janet so I walk Gran over to a comfortable-looking seat in the waiting-room. I can see my green armchair unoccupied in the corner. It's funny, until this moment I'd forgotten all about the puzzle book. I wonder if there will be a message explaining why he couldn't come to the conference.

'Miss Brookes?' Janet's voice brings me back to the present.

I smile and walk over to her, ignoring the suspicious look on her face.

'What can I do for you today?'

'My gran isn't very well. I was hoping Dr Danes could take a quick look at her?'

'There are no free appointments today. Is it urgent?'

'Yes. I left work because my gran rang to say she was,' I lower my voice, 'having a funny turn.'

Janet looks over at my gran who is now having a bubbly chat with one of the other patients waiting to be seen. Then she gives me the look I've grown accustomed to over the past few weeks. But this time I'm not lying, Gran really does need an appointment. I hold my ground (by that I mean, I continue to stare back at Janet with equal determination).

Janet glances over at my gran again and relents.

'Dr Danes is between patients at the moment. I will see if she can fit you in. Please wait with your gran.'

Janet walks down the corridor towards Dr Danes' room while I go over to sit with Gran.

'The doctor's going to fit you in now,' I say to her.

'I really am feeling much better, pet,' Gran says to me. Gran carries on chatting to the woman next to her while I try to listen to the distant voices of Janet and Dr Danes. They exchange a few hushed words and then I hear a door close but Janet doesn't reappear.

'Maybe the doctor is too busy. We should go home,' Gran says to me ten minutes later.

'No, it's fine. She's just talking to the receptionist. When they are done, Dr Danes is going to see you.'

Just as Gran is about to protest, Janet appears.

'You can go in now, Mrs Brookes.'

Janet gives me a strange look before returning to her desk. After helping Gran up and into Dr Danes' room I make my way back to the waiting-room. This time I go over to the armchair.

I try not to get my hopes up as I pick up the puzzle book. The invitation is gone so he definitely knew about it. Maybe inviting him to the conference scared him away.

Adrenalin rushes through me. A new page is folded over. I feel like I did the first time I opened my bonus payslip and thought I'd won the lottery. I place my finger and thumb over the folded edge and open up the puzzle-book. My eyes are half open and half closed as I try to prolong the anticipation but I'm too excited to wait.

Horoscopes.

He's left me a message, it says:

I hope you are an Aquarius.

Actually, being an early February baby, I am an Aquarius. I am apparently 'clever, sarcastic and original' but my stubbornness and independence can make me seem cold and impersonal. I wouldn't normally read my horoscope, but I'm curious. Puzzle-man must have read something in this that he wanted to come true.

You are soon going to meet a mysterious stranger and get a nice surprise.

Wow! He wants to meet me too! Maybe he really is my true love. Underneath he has written:

See you at the conference.

My heart sinks. He really did stand me up. He must have changed his mind.

'Miss Brookes? Could I have a word, please?' Dr Danes is standing in front of me with Gran beside her. I don't have time to hide the puzzle book so I just put it back on the pile as casually as I can. Gran takes my place in the armchair as I follow Dr Danes into her room.

'Gran's OK, isn't she?' I ask once we are inside, my personal panic button feeling like it is about to go off.

'She is quite well.'

'Thank God! So what did you want to talk to me about? Does she need new medication?'

'No,' Dr Danes sighs. She takes off her glasses. 'May I call you Cassidy?'

'Cassy, please.'

'Cassy, this isn't an easy conversation to have but it is very important.'

Oh God, something is wrong with Gran.

'Cassy?'

'Yes? Sorry. I am listening. I'm just worried about Gran.'

263

Dr Danes sighs again. 'This is not about your grand-mother. It's about you.'

Her tone makes me want to squirm in my seat the way a child does when they are called to the headmaster's office after they've been caught smoking. (Not that I have any first-hand experience of that, obviously.)

'This isn't the first time a case like this has occurred and that is partly why Mrs Jones picked up on it.'

Mrs Jones?

Who is Mrs Jones? Janet?

Janet Jones?

'Cassy?'

'Yes? Sorry, I am listening.'

'Good, because wasting doctors' time is extremely serious.'

I go still.

'Mrs Jones has told me about the frequency of your visits…'

My mind starts playing a personal video of all the outings I've had to the walk-in centre.

Cassy Brookes nicked for Puzzle Book Stalking… Lost property… Sleeping pills… Flu jab… STDs…

But… I mean… lost property isn't so bad. I didn't see the doctor and I do think that getting a flu jab was important and then I only saw the nurse. OK, you shouldn't waste nurses' time either but I did really need a jab if I was going to be staying with my gran. OK, I wasn't really living with my gran but I am intending to see her more often…

Oh God. Listen to me! What the hell have I done?

'Miss Brookes, this is serious.'

'Sorry. I'm sorry.'

Dr Danes' expression softens. 'It can be hard to ask for help. We all struggle sometimes and mental illness is nothing to be ashamed of. Your need to create reasons to come here, while it cannot be condoned, suggests that—'

'You think I lied about Gran being sick?'

'Your grandmother told me she is feeling fine.'

'But she wasn't earlier. She rang me to say she had a funny turn,' I say, feeling defensive. I might be a white-liar but I really was concerned about Gran.

'She also told me that you don't live with her.'

Oh crap. That is true.

Silence fills the room and suddenly 'The Boy Who Cried Wolf' comes to mind. With every second that passes guilt weighs a little heavier. I can't meet Dr Danes' eyes. I'm supposed to be a grown-up but I've been behaving like a teenager with no thought for anyone else or respect for the rules we all live by.

'The important thing is that you take the right steps from now on.'

For a second I think about trying to explain myself but the truth is even worse than what I am being accused of and I don't have the guts to admit it out loud.

Instead I nod, keeping my eyes firmly fixed on my shoes.

'You will need to register with a local doctor's surgery near where you really live. They will be able to refer you for counselling. Mrs Jones can give you a leaflet with London surgeries. You do live in London?'

I nod again. The reality of what I've been doing over the past few weeks has hit me like a splash of cold water.

'OK. Well, hopefully we can put this behind us but I must stress the seriousness of what you have done.'

'I understand. I'm extremely sorry. If there is anything I can do to make up for it—'

'That won't be necessary but please do take on board what I have said and treat doctors' time with respect in future.'

'I will,' I say, getting to my feet.

I want to shake her hand and have a physical sign that my stupidity has been forgiven but instead I just make my way back to the waiting-room. Out of the corner of my eye I see Janet look up from her paperwork and quickly avert her gaze so as not to make eye contact with me. What have I been thinking of?

'Come on, Gran, time to go.' I do my best to smile and look normal.

'Some of these magazines are so old,' Gran says, more to herself than me.

Gran's training at a London hotel has never left her. She is still obsessed with everything looking perfect and presentable. She stands up and throws a few magazines in the bin. I catch sight of the puzzle book. I dive to try and save it. My bag falls to the floor, my things scatter everywhere. I'm too late. The puzzle book is dumped in the trash.

It's probably for the best, I think to myself as I start to pick up my stuff.

Mystery puzzle-men... Wasting doctors' time... Horoscopes... It's not me.

It's not me anymore. It's over.

Twenty-One

By the time I have settled Gran back into her house, made her some lunch and watched *Countdown* it's approaching two o'clock.

'Bye, Gran, I'll see you again soon,' I say and reluctantly close the door behind me.

The street feels cold and uninviting as if it is telling me to go back inside and wait a bit longer before facing the world. But I know I can't put it off any longer. I need to go back to the office and do the one thing every atom in my body is currently rebelling against. I need to congratulate Martin.

The bars and pubs are already getting crowded. I stumble over the feet of some idiot standing on the street smoking and sipping a lager.

'Cassy?'

I don't believe it. It's Rupert Rufus, Head of Logistics at Holywells (who is definitely an idiot but also a very important partner and whose foot I have just trodden on).

'Mr Rufus, hello. Sorry I—'

'Oh, it is you. Come in here, we're celebrating. How is your aunt?'

'It was my gran. She's fine th—'

'Martin! Look who I found lurking outside,' says Rupert.

Martin breaks his conversation at the bar and looks over. I see his body tense when he realises it's me but he recovers himself, smiles, and beckons the pair of us over. I can feel Rupert's slimy arm on my lower back guiding me further into the pub. I walk towards Martin and force myself to smile back at him.

'Cassy, I—'

'Congratulations!' I say loud enough for the surrounding party to hear and I give Martin a kiss on the cheek. 'I'm so sorry I had to rush off earlier before I had a chance to speak to you properly. Here, let me buy you a drink.'

'I've just got one, thanks.'

'Ah, you can never have too many drinks when you're celebrating.'

Martin nods and I brush past him to get to the bar, thankful that I'm going to have a few minutes of solitude to prepare myself for the hours ahead of faking being happy for him.

'Hi, could I get a lager, a vodka shot and a double vodka with a little bit of lemonade, please?'

I make sure my back is turned to Martin and his puppets as I pour the vodka shot into my drink. I dread to think what damage I'm doing to my liver but tonight a triple is definitely needed to keep me smiling. Besides, I need to catch up with them!

–

'Cassy,' Martin says, pulling me over to the side of the room. 'You're drunk.'

'I most certainly aren't.'

'You're swaying.'

'Marrrin. I am fine.'

'You're not fine.'

'You're right. I'm not. I'm better than fine. I'm having fun. Networking. Apparently that's what you need to do to get promoted, you know, if you're not the offspring of a knight. Hey! Get your arm off me.'

He looks deep into my eyes. His face is full of sadness. He opens his mouth but no words come out. He takes a deep breath, stands up straight and whatever he was planning on saying has been scrapped.

'Let me order you a taxi.'

'No,' I say and shrug out of his grip. 'I know what you're doing. You're trying to pushhhh me out.'

'What?'

'You're trying to get me to go home so you can hog all the time with the partners and shut me out. Wasn't getting promoted enough for you?'

'Cassy—'

'Isn't centre stage big enough for you?'

'Stop it. I'm trying to do you a favour.'

'Ha,' I say and burst into a fit of giggles. 'You're trying to do me a favour, are you? Well, why don't you do me a *real* favour and die!'

I push through the crowds and stumble onto the street. The fresh air slaps me in the face. I clutch my head which suddenly feels ten times its normal weight.

'Taxi!' I say and raise my arm but there is no need, there is one right in front of me. I take several attempts to open the door. The driver keeps mouthing something about waiting for it to unlock before trying to open it, but why would he lock it when I'm trying to get in?

'Where to, love?' he asks when I finally fall onto the back seat.

'Home.'

'And where might that be?'

My stomach feels like it's in my throat.

'Hey, what you doing?'

'Train,' I say and stagger back onto the pavement. I pull off my shoes and start walking towards Bank station.

Ah, a corner shop.

'Water,' I say, unable to manage an actual sentence.

'That's a pound.'

I try hard to count the coins in my purse but in the end I give the guy a ten-pound note.

On the station I stay well away from the yellow line which is very wobbly. I sit down on the hard metal bench and gulp down my bottle of water. My stomach feels full but also empty. I need food. But if I eat I'm sure I'm going to throw up. In fact, I think I'm going to throw up either way.

The next train at platform nine is for Woolwich Arsenal.

I make it to a forward-facing seat just before the DLR starts moving and rest my head on the window. Every bump of the train rocks my body so much I feel like I'm going to be propelled forward onto the guy sitting opposite me. He has a long nose, beady eyes and he keeps giving me funny looks over the top of his *Metro* paper.

The next station is Shadwell.

The stern-looking man has got up and sat further down the carriage but still keeps giving me funny looks. I think about giving *him* a funny look but I don't. I stare at my empty water bottle instead. My headache is getting worse.

Random snippets of conversation from earlier keep popping into my head.

The next station is Limehouse.

I think I told Martin to die. I actually said those words out loud. I bang my head on the glass. I should never have lost it like that. I can't believe I had so much to drink.

What must Martin think of me? What must they all think of me? I'm sure some of the others must have overheard what I said. I wasn't exactly whispering.

What if Mr Samuel heard and he thinks it's best I don't work with Martin anymore? What if he fires me?

The next station is Westferry.

Maybe I should resign.

What's left for me there anyway? Mr Samuel is disappointed in me. My new boss hates me (or if he didn't he does now I've told him I wish he was dead). God, why the hell did I say that? I'm ninety-nine per cent sure I said that out loud. Maybe I should email Martin now and apologise?

The next station is Poplar.

From: Cassidy Brookes
Sent: Tues 21:38
To: Martin Robertson
Subject:

Hey Martin,
It's Cassy (Cass). I'm really sorry about earlier, totally joking obviously. We got on great at Le Papillon last

week and I hope we can continue to have a good
working relationship.
See you Monday.
Cassidy (Account Director)

PS: I just thought of the most apt cryptic clue.
Guess what station I'm at? I'm liked by many without
including u.

The next station is Blackwall.

That's made me feel a bit better. Although Martin hasn't
emailed back yet. He's probably still in the pub.

I'm sure he's fine. He's not dead.

I'm mean, I know I wished him dead, but it was only
for a second. Besides what are the chances that of all
the wishes I've made – becoming a millionaire, getting
promoted, marrying Will Smith – my rash comment
about Martin is the one that comes true.

No. It's just drunken nonsense. Martin is fine.

The next station is East India.

Maybe I should email Dr Danes too and say sorry again.
No, she'd probably just think I'm wasting more of her
time. The best thing to do is never to go back there. In
fact, I'm going to make a vow.

*I, Cassidy Ann Brookes, do solemnly swear never again to
step even one foot inside the Threadneedle NHS Walk-in Centre
for any reason.*

I had to write it on my arm as I couldn't find my
notebook in my bag. I hope I haven't lost it.

The next station is Canning Town.

One stop to go…

The next station is Royal Victoria. Please
remember to take all your belongings with you.

I step off the train and onto the platform. I think I'm
starting to sober up a tiny bit. I still feel like I'm going to
throw up and my head is pounding but at least my vision
seems to be back to normal. Home is in sight. But then I
remember what a mess I've made of that too. Dan won't
be there.

–

I fall to the floor of my flat, my bag falling with me. I catch
my reflection in the hall mirror, my mascara has streaked,
my hair is everywhere, there are holes in my tights and
I'm a mess.

'A big mess, just like my life,' I call out to the empty
room. I'm crying as I sit curled up in a ball with my back
pressing on the front door. Every now and then I look at
the intercom, willing it to buzz and for Dan magically to
be outside, waiting to come home.

But it doesn't buzz and I don't think it's going to.

I've screwed up the one good relationship I had left. I
dive into my bag in search of my mobile. I need to call
Dan and explain. I need to tell him to come home, that
I'm sorry and that I'm going to be a better friend from
now on.

My mobile is lost under the collection of receipts in
my bag that I never get around to shredding. I see the Tea
business card I picked up and I start to feel sick again. How
have I let my life spiral so out of control?

I know it's pointless calling Dan, he won't pick up until he's ready. What if he decides never to pick up to me again? The thought is enough to break me and I burst into uncontrollable tears.

It's not just about Dan. It's about everything. Seph having a double life. Martin getting promoted. Obsessing over a puzzle book. Dan was right. I've lost sight of what really matters.

Hard, heavy rain drops bang on the window. It's like the world is crying for me: sad, self-destructive Cassy Brookes. I wish I could go back and do the last few weeks differently. Still clutching my phone, I do the only thing I know to do when things are as bad as they can possibly get.

'Mum? It's me... No, I'm not OK.'

> From: Thomas Samuel
> Sent: Tues 22:32
> To: Cassidy Brookes
> Subject: Meeting
>
> Dear Cassidy,
> Please could you come to my office at 9 a.m. tomorrow morning as there are a couple of things I would like to discuss.
> Kind regards,
> Thomas Samuel (Partner)

> **From: TimTim Taxis Weds 06:59**
> Your taxi has arrived. It is a BLACK FORD GALAXY. Thank you for using TimTim's Taxis.

I wake up in my room with a terrible headache. I can hear some sort of bell chiming in the background. It must have woken me. Switching on the bedside lamp, I see familiar black, super-water-resistant mascara face prints on my pillowcase.

My alarm clock says it's 07:11 which is weird. Why would a bell-clock be chiming if it's not on the hour? Hang on, that's not a bell, it's the door! It's Dan. I knew it! He can never stay mad at me for long. Several things happen at once, my body goes forwards, the wine glass by the bed tips over and my feet stay cocooned in the duvet. The end result being I fall to the floor with a thud. I ignore the pain of the very large bruise I can feel forming on my hip and run-hop-hobble down the hallway to the door.

'Dan, I'm so sor—'

'Hello, it's your taxi driver.'

Scenes from last night come flooding back to me. I remember reading the email from Mr Samuel and booking a taxi so I wouldn't be late.

'Oh, sorry, I'll be down in five minutes.'

'OK, the meter is running.' I hang up the intercom and sprint round the flat. There's no time to shower, I splash my face with cold water, throw on a clean shirt and yesterday's skirt, quickly tie my hair back and grab my bag.

I dive into the back of the taxi, the meter already at £10 and try my best to respond politely to the taxi-driver's morning chit-chat as we begin to make our way to Holywells.

I fumble in my bag for my notebook. I remember making notes to pre-empt this morning's meeting. I had to start a new notebook because I seem to have stupidly left my old one in the office. Still, I guess it symbolises a clean slate? I wish it felt like a clean slate. I keep coming back to the same question: Why did my life have to start malfunctioning the month before promotions? But I can't blame life: I'm the one who took up a crazy correspondence in a puzzle book and I'm the one who manipulated Martin's father. The only person to blame for me not getting promoted is me and now I have to face the consequences. The truth is none of that really matters anymore. I just miss Dan. I throw my notebook back into my handbag. Being in the back of this taxi is starting to make me feel nauseous. My handbag begins to vibrate and then the familiar words of ABBA fill the back of the taxi.

'Hi, Mum.'

'Hi, darling, how are you feeling this morning?'

'OK, I guess,' I say, thinking back to my outburst on the phone last night. 'Thanks for listening yesterday.'

'That's my job, sweetheart. I'm your mum.' There's hesitancy in her voice, like she wants to say more. 'I know things weren't easy for you growing up and—'

'None of this is your fault, Mum. I got myself into this mess. I had a great childhood. You were – you are – an amazing mum.'

'But I had to work a lot and you had to be independent.'

'You taught me that anything is possible if you try your best.'

'Yes, but that doesn't mean you have to do it alone or at the speed of lightning for that matter.'

My bottom lip begins to tremble.

'Darling, you have done so well for yourself and I'm so proud of you. But you have put yourself under so much pressure to get this promotion and… and lost sight of what really matters.'

A silence grows between us but I don't fill it. I don't know what to say.

'Do you want my advice?'

'Yes, please,' I mumble.

'This guy, Martin, sounds like any other bloke. Don't let him get to you. So he has a rich dad and got promoted a bit quicker than you? So what? Will it matter in the grand scheme of a forty-year career? OK, you made a scene yesterday. Apologise and move on. Life is too short to get worked up over a job. And, as for Daniel, he's feeling hurt. My advice is that you stop asking him for forgiveness and show him how sorry you are.'

'You make it sound so simple.'

Mum does a little sigh as if to say, 'isn't it?'

'I'd better go, Mum. I'm at Holywells now. Keep the change,' I say to the taxi driver and step out onto the pavement.

'OK, darling,' Mum says. 'You have a good day now and remember, it's your life, your job and your future, so do what you need to do.'

'Thanks, Mum.'

'You're welcome, sweetheart, and call me anytime. You know you can always pop over for a catch-up or dinner. I can make you lots of vegetables.'

'I know,' I say, a smile creeping on to my face. 'I love you, Mum.'

'I love you, too. Bye, now.'

That was exactly the pep talk I needed. I walk through the revolving doors with my head held high.

'Morning,' I say to a random person in the lift and give them a genuine smile.

Mum is right. Just because Martin has been made Head of Accounts doesn't mean he's now my boss. It simply means he has a new title. He still has his accounts. I still have mine. Nothing has really changed. (Except that he now earns twice as much as I do for doing the same job and I now need his seal of approval every time I want to take on a new client.)

Level Seven.

'Hello, Cassidy, I was just on my way to the meeting. Shall we walk together?'

Martin's going too?

'Sure,' I reply, trying to look casual. *It's not like it means anything.*

'Good morning, both,' Mr Samuel says when we reach his office. 'Please, do sit down.'

Martin takes a seat next to him and I face both of them. We exchange pleasantries as Mr Samuel begins to look more and more nervous. Am I being fired?

'Now, Cassy. Martin and I have agreed that after everything that has happened you could probably do with a couple of days off.'

'I'm sorry?'

'You haven't had a vacation in over nine months and with all the stress you have been under we think it will do you good.'

'But I'm fine.'

'I got your message by the way,' Martin interjects. 'If you feel that there is hostility towards you in the workplace, we should discuss it.'

'What?'

'Poplar, popular.'

The palm of my hands clap onto my forehead as if pulled by a magnetic force. *How* could I have forgotten about that email?

'About that,' I say and give a pleading smile to Martin, hoping that he won't fill Mr Samuel in on the details. 'I'm sorry. It wasn't meant to be taken seriously.'

'This is a serious issue, Cassidy,' Mr Samuel says with genuine concern. 'And this holiday is mandatory.'

The three of us sit in silence for a moment. 'I have some paperwork here on the work-life balance and wellness services we offer in our employee-benefits package and please remember Martin and I are always available if you need advice or want to talk.'

'Thank you,' I say, trying to hold on to the small ounce of dignity I have left. 'A few days off will do me the world of good and I will come back fresh and ready to be an asset to the team.'

'I have no doubt,' Mr Samuel says and gestures for me to follow him out.

Five minutes later and I'm back on the spot where the taxi dropped me off. Part of me wants to scream and yet something is making me smile. It could be a breakdown but I actually think it's a eureka moment. This is a sign that my time at Holywells has come to a natural end. It's the push I needed to take the leap and follow my dreams. Thoughts fight for space in my brain as I hail a taxi. It's all a blur at the moment but I think I know what to do. Mum's words replay in my head. I need to show Dan how much he means to me and I think I know exactly how to do it.

Twenty-Two

With no way to contact any of my clients (old or existing)
while on mandatory leave, I was forced to tackle Dan's
dilemma on my own. After a day and a half of dead ends
and procrastination, I hit the jackpot. There was no way
I could prove Luke's foul play but I didn't need to. It was
the procrastination that held the key. I spent a fair number
of hours stalking Seph and discovering all the women he
had cheated on. (A little psycho but no one could deny
it gives you closure.) The more digging I did, the more
work-related affairs I came across and I realised there was
an easy way to help Dan. I put on a suit and make-up and
fixed my hair and I was in Canary Wharf twenty minutes
later, standing outside the country's leading legal firm.

I'd taken several deep breaths. I knew that in a few
minutes I was going to be face-to-face with Seph. *Stay
calm, Cassy*, I told myself, *you can do this.* I reminded myself

that I had been planning to confront him at some point. What was wrong with today?

'Hello, I'm here to see Sep – Mr O'Carroll?' I said confidently to the girl on the front desk.

'I'm afraid he was just on his way out to meet some associates. Can I help?'

'Please tell him it's Cassidy Brookes and I'm sure he'll find the time.'

It only took three minutes before the receptionist ushered me up to the fifth floor. The corridor was lined with modern art. I turned the corner and saw him sitting at his desk, watching me approach.

'I suppose you're wondering why I'm here.' I said, sitting down in the chair opposite him. He looked so calm and collected and it made me smile. I think he thought I was there to ask him back. 'I've been talking about you a lot lately.'

Seph smirked.

'I spoke to Jess. She was your assistant three years ago, remember? We had a lovely chat.'

That made him sit up straight.

'Then there was Melanie, an intern here last year, I believe. And I had a Facebook chat with Lauren, your boss's seventeen-year-old daughter. I also spoke to her sister—'

'Enough, Cassy, what do you want?' Seph's voice had lost its usual smoothness.

'You know, I've thought a lot about that. I could say nothing, let it go, be the grown-up but where's the fun in that?'

I watched Seph squirm in his seat.

'Alternatively I could ruin your career, tell your boss you've slept with both his daughters and that there's a rumour you've done his wife too. But then I thought that knowing a lawyer who will owe you favours for ever is probably more satisfying.'

'You really think you can blackmail me?'

'No. I think I can ruin you and we both know you are nothing without this job.'

Seph loosened his tie and ran his hand through his hair.

'Here's what I want you to do.'

I explained Dan's situation. I could tell Seph was nervous because he didn't once give any outward sign of enjoying that Dan was in trouble. Then I hit him with it. I wanted him to write a letter to Luke threatening legal action. I knew there wasn't enough evidence for a case but with any luck the letter would be enough to get Luke to back down and give Dan his money back.

'You can't be serious,' he said when I was finished.

'Do you think I'd have bothered to see you if I wasn't?'

'My reputation—'

'I think we both know you don't have a reputation worth keeping. Or at least you won't once I'm finished enlightening your boss about your... extracurricular activities.'

'I'll send it this afternoon.'

'I thought you might. Goodbye, Seph.'

> **From: Dan Mobile Sat 11:44**
> OK. I'll meet you at the Royal Exchange at two.
> PS: yes I did pick the Royal Exchange because it's the most expensive place I could think of.

I shake off my umbrella and tidy my hair as I walk into the Royal Exchange. I make my way over to a table for two near the middle and take off my coat.

'Hello. Welcome. Can I get you something to drink?'

'Could I get a tea, please? Actually, no. Could I get a skinny latte, please?'

I haven't drunk a cup of tea since I quit the Puzzle-man saga. It just makes me think of the Tea café.

'Will you be eating as well?'

'I'm waiting for someone.'

'OK, I'll come over to take your order when you're both ready.'

'Thanks,' I say.

A horrible thought runs through my mind. What if Dan doesn't show up? No, he wouldn't do that, he's not like that. I scan the room in case he's already here and I haven't noticed.

I gasp and quickly pull the menu up to my eye level. What's Martin doing here? And why is he wearing a suit at the weekend? He's mid-flow in a bubbly conversation with a fifty-something-year-old man who is wearing a plush suit, probably some partner I've never even been introduced to. A little irritating voice in my head just keeps saying, *Head of Accounts, Head of Accounts, Head of Accounts.*

Oh, Dan's here.

'Dan, I—'

'Before you say anything, I'm only here as a favour to Ann.'

'Thanks for coming,' I say as he sits down opposite me. (I need to remember to thank Mum later.)

'Where's the body?'

It takes me a couple of seconds to realise he means Luke's.

'Right here,' I say and pass Dan the cheque Seph had couriered to me earlier that morning.

'Wow,' Dan says and takes it from me. 'But how?'

I take a swig of latte and then give Dan a scene by scene account of everything that had happened.

—

'What a spineless idiot,' he says. I'm not entirely sure whether he is referring to Seph or Luke. I think the description applies equally to both. 'I can't believe you confronted Seph just to help me get the money back off Luke.'

'I'd do anything for you,' I say softly and take his hand in mine.

'I guess I'd better make sure I invest my money properly next time.'

'Well, I'm hoping you will like the look of this *alternative* investment opportunity I have for you.' Dan raises his eyebrow. 'Here, take a look at this.'

'What is it?'

'A business plan. Our business plan. Our very own digital agency.'

'Cassy, I'm a gaming tester.'

'Don't give me that. You're a better programmer than most tech guys out there. You just don't like hard work. You could easily build social-media platforms and client websites.'

'But I don't want a job.' He holds the plan out.

'Turn to page seven and look halfway down. That's how much I predict we'll make in years one, two and three.' I carry on talking as Dan flicks through the plan.

'If we share the start-up costs fifty-fifty our return after three years should—'

'Bloody hell!'

'So are you in?'

Dan grins. 'One thing I don't get. I thought your ten-year plan involved staying at Holywells and making partner.'

'A girl can change a plan, can't she?'

'And it's really over with the Puzzle-man mystery? You're moving on?'

'Yes,' I say. I'm so relieved he finally believes me that I bang my arms on the table and the sound echoes around the magnificent walls of the Exchange. Urgh, I think Martin has spotted me, although, he looks more nervous about being caught out than I am.

'I'm sorry,' Dan says. 'I overreacted.'

'No, I'm sorry. I should have noticed what was going on with you.'

'And you're really going to resign?'

I nod. I find myself looking over at Martin.

'Cassy, you're ringing.'

'What?'

'Your phone, it's ringing.'

I fumble in my bag and pull it out.

'It's the Threadneedle Walk-in Centre.'

'What do they want?' Dan asks.

I shrug.

'Hello?'

'Hello, is that Miss Brookes?'

'Speaking.'

'Hello, it's Mrs Jones calling from the Threadneedle Walk-in Centre. Is it possible for you to pop by the centre?'

There's a trick question, if ever I heard one.

'I've actually registered with a doctor's surgery that is closer to home.'

'I understand. However, I believe I have something of yours.'

'Mine?'

'Yes, a notebook.'

I think I'm going to need a defibrillator. I never did find my missing notebook. Could it be I left it there?

'Miss Brookes? It has your name in the front and I happened to open it up on a page where there was a list of reasons to go to the doctor's?'

'Yes,' I say, the blood draining from my body. 'Yes, that sounds like mine. Wicked sense of humour I have, eh?' I say with a nervous laugh.

'We're closing in an hour. Do you want to collect it on Monday?' Janet asks, coolly.

'Yes, that's fine,' I murmur. My hand falls to the table and I hit the red end-call button.

'Cassy?'

'Oh my God,' I say as the reality of what just happened sinks in. My mind runs through all the things I have written in there.

'*Cassy*, what the hell is it?' Dan whispers, three long worry lines etched on to his forehead.

'I left my notebook in the walk-in centre. All my lists about Puzzle-man and Martin are in there.'

'Well, that's a turn-up for the "note"-books.'

'It's not funny,' I say and kick him under the table. He is laughing so much it has brought tears to his eyes.

It must have fallen out of my bag on Friday when I took Gran there. But I was sure I picked everything up. Oh God, what a disaster.

'So what are you going to do?'

'Janet said I can collect it on Monday.'

'*Monday!* But, Cassy,' Dan says and dramatically brings his hand to his mouth, 'Janet could have read every list by then.'

He's right.

'I'd better go now.'

Just as I beckon the waitress over to ask for the bill, I catch Martin heading in our direction. That's all I need.

'Well, hello again, social visit, is it?' he says to Dan.

'We're having lunch,' Dan says plainly, not reacting to Martin's childish tone.

'Oh, that's nice. For a moment I thought I was going to be able to enjoy another role-play.'

'So what brings you here?' I ask, changing the subject.

'Just finalising a bit of business,' he says and taps his Armani briefcase.

'Can I get you any dessert?' asks the waitress, appearing at Martin's side.

'Enjoy the rest of your vacation,' he says and makes his way out.

I nod and turn to the waitress, 'Actually, can we just get the—'

'Yes,' Dan interrupts. 'I would like the… cheesecake, please.'

'Certainly, sir. And anything for you?'

'I'm fine, thanks,' I say and glare at Dan.

'This is my make-up lunch,' he says when the waitress has gone. 'I'm not cutting it short over a notebook of lists.'

'Fine,' I say and huff loudly.

I guess in the grand scheme of things, it doesn't really matter… How long can it take to eat a piece of cheese-cake?

'OK, Dan, you're seriously taking the piss now,' I say, *forty-five* minutes later. The centre will be closing soon.

'What?' he asks innocently.

'Ordering an espresso? You don't even drink coffee!'

'Are you sorry or not?' He grins.

'Oh, whatever.'

'So, tell me more about our new business venture.' Dan smiles and suddenly my notebook shrinks into insignificance.

Twenty-Three

Warm Monday morning sunshine streams through the gap in the curtains. I roll over and enjoy the full width of my double bed. Today is going to be the beginning of the rest of my life. Dan and I spent the whole weekend working on our business plan and in a few hours (after I've resigned and picked up my notebook and destroyed it) we will start our new life together.

I take my time getting ready. I've decided I need to be kinder to myself and lower some of my personal expectations. I've had a bit of a shredding session of all my millions of lists and I came across the one I made on the back of a leaflet about cognitive behavioural therapy a few weeks ago. Maybe I should have looked into it more. All these so-called thinking errors: blowing situations out of proportion; trying to mind-read everyone; seeing the world in black and white; and striving for unrealistic goals. I do all that stuff and it stresses me out. It is time I took a large chill pill.

When I finally leave the house, I enjoy the crisp morning air as I make my way to the station. I don't care which train I catch, I'll still get to work in time. I pull the plastic lid off my coffee as I stand on the platform at Royal Victoria and breathe in the soothing smell of fresh coffee. When the DLR arrives, I let the other passengers get on first. I sit down on one of the sideways-facing seats by the door and sip my coffee.

I wait patiently for the other commuters to sprawl onto the platform at Bank before I get up. I let the escalator gently lift me up to ground level and I smile to myself as I picture the state I was in when I almost got killed by a cyclist. I walk at a steady pace from the station to Holywells and through the revolving doors into the lift.

'Morning, guys,' I say to the graduates as I walk past them. 'Morning, Sally. No Sofia still?'

'Oh, you haven't heard?' Sally rushes up to me. 'She was fired and I've been promoted.'

'Poor Sofia!' I say before I can stop myself. She didn't deserve to be fired. 'Congratulations to you, though,' I add. 'Actually you don't happen to have her home address do you? I'd like to send her a card.'

'Aww, that's so sweet. I've got a friend in HR who can probably get it for you. I'll ask her.'

'Thanks, I appreciate it.'

I leave Sally calling her friend in HR and walk into my office for the last time. Sitting at my desk I begin to shred the endless, pointless lists I have on bits of paper, tissues and old envelopes. I think I will keep my to-do list, though, that one is actually useful. I start to put into my bag a few things that I want to take with me. Once I resign things are likely to get ugly.

–

Before I know it, the clock on my computer says 10 a.m. and my stomach gives that little gurgle to tell me it's time for a drink. I think I will have a coffee before I confront Mr Samuel. Unfortunately coffee and Mr

Samuel seem destined to coincide; I see him just as I get to the kitchenette.

'Morning, Thomas.'

'Sorry, Cassy, talk later.'

Mr Samuel almost knocks me off balance, he darts past me so quickly. He goes straight into Martin's office without knocking and firmly shuts the door. I carry on making my coffee but my mind is wandering. What does he need to talk to Martin about so urgently?

–

My coffee has gone cold. I can't concentrate. I keep looking out of my office window. They're happening again, the secret conversations. I've counted nine so far, partners that is. Nine have gone in and out of Martin's office, all whispering and wildly gesticulating to one another.

I know what it's about.

It's me. They're going to fire me before I get a chance to resign. I should have known. Martin wants me gone and now he is Head of Accounts he has the clout to do it. I know it shouldn't bother me – I was going to quit anyway – but it's the principle.

I watch as Mr Samuel leads Martin from one meeting room to the other. The graduates have all stopped working, too, but there's no point asking them what's going on, their faces look as perplexed as I feel.

I pace up and down the room, resisting the urge to make a list of all the possible outcomes. I stop and take a couple of large, deep breaths. Thinking about it, there is no way it can be about me. I'm being stupid. They can't fire me. On what grounds could they? Going through a hard time in my personal life? I could start a lawsuit. No. It can't be about me.

Mr Samuel does look really stressed out though. He has undone his tie and taken off his jacket. Maybe the company has lost money? Maybe Martin screwed up on one of his accounts? Maybe *Martin* is being fired? No. That's just wishful thinking. They only just promoted him. They wouldn't fire him a week later. It can't be about Martin. But then... Oh, what the hell is going on? Sally isn't at her desk anymore. I bet she knows.

> From: Cassidy Brookes
> Sent: Mon 10:57
> To: Sally Lawson
> Subject: ????
>
> Hey,
> Have you got any idea what is going on?
> Cassidy (Account Director)

The phone rings; I snatch it.

'Holywells, Cassidy Brookes, Account Director, speaking.'

'Cassy, pet, is that you?'

'Hi, Gran, I can't really talk at the moment.'

'Not to worry, pet. I was just calling to let you know a letter arrived for you in the post today from the Thread-needle Walk-in Centre.'

'Oh really,' I say, only half listening.

'Yes, pet, I opened it by mistake.'

'Don't worry, Gran. It was probably junk mail.'

'Oh no, pet, it was confirming your careers consultation.'

'Oh I see.' I'd completely forgotten about that. 'Just bin it, Gran. I'm going to cancel the appointment anyway.'

'OK, pet.'

The partners all seem to have gone now. Suddenly, I see Sally scuttle around the corner and start jogging towards my office on tiptoes to stop her heels clapping on the floor.

'I'd better go, Gran. I'll talk to you soon.'

'OK, pet. Bye-bye.'

I put the phone down as Sally enters the room. She's huffing and puffing so much she curls over in a heap.

'It's Martin,' she manages after what feels like five minutes, her cheeks ruby red.

'Well, I figured out that much. What about Martin?'

'He's...' Sally looks out the window, back towards Martin's office, as if looking for clarification.

'He's what? Sally?'

Surely he can't have got a double promotion to partner!

'He's quit.'

'*Quit!* That can't be right!'

'It is. I overheard a couple of the partners. They tried to offer him more money but they couldn't match the counter offer.'

'Seriously?'

'Seriously.'

'Oh my God.'

'I know. Look! Here comes security to escort him off the premises. Hey! Where are you going?'

'I have to talk to him,' I call back to Sally. I run over to Martin's office.

'Excuse me,' I say to the security guard who is watching Martin like a hawk as he packs a box of his belongings. 'I need a word with him.'

Martin looks up but doesn't say anything. He just carries on packing.

'So that's it. Five years working together and you're not even going to say goodbye, have a nice life?' I don't know why I'm suddenly so choked up.

'I thought you'd be delighted to see the back of me,' Martin says, coolly.

'So where are you going?'

'Patterson sorted me out. I signed on the dotted line over the weekend. You saw me with my lawyer on Saturday. The guy I was having lunch with in the Royal Exchange.'

Of course, everything makes sense now.

'How long have you been planning this?'

'Well, since you decided to make my genetics public knowledge you left me little choice.' Martin glares at me. I've never seen him so angry before. 'You know, Cassy, I worked hard to get to where I am. On. My. Own. And then you swan in and make me look like a joke.'

'I am genuinely sorry.' My eyes start to sting.

Martin relents. 'Forget about it. Enjoy your promotion.'

'What?'

Martin laughs. 'Don't tell me you're so naive you can't see the fantastic position you're in now?'

I look at him, awaiting his infamous wisdom.

'Tom has no choice but to ask you to take over as Head of Accounts.'

How is it that I'd never even thought about that?

'And on that note,' he says, lifting up his box of possessions in his now soulless ex-office, 'have a nice life, Miss Cassidy Brookes.'

Martin walks over to the door.

'You too,' I call out to him. He looks back at me, disappointment flashing across his face. He nods and then disappears down the corridor towards the lift. I stand in his office for a few moments longer. My body aches as if it's lost something more than just a colleague.

My phone starts vibrating in my jacket pocket and a sickening sensation runs through my veins.

It's time.

–

I may have been drunk but I remember what I wrote on my arm last Tuesday evening on the train home. (Mainly because it took a while to scrub it off in the shower.) I swore that I would never go back to the walk-in centre and, while the purpose of that promise was to never again waste doctor's time and on this occasion I have actually been given permission to go and collect my stupid notebook, the fact remains... I don't want to go!

My muscles are fighting every demand of my brain to move forward. I drag myself along Cornhill so slowly that tourists overtake me for a change. The clouds in the sky look ominous but at this moment I think I would rather get drenched than step one foot closer to Threadneedle NHS Walk-in Centre.

I know I sound like I am overreacting, but I'm not! If I collect that notebook, I have to look Janet – protocol-loving – Jones, in the eye and admit to everything I have done over the past month. All those times I went to the walk-in centre, looking for Puzzle-man. She'll know everything. She'll know how stupid I have been. She'll have seen all those lists I made about Martin, too. What if she thinks I'm insane? What if the police are there, waiting for me?

My legs are starting to cramp. I've reached the huge junction at Bank station. There are taxis and buses everywhere. I could hop on and be driven far away. I give myself a mental slap around the face. There's no need to be melodramatic, the chances are Janet won't have read any of my lists. I mean, I'm sure she has much better things to do with her time. It's not like she's ever tried to snoop around to find information about me before…

OK. I need to stop thinking about Janet or I really am going to do a runner and change my name.

OK, Cassy, start thinking about other things…

I don't know what to do about what Martin said. The career-focussed part of me is telling me Martin is right: I should use this situation to my advantage, take the promotion and squeeze out the perks. But what about my new business plan with Dan? Would he understand?

Crap. I got so excited about the prospect of being Head of Accounts that I sped up and I'm now standing about four paces from the door of the walk-in centre.

I don't know if I can do this. I don't know if I can face Janet again.

Oh, get a grip, Cassidy, I say to myself. At that exact moment, a tall, mid-forties, well-dressed man walks out of the centre and holds the door open for me. I guess there is no escaping now anyway.

'Thanks,' I say, probably too quietly for him to hear, and step inside.

The warm, antiseptic smell seems stronger today and it feels so familiar. Janet is there, tapping away on her keyboard and booking someone an appointment over the phone. She's wearing the same M&S shirt I saw her in that first day I came in with a twisted ankle.

She's seen me. I want to smile, but I'm too embarrassed and also a little scared of what she might say. I can see the old armchair from where I am standing in the queue. It's strange looking at it from a distance. I'm having one of those movie-style flashbacks, when you see everything that happened in a particular place over time, sped up. I see myself sitting there, hiding there, getting excited, being sneaky. It feels like a film of someone else's life. What on earth came over me?

Argh!

I'm still doing it and I can't help it. My mind is going into overdrive about who Puzzle-man is. I can't deal with the unknown. Someone wrote back to me, on multiple occasions. They even gave me tea-shop advice! However nuts I have been, there is no denying that this person exists. They are out there somewhere and they wanted to meet me.

Who.

Is.

Puzzle-man?

I bang my hand against my leg.

It's irrelevant now, I remind myself and try to calm my racing heart. The puzzle book is gone. There is no way I'll ever know. I am going to have to live with this forever.

'Hello, Miss Brookes,' Janet says when I reach the front of the queue. 'I believe this is yours?'

There it is, my notebook, in the pale, bony hands of Janet Jones.

'Yes,' I say and reach out to take it from her.

I hold it tight, almost as though, if I hold it tight enough history may be changed and it will disappear, as if I never wrote it. I'm still standing in front of Janet, I realise. I feel I need to say something, but I don't know what.

'Thank you for keeping it safe. Also, what I wrote in here about—'

'I hope you are not insinuating that I read any of it,' she says, 'because that would be totally against the Thread-needle Walk-in Centre's lost property policy.'

'No, of course not,' I say quickly. *Could I make the hole any deeper?* I stop myself from saying anything else and just give a small, awkward bow of my head, before turning to make a speedy exit.

'Did you ever find Puzzle-man?' Janet blurts out, her voice a little frantic. I look back, her face is flushed. So she did read it!

'No,' I say quietly and disappointment spreads over her face. She smiles at me, a genuine smile I think, partly out of sympathy and partly out of gratitude for not calling her up on breaking protocol! I can't help but smile back. In a funny way, I think I'm going to miss Janet.

'Bye,' I say and head for the door a second time. 'Oops.' I bump straight into Lucy. 'I'm so sorry,' I say, but she doesn't notice, she just stands still, in a trance-like state. 'Are you OK?' I ask.

She doesn't answer.

Suddenly she starts crying. Actually, crying is an understatement, she is wailing. I stand there, unsure of what to do. I can't just walk out.

'Nurse Clarkson? What's wrong?' Janet asks, appearing at her side. She's looking at me as if I should know what's wrong, along with all the patients sitting in the waiting-room. She puts her hand, uncomfortably, on Lucy's back and whispers something in her ear but that only makes Lucy sob louder.

'It's… it's Simon,' Lucy sniffles, before balling her eyes out again.

'Perhaps you should get some fresh air?' Janet suggests but Lucy doesn't look capable of finding the exit.

'Why don't I take her?'

Janet looks at me and then back at Lucy. I don't actually know why I said that, given Lucy drives me completely and utterly nuts. Not to mention if this rich-kid has dumped her, (which is the only thing I can think has happened) frankly, good for him. Oh, whatever, maybe being a Good Samaritan is part of the new Cassy. Besides, if I can make up for all my recent malarkey, even if only in some small way, I should try. I reach out to Lucy and she takes my hand. She's managed to turn the crying into small hiccup-like sobs, at least.

'Are you feeling a little better now?' I venture once we've been standing outside for a couple of minutes.

Lucy nods but her face starts to scrunch up and then the piercing wailing starts up again. People are walking past us, gawping. This is so embarrassing.

'Come on, Lucy, it can't be that bad.'

Unbelievably her cries get even higher pitched, making me wince.

'How about we go and sit down somewhere and have a chat? You can tell me all about it?'

She seems to perk up at the sound of someone being willing to listen to her and, after a few more seconds deliberating, nods her head. I lock arms with her and guide her towards Bank, we can sit outside the Bank of England on one of the benches. She's shaking a little and for the first time I feel a little worry creeping into me. I thought she was just making a scene but maybe something bad has happened.

'OK, let's sit here. Do you want to tell me what happened?'

I put my hand on her arm and give her an encouraging squeeze as I wait for her to calm down a little.

'It's… It's Simon.'

'Did you have a fight?'

Lucy has gone very still, her eyes are wide open. I think she might be in shock.

'Lucy? Did he… did he hurt you?'

'No!'

Thank God.

'So what happened?'

'He's… he's cheating on me.'

Lucy bursts into tears again, scaring quite a few pigeons away in the process.

'Oh, Lucy, I'm sorry,' I say and put my arm around her. 'Are you sure?'

Lucy nods. 'The little things gave it away,' she says and looks on at the busy street.

I think about Seph. There must have been so many things I missed.

'The car for a start.'

'The car?'

'He kept being late picking me up and, when he did arrive, the car smelt of different perfumes.'

'God, what an arse.'

My phone starts vibrating. I quickly read the email, Lucy carries on staring at the commuters.

From: Thomas Samuel
Sent: Mon 13:34
To: Cassidy Brookes
Subject: Urgent

'I'm really sorry but I have to go now. Lucy?'

She turns to me. She looks lost, helpless.

'Listen to me, Lucy. I really do understand what you're
going through. A very similar thing happened to me
recently and, I'm not going to lie, it was tough. But I
got through it.'

'How?'

'By forgetting the moron existed and moving on,' I say
as we stand up. 'In fact, I'm just about to go back to my
office and quit my job. I'm starting a whole new chapter
of my life. And remember, it's his loss, OK?'

I give her a quick hug.

'I'm not so sure it is,' she sniffs.

'It is, Lucy, trust me. You're sweet and kind and good
at your job. He was an idiot to lose you.'

'I guess,' she says and then laughs gently. 'At least he
lost his puzzle book anyway.'

The hairs on the back of my neck stand up and my
arms cover themselves in goose bumps.

'His puzzle book?'

'Yeah, that's how I knew for sure.'

'I don't understand.'

'It was yesterday when he came to pick me up. I'd
booked us a table at The Ritz but he didn't want to go. He
said he was looking for a puzzle book and kept frantically
sifting through the centre's magazines.'

'Oh my God!' I clamp my hand to my mouth. *I feel sick.*

'Exactly.'

It can't be. He probably just wanted to do a puzzle while he waited for Lucy. She probably misunderstood what he said. But then...

'Why did he care so much about finding the book?'

'That's my point exactly.'

Maybe he had seen there was a new edition puzzle book a few days ago, but how could he? It was inside the jacket of an old copy? If he was looking for it then...

'He has to be...'

'Stalling because his "other woman" is at The Ritz.'

Puzzle-man. I mean...

'It's the only possible explanation.'

'I know, right? God, what you said is so true. It is his loss.'

There's a couple of high-pitched beeps and I look around wondering what it could be, my mind still trying to process what Lucy just said.

'Oh look, he's texted me. He wants to rearrange our dinner at The Ritz for eight o'clock tonight so we can talk things through. Look,' she says and holds the phone up so I can see. 'Well, he can forget it. There's no way I'm giving him another chance. Oh, Cassy, thank you. You've made me feel so much better.'

'Hmm?'

'I know exactly what I'm going to do to get over him.'

'Good... that's good,' I say and swallow hard.

Lucy turns and starts making her way back to the centre.

'Thanks again,' Lucy calls out to me. I lift my arm up, I think to wave but I'm too numb to gesture.

ABBA starts singing in my pocket. On autopilot I take out my phone and hit the green button.

'Hello?'

'Cassy? It's Sally. Where are you? Thomas is looking for you.'

'Yes. Sorry, I'm coming. I'm about ten minutes away.'

'OK, good. Are you all right? You sound kind of weird.'

'Yeah, no, I'm fine. It's just...'

'Yeah?'

'I think I know who – Never mind. I'm on my way in now.'

Twenty-Four

OK, I can do this. Anything Martin can do, I can do better, right? I just need to play it cool and stand my ground.

I'd ended the call with Sally pretty abruptly. There was no way I was going to fill her in on everything. Besides I knew I needed to stop thinking about Simon being Puzzle-man. I can think about that later. First things first. I need to deal with Mr Samuel and my promotion. I wiggle my body and adjust my posture as I stand in the lift.

The air con is turned up high when I reach level seven and a tingly shiver runs over my arms. I ignore it and walk towards Mr Samuel's office.

'Ah, Cassidy, there you are,' says Mr Samuel after I give two light taps on his half-open office door.

'I'm sorry I kept you waiting. I had an appointment I couldn't cancel.'

'Not to worry. Please take a seat.'

His office is huge but has a homely feel that puts me at ease. He has pictures of his two children all over the walls and one of his wife Veronica on his desk. He doesn't have a computer, just a small laptop which is closed; he has several stacks of papers dotted around the place. We both sit down, opposite one another, on armchairs by a little coffee table in the corner and then Mr Samuel puts on his serious, business face.

'I assume that you heard about Martin before you left for your appointment,' he says in a low, grave voice. He looks tired and worn out as he sits there, shifting about in his seat.

'Yes, I spoke to him briefly.'

'Did he tell you what his new role is?'

'He just said Gregory Patterson helped him out.'

Judging by the mixture of indifference and annoyance on Mr Samuel's face that was all the information Mr Samuel got out of Martin as well.

'Cassy,' Mr Samuel says and leans in closer. 'I would appreciate it if what we discuss doesn't leave this room.'

I nod.

'The truth is Martin rather pulled the wool over my eyes these past few months. In my conversations with Martin today, it came to light that you were the main catalyst for the MediaTech strategy, is that right?'

Martin told him that?

I nod, too confused to find words. Mr Samuel sighs.

'I thought Martin had been trying to demonstrate his leadership skills by helping you when you were having quite a... turbulent time in your personal life. I misjudged him. The partners and I think extremely highly of you. As you know, we were also considering you for the Head of Accounts role but I felt that it wasn't right to add stress if you weren't coping. It was my misjudgement and something I should have spoken to you about in person. For that, I am sorry.'

I can't even nod, just stare.

'We think Martin leaving the firm is for the best and we haven't countered the offer from MediaTech. More importantly, we think the Head of Accounts position would be a great opportunity for you.'

This is it. It's a promotion or Dan.

'Thank you, it means a great deal to me that you and the other partners have faith in me.' Mr Samuel just gives a polite bow of the head and smiles. 'However, I won't be accepting the position. Here is my letter of resignation.'

I don't know who is more stunned by what I said, Mr Samuel or me. I watch as he shuffles in his seat.

'Now, Cassy, I know the past week has been very unorthodox but I assure you this promotion will be the affirmation of your great career and future here at Holy-wells.'

I stand firm. 'Thank you for the opportunity but I have re-evaluated what I want from my career and leaving Holywells is the right thing for me at this time. My decision is final.'

'And there is nothing I can say to change your mind?'

'I'm afraid not.'

'You will be missed,' Mr Samuel says, already leaning over to call security.

–

Standing outside Holywells with only a cardboard box worth of possessions to show for the last five years, I know where I'm going next. I hail a cab and give him a pink post-it that Sally had discreetly placed in my hand as we said goodbye.

It doesn't take long to get there. I knock on the door and wonder if I should have asked the taxi driver to wait.

'It's you.'

'Can I come in?' I ask.

Sofia moves aside to let me in, staring at my cardboard box.

'Drink?' she asks.

I sit down on the sofa. She has a nice ground-floor flat in Crossharbour. It smells of Italian herbs. I try to imagine Seph living here, lying on the sofa watching TV on such a small screen. His bare feet on old red carpet; he would have moaned so much. At least the Seph I knew would have, perhaps Sofia brought out a different side of him. I take a deep breath. *I can handle this*. I do my best to block out thoughts of Seph as Sofia returns holding two mugs of hot chocolate.

'No poison, right?'

'I'm all out,' she says but doesn't manage a smile. Her eyes are fixed to the floor. I won't lie, looking at her now, she seems different to me. She's not the loyal, bubbly creative designer I liked, but the woman who was sleeping with my boyfriend behind my back. I can feel my body begin to heat. I take another deep breath. What I thought may be true, but I am also the woman that was sleeping with *her* boyfriend behind *her* back. We were both used. This isn't Sofia's fault any more than it is mine.

'I'm sorry you were fired.'

'I deserved it,' she says and sips her hot chocolate.

'No you didn't. It's Seph—' Sofia flinches. 'Joey, that deserves to be punished.'

'Maybe but I still threw wine over a partner at a conference in front of all the firm's major clients,' she says, her eyes still firmly fixed on the carpet. 'I have no idea how I'm going to afford the rent on this place anymore.'

We sit in silence for a while as I pluck up the courage to say, 'I miss you.'

For the first time, Sofia lifts her head and looks at me. It's like she reached out and pinched my heart. The pain she is feeling is etched over her face.

'I'm so sorry,' she says and a tear falls down her cheek. 'You'd been dating him for seven years. It was me who was cheating and I blamed you in front of everyone.'

'Oh, Sofia, it was Seph who was cheating. In fact, in hindsight, watching you throwing wine over Seph was one of the funniest things I've seen in the past seven and a half years. Don't get me wrong,' I say, looking around the room again. *I wonder if they had sex on the sofa.* 'It still hurts, and I feel like a complete idiot for not realising—'

'No, I'm the idiot. I feel so *stupid*!' Sofia breaks down in tears and on instinct I pull her into my arms. Tears begin to run down my cheeks as well.

'OK, OK, enough,' I say. 'We are not ruining our make-up or crying another tear over that loser, all right?'

She sniffs and nods. Then she smiles at me and suddenly everything feels a little bit better.

'So listen,' I say in my stern voice. 'I didn't come here to cry. I came to offer you a job.'

'What?'

'I've quit Holywells,' I say, nodding towards the cardboard box. 'Dan and I are starting our own digital-marketing agency and we're going to need a creative director.'

'Are you serious?'

'I don't want that moron to ruin our friendship and you're the best creative designer I know. Will you consider it?'

'*Consider it?* I'll take it! Thank you.' Sofia hugs me and suddenly I know I've made the right decision about everything.

'So what exactly is the company's point of difference?'

I run through the basic concept and we arrange to meet for lunch at my flat tomorrow so Sofia can meet Dan and we can go through some details.

'We should open a bottle of wine to celebrate our new jobs,' she says afterwards.

'I'd love to but I'd better get home and tell Dan.'

I text Dan while Sofia orders me a taxi.

To: Dan Mobile Mon 15:13
Martin quit and I got promoted!!!! But don't worry I still quit and Sofia agreed to be our creative director. On my way home. Order in stuffed crust, we're celebrating in style tonight.
PS: I found out who Puzzle-man is.

From: Dan Mobile Mon 15:23
Oh my God! Who is it?
PS: Great about Sofia.
PPS: Why did Martin quit???

To: Dan Mobile Mon 15:25
Gregory Patterson offered him a position at MediaTech.
PS: Tell you when I get home, it's complicated

I turn the key and for the first time walk into my flat as a business owner. I can't wait to see –

'Dan! What are you doing? Get down from there.'

'Nope,' Dan says, panting a little as he continues to jump up and down on the sofa. 'I'm not stopping until you tell me. I've been doing this for twenty minutes.'

'You have not.'

'I have so.'

'Well then, you are buying me a new sofa,' I say and fold my arms pretending to look angry.

'Can't,' he says and pokes his tongue out. 'I'm penniless remember?'

'Not for much longer. Your cheque will clear soon.'

'So who is Puzzle-man?' Dan asks and jumps again.

'Can't we just enjoy going into business together tonight?'

'Sure. Right after you tell me who Puzzle-man is.'

I let out a sigh.

'Well if you sit down, I'll tell you.'

I think back to all my crazy lists about who Puzzle-man might be. What I'd give for it to be a woman or a gay guy now. Anything instead of the truth. Dan is looking at me expectantly. I suppose I'd better get it over and done with.

'You're joking me,' Dan says once I've relived my conversation with Lucy in excruciating detail.

I shake my head. 'I wish I was.'

'The hot, rich guy?'

'Yep.'

Dan's eyes flicker over my face looking for any sign that I'm having him on.

'You can't blame yourself,' he says eventually.

'Really? Because I kinda am.'

'You didn't know who it was! He was the one being dishonest. It's a bit like how...'

'You can say it.'

'No, it's nothing.'

'No. You were going to say it's a bit like how Sofia had no idea Joey was Seph.'

'Well... It sort of is, isn't it?'

I sigh. 'It doesn't make me feel any better about it.'

The intercom buzzes. 'I'll go,' Dan says, 'it's the pizza. I ordered wedges, garlic bread and... Pepsi Max.'

'Wow. Let's get this party started!' I say, heading into the kitchen, happy to change the subject.

I start gathering the plates and glasses and do my best to forget about Simon and Lucy.

'Have you got lost in there?'

'I'm coming, keep your hair on. Here,' I say and give Dan a plate. I pour the drinks as Dan divides up the pizza and sides.

'Right, let's have a toast,' Dan says, raising his champagne glass of Pepsi Max. 'Here's to you, Cassy.'

'No. Here's to you, Dan, for being such a good friend.'

'To us,' he says.

'To us. The cheesiest twenty-something-year-olds alive.'

'Stop it. You'll make me snort bubbles! Ah, this is the life. So how does it feel, Cassy?'

'How does what feel?' I ask, leaning back and sinking into the sofa.

'Being sorted. No more worrying about wanker-colleagues or wanker-boyfriends. No more puzzle mysteries or elaborate white lies. How does it feel to be normal?'

'I – I don't know. Nice?'

'OK, Princess, come on.'

'What?'

'You should be on cloud nine right now and instead you look like you ordered a Hawaiian but got Pepperoni instead.'

'Pizza analogies? Really?'

'Stop deflecting.'

'It's Simon.'

Dan opens his mouth but I speak first.

'Before you say anything, I know nothing really happened. It was just a few silly messages in a puzzle book, but—'

'But nothing. Puzzle-man could have been anyone. The only reason you started replying was because you needed a distraction from what was going on in your life. Maybe it was the same for Simon. You don't know what was really going on between him and Lucy.'

'I know. You're right. I know you're right.'

'I can sense another, but, coming.'

'It's just… I hate that he had a girlfriend.'

'Because he was going behind her back or because you wanted to be his girlfriend?'

'I won't deny it, however crazy it sounds, I really did think we had a connection and part of me thinks there must be some kind of mistake.'

'But?'

'But… the other part of me knows that I missed all the signs with Seph, and Simon is just another jerk, and it's no wonder I missed them all again.'

'You always knew it was a possibility. It was even on your list.'

'I know and that's why I feel so guilty. But it's more than that. I feel let down. Again.'

'OK, well,' Dan looks at me solemnly. 'Maybe you should do something about it. Confront him. Tell him how you feel.'

'I am not going back to the walk-in centre if that's where this conversation is leading.'

'But—'

'*And* even if I did, the puzzle book is gone.'

'But—'

'*And* Lucy's dumped him so he won't go back there. Especially not after she stands him up tonight.'

'Finally,' Dan says and holds his arms out as if to say 'Hallelujah'.

'Huh?'

'I thought you were never going to realise.'

'Realise what?'

'How to see him again.'

I stare at Dan to see if he's making fun of me.

'You couldn't have asked for a better opportunity.'

'What the hell are you talking about?'

'The Ritz, Cassy. The Ritz.'

It takes me a few seconds to realise what he means.

'You can't be serious.'

'Why not?'

'And what reason could I possibly give him when I turn up and he sees that I'm not Lucy.'

'The truth. You knew Lucy was going to stand him up and you know why.'

I stand up and begin to pace around the room. *This could work.*

'All right,' I say and roll my shoulders back. 'I'll do it.'

Twenty-Five

The last time I was at The Ritz was for Gran's seventieth birthday. Mum, Dan and I had arranged for a surprise afternoon tea. Gran had loved going back into a hotel and had been quick to tell us what she thought of The Ritz's chinaware. I doubt this time is going to be so enjoyable. I did a lot of thinking on the train and more than once thought about calling the whole charade off and going home. God forbid Lucy has changed her mind and I just butt in on their reunion meal. In the end, I decide it is a risk worth taking. I deserve a bit of closure and Simon deserves to hear a few home truths. I'm not going to make a scene. The Ritz is no place to make a scene. I'm going to deal with this like a grown-up.

I make the short walk from Green Park station to the grand entrance of The Ritz. Once inside, I am directed towards the restaurant. It really does feel like a palace. It has floor-to-ceiling windows with gold curtains that accentuate the large chandeliers. One of the restaurant staff takes my coat. It's only then I realise that I don't know what name the table will be booked under. Luckily I spot Simon. He's sitting at a table for two by one of the windows. I gesture towards him before I'm asked for my name and walk over to him. I take large confident strides. I know exactly what I'm going to say to him.

'Simon?'

He looks up at me.

'Yes, I'm Simon,' he says very politely but with a quiz-zical look.

Oh crap, I've lost my nerve.

'I'm sorry. I'm Cassy? You probably don't remember me but we met once? At the Threadneedle NHS Walk-in Centre? I'd twisted my ankle? And I bumped into you?'

I realise I'm finishing every sentence with a question and speaking rather fast but I see him register who I am which relaxes me slightly.

'I do, remember, yes. How are you? How's the foot?'

'Oh fine, thanks,' I say and sit down without really thinking about it.

'Oh,' he says and shuffles in his seat. 'I'm sorry but I'm actually expecting someone.'

'Lucy,' I say.

Simon suddenly looks very uneasy.

'I saw Lucy earlier and she told me... She told me everything.'

'Ah,' he says and dips his head. 'She's not coming, is she?'

He looks so upset, I'm momentarily thrown.

Maybe there has been some kind of mistake?

Then I remember the flirty messages he wrote to me in the puzzle book.

'No,' I say sternly. 'The reason I came here was to tell you that—'

'May I get you something to drink?' The question startles me. I look up at the waiter.

'I'm fine, thank you,' I say.

He nods but picks up the bottle of still water on the table anyway. He seems to take an age pouring me a glass but I am determined not to get thrown off course. Simon needs to own up to his mistakes.

'I came to tell you,' I say once the waiter has gone, 'that I know you were going behind Lucy's back and—'

'I wasn't.'

'Simon, cut the crap. OK? I know. I know everything. I know about the car, the puzzle book—'

'Damn that bloody puzzle book,' he says and slams his hand on the table. 'It's got nothing to do with it.'

The people around us look over but I don't care.

'It's got everything to do with it. You were going behind her back, lying about—'

'The only thing I've lied about is being rich.'

OK. I wasn't expecting that.

Simon runs his fingers through his hair. He holds his hand up apologetically before covering his face with his hands. I sit silently, trying to think of all the possibilities.

'The only thing I'm guilty of,' he says, softly, 'is covering up the fact that I'm broke.'

'Lucy said you were loaded. That you didn't work, you just played golf with your father.'

'I used to,' Simon says, wistfully. 'Until he went bankrupt last year. My father owned a chain of car dealerships, specialising in high-end vehicles. Lamborghinis mainly.'

'Right. I saw yours once, when you came to pick up Lucy.'

'How well do you know Lucy?'

'We've become friends recently,' I say and realise how weird this whole situation is.

'It's odd she's never mentioned you.' He studies me for a while. 'The car isn't mine.'

'OK, I think I'm going to go. I've heard enough. I'm not going to listen to this nonsense.'

'It's the truth.'

'Lucy told me she bought it for you.'

'Did she also tell you she put it on my credit card?' *Actually I think she did mention that.* 'You can't buy a car on a credit card.' *That's a valid point.*

'OK. So, if it's not your car… explain it to me.'

'When my dad had to sell the business, I realised I needed to work if I was going to be able to buy Lucy all the things she wanted. I went to the careers advisor at the walk-in centre and he helped me to convince the new owner to let me be a salesman at one of my dad's old dealerships. Everything was going fine. With the commissions I made, I was able to take Lucy to restaurants we used to go to and I could still buy her gifts. But then Lucy decided she wanted to get me something for my birthday.'

'The car.'

He nods. 'Thankfully she went into my branch. I saw her coming and got one of the other salesman to serve her. We convinced her to buy one a couple of years old, said it was a limited edition colour. We made her fill out all the correct paperwork. She really thought she'd bought it. Then, a few weeks later, she came back with me and we drove the car away. I just booked it as a test drive and drove it straight back afterwards.'

'That's a pretty elaborate lie, don't you think?'

'You don't know what it's like where we live, the lifestyle I used to have. I can't just ask Lucy to give up on all her luxuries and I can't lose her. I'd do anything to make her happy.'

'That still doesn't explain how you could pick her up every day?'

'The guys in the dealership knew what was going on. They felt sorry for me. And they agreed to let me take the car out on fake test drives in my breaks. I timed them as best I could to pick her up but sometimes someone else was test driving the car when I needed to leave.'

'And that's why you were late sometimes.'

He nods again. 'The car smelt of different perfumes because there were always different people in it.'

'And the puzzle book?'

'It was nothing. A misunderstanding. Lucy was just so suspicious by then she wouldn't let me explain. She knew I was lying about something. I've never been good at hiding things from her. Watching my parent's world crumble… it's been so hard and the one person I want to talk to about it, I can't.'

'But, why not just tell her the truth?'

'Do you think Lucy would want to be with me if she knew I was broke?'

'I think she deserves to make that decision for herself.'

The waiter comes back over, he's holding two plates of what looks like stuffed crab claw and salad. He places one in front of each of us.

'Please,' Simon says and gestures, 'help yourself. It's a three-course set menu and I've already paid.'

'It's the cheapest way of eating in this place,' he adds quietly, once the waiter has gone.

We eat the first course in silence. Everything he's said makes sense. It's completely nuts, but then everything that's happened at the Threadneedle Walk-in Centre has been nuts. Why should this be any different?

'I'm sorry, you don't have to stay,' he says once the waiter has cleared the plates. 'Thanks for letting me know she wasn't coming. It was kind of you.'

'It wasn't really,' I say. 'I actually came here to tell you that I thought you were a super loser and that you couldn't blame it on your toothpaste.'

'Oh,' he says and looks confused – he doesn't seem to get the reference to the crossword clue. 'Well, I guess I've gone from super loser to super idiot?'

'You're not an idiot, you're just… A fool in love.'

–

I don't think I quite appreciated how much in love with Lucy Simon really was until the main courses had been served and finished. I decided against telling him I was the one he had been messaging in the puzzle-book. There was no need to complicate things further. I'd dropped in a few more hints from the puzzle book but he hadn't taken the bait. All he could talk about was Lucy and how difficult it had been not being able to confide in her. The stress of keeping secrets from Lucy seems to have taken its toll on him and sitting here with me, in this rather surreal situation, has given him a chance to offload. I admit, I have switched off on occasion during his monologues but at least the evening is drawing to a close.

'It really was love at first sight. For me at least,' Simon says as the desserts are served.

Having recounted most of their relationship, he has now decided to tell me about how they met. I think.

'It was that moment. When your eyes lock and it's like you can see right through each other. D'y'know what I mean?'

A memory comes to me. Not of Seph. Of Martin. Standing outside my flat, when I'd finally cracked his cryptic clue after our date. Well, the date that wasn't really a date. 'Love,' I'd said and our eyes had met, just like Simon had described. I suddenly realise I have no idea what would have happened that night if Seph hadn't interrupted.

'Sorry. I'm boring you.'

'No, not at all,' I say, realising I haven't heard anything he's said while we've been eating dessert.

I find myself comparing The Ritz to Le Papillion as the waiter helps me into my coat. There isn't much of a contest. Le Papillion wins hands down. The food and the company.

'Here, take this, for the food,' I say when we're in The Ritz entrance hall and I hand Simon a few notes.

'No, it's fine. You've had to listen to me ramble on all night.'

'Please take it. I insist.'

'Thanks, but, I'm not a charity case.'

I put the notes away. We say goodnight and I make my way back to the train station. Sitting on the tube, I feel deflated. Perhaps it's just because Puzzle-man didn't turn out to be my dream man but, let's face it, it had always been a long shot. Dan had been right. I had been using the Puzzle-man mystery to escape my life and Simon was doing the same. Perhaps I'm simply feeling deflated because the mystery is solved and I have to face up to my problems. But it feels like more than that. I can't shake the feeling and even when I've updated Dan on all the night's revelations the feeling stays with me.

–

The feeling is still there when I wake up the next morning only now I think I know what it is. It's not just about the mystery. I feel sorry for Simon and Lucy. Had my ridiculous saga with the puzzle book really played a part in their break-up? OK, Simon had lied to her and Lucy seemed too focused on material things but she always spoke about him with admiration and Simon is clearly devoted to her.

'If only there was a way for the two of them to work things out,' I say to Dan while we eat breakfast: scrambled eggs on toast.

'It's not your problem,' Dan says and gives me a stern look that says, 'don't-get-involved'.

'But I'm already involved,' I say to him.

I pick up my mobile phone. Dan lets out a sigh, deliberately loud, but I ignore him. I dial a number that I really shouldn't know off by heart. It begins to ring.

'Threadneedle NHS Walk-in Centre, how may I help?'

'Hi, Janet, it's Cassy Brookes.'

The line goes quiet.

'I know I shouldn't ask but I really need a favour.'

I'm not entirely convinced Janet is still on the line but I carry on anyway.

'Is it possible to speak to Nurse Clarkson?'

'I'm afraid she no longer works here,' Janet says very matter-of-factly.

'What?'

'She resigned this morning.'

'I don't believe it.' Even as I say it, I do believe it. Hadn't I told her to start a new chapter in her life and that I was doing the same by quitting my job?

'Well, believe it or not, it's true,' Janet says, irritably. 'She is coming in to collect her things in an hour.'

'Thanks,' I say but Janet has already hung up.

'What?' Dan asks.

'Lucy's quit.'

'Well, if that's not a sign from the universe telling you to keep your big nose out of it, I don't know what is. Hey, what are you doing?'

'Turning on your laptop.'

'I can see that. Why?'

'I need to find the address of a car dealer.'

Five minutes later, I'm putting on my shoes and heading for the door.

'Don't forget that Sofia is coming over for lunch,' he calls out to me.

'I won't,' I say and blow him a kiss on my way out.

–

The car dealership is just as Simon had described last night. I'm not sure which one of us spots the other first but by the time I reach the door he's already opened it. His expression says, 'what are you doing here?' but before he has a chance to ask in words, I say, 'It's Lucy. She's quit her job but I have a plan.'

Simon doesn't ask for too many details. I wait for him in the entrance of the dealership while he speaks to his boss. I watch them talking in hushed voices for a few minutes before Simon looks over at me and nods.

'Meet you out front,' he mouths at me before exiting himself out of a back door.

I feel a burst of excitement run through me. I actually think this is going to work.

A few minutes later, Simon pulls up on the roadside in front of the dealership in the same Lamborghini I saw him driving a few weeks ago. I get in the passenger side and we're away. Now I am most definitely a vintage-car girl over a modern revving monster but, I have to admit, driving through central London in a state-of-the-art Lamborghini is pretty cool. I glance down at my watch as we cross London Bridge. If Janet was right about Lucy collecting her things in an hour then she should be arriving at the walk-in centre now. I just hope we don't miss her.

Simon pulls into the small staff car park behind the walk-in centre. We both look a little nervous, though Simon perhaps more justifiably. We get out and walk towards the entrance. I guess my work is done. I should leave the rest up to Simon. I should say goodbye and wish him luck.

Curiosity killed the cat, I remind myself.

I'm just about to speak when Lucy walks out of the building carrying a designer bag. She stops in her tracks.

'What are you doing here?' she asks, looking from Simon to me and then back to Simon.

'If you're here to tell me I should keep my job forget it.'

'But you're good at your—'

'You can talk, you don't even have a job.'

'Well, actually…'

'Actually, what?'

'Actually…'

He can't do it.

'Lucy,' I say. 'I know this isn't really my place but I think you're both about to go round in circles. The truth is, Simon *does* have a job. His family don't own the business anymore and Simon has been working for the new owners so that he has enough money to buy you gifts.'

Lucy looks from me to Simon.

'I'm sorry. I didn't know how to tell you.'

'But all those dinners. The car?'

'I borrow a company car at lunchtimes to pick you up.'

Lucy drops her bag to the floor.

'I'm sorry. You deserve someone who can treat you like a princess.'

'That's what you've been hiding from me, isn't it?'

Simon nods.

'Si, I don't care about money. I care about you.'

Simon dips his head. 'I'm sorry I lied to you.'

Lucy draws closer to him and I take a few steps back as they embrace. A weight seems to lift from me. For the first time since I broke up with Seph I don't feel angry or jealous seeing a couple in love kiss. I'm happy for them.

Lucy suddenly turns to me.

'How did you know?' she asks.

'I went to the Ritz to tell him you were going to stand him up and, err, give him a good talking to,' I say and raise my fist in an attempt to show sisterhood solidarity.

Lucy looks a little confused.

Time to go, Cassy.

'Anyway, it's great that you two have sorted things out after the whole puzzle-book thing.'

Oh God, I'm digging myself into a hole.

'Which, obviously, turned out to be a big misunderstanding.' I let out a nervous laugh.

'Yeah,' Simon says, coming to my rescue. 'I guess it was lucky I helped my careers advisor look for it after all.'

'Exactly, right. Your careers advisor. Wait, your *careers advisor*?'

'Yeah,' Simon says, gazing at Lucy, oblivious to the urgency in my voice. 'He'd been so good to me. I wanted to help—'

'That's sweet,' I say, cutting him off short. 'So *he* was the one looking for the puzzle book?'

'Yeah,' Simon says and kisses Lucy's forehead. 'I'd been waiting for this one,' – Simon squeezes her and she giggles – 'to finish her shift when I saw him looking flustered. He kept going on about finding some old puzzle book.'

I feel the hairs on the back on my neck stand up on end.

'When he couldn't find it he got really stressed out. It was his last day and he said he wanted it as a souvenir. He looked as if he was about to cry so I said I'd help him.'

'You really are so kind,' Lucy says and gives him a big wet kiss.

'Well, we'd better get going. I need to get the car back. Ready for one last ride in the Lamborghini?'

'Yes, please,' Lucy says and smiles. 'Bye, Cassy.'

'Bye,' I say, already reaching for my phone. It beeps as I take it out.

> **From: Dan Mobile Tue 12:05**
> Sofia's here xx

I don't bother to reply. I quickly dial Gran's number.

'Hello?'

'Hi, Gran, it's me.'

'Cassy, is that you?'

'Yes, Gran, it's me. I just had a quick question, did you throw out that letter about my careers consultation yet?'

'Oh yes, pet, don't worry, I ripped it up so no one can steal your details. It's awful the things you hear on the news about fraud. One of my good friends—'

'Do you think you could put it back together, Gran?' I ask, power-walking towards Leadenhall Market.

'Well, I suppose. Hold on, pet.'

I'm almost at Gran's front door by the time she comes back to the phone.

'OK, pet, I've sellotaped it back together for you.'

'Thanks, Gran. Does it say the name of the consultant on it?'

'Yes, pet.'

My heart is pounding so hard I can barely hear my own voice say, 'What's their name, Gran?'

'It's a Mr Martin Robertson.'

Twenty-Six

'Sorry, I'm late,' I say when I get back to the flat.

'No worries, Dan filled me in on your latest Thread-needle mission. Did everything get sorted? Cassy?'

'I'm not sure how to answer that. Yes? Yeah, I suppose it did.'

'OK,' Dan says and pulls me over to the sofa. 'Spill.'

I slowly recount everything that had happened. Meeting Simon at the car dealership. Stepping in and telling Lucy the truth about Simon's financial situation. I make sure not to leave a single detail out. Not for their benefit but mine. It's the only way the whole thing seems real. I tell them about Simon and Lucy's kiss. How I felt pleased for them rather than jealous. Then I tell them what Simon said about the puzzle book. How I found out it was really the careers advisor who had been leaving me messages.

'But didn't you have a careers session yourself?'

'I didn't get round to it. The letter only arrived at Gran's a few days ago.'

'So the letter,' Dan says, 'won't it say on it who the careers advisor is?'

I nod. This is the part that doesn't seem real.

'So can't you just ask your Gran what name is on the letter?'

'I already have.'

'And?'

They've both leaned forward, intrigue pulling them closer to me. I gulp.

'Martin Robertson.'

'No way!' Sofia says, her hands clamped to her mouth in disbelief.

'Who?' Dan says looking from Sofia to me.

'It's Martin,' I say again.

'Martin?' Dan asks and then his eyes widen. 'As in *the* Martin, your nemesis, who stole your promotion?'

I nod.

'But how?' Sofia asks.

I hunch my shoulders and shake my head. 'I don't know. I knew he did some mentoring. I even bumped into him there once. Remember? But I didn't click that he was the careers advisor.'

The three of us sit in silence.

'Bummer,' Dan says eventually and begins to laugh.

'I really don't see how this is remotely funny.'

'Oh, come on,' Dan says. 'This is the guy whom you loath and whose chances of getting a promotion you have been doing your level best to destroy and all the while you've been sneaking out of work to send him secret flirty messages.'

Sofia lets out a small, feminine snort and begins to laugh too. Dan wipes a tear from his eye.

'You've got to admit,' he says. 'It is pretty—'

'Don't you dare say ironic.'

Dan and Sofia stop laughing. They look at each other and then, in unison, start singing, 'Ironic'.

'You know, I really hate that song,' I say and slouch back in the chair.

'So what are you going to do?' Sofia asks once they've finished their rendition.

'I have no idea. Nothing? I mean, Martin was pretty pissed that I went behind his back about his dad. He probably wants nothing more to do with me.'

'I guess. It's not like you liked him anyway,' Sofia says.

'Yeah, you're right,' I say.

Except that lately I've seen a different side to him.

'Uh, oh, that didn't sound very convincing,' Dan says.

'Oh, I don't know. It's just... What if I was wrong about him?'

'We are talking about the same Martin Robertson, right?' Sofia asks. 'The chauvinistic pig?'

'Yeah,' I say, softly.

Except that he told Mr Samuel I came up with the MediaTech strategy.

'Who cares about no one but himself,' she continues.

'That would be the one.'

Except when he helps out the kids in Rose's youth group and volunteers at soup kitchens.

'The slick womanizer.'

'Yep.'

Except when he acts like a complete gentleman on a blind date.

'The cut-throat opportunistic snake who'll do anything to get ahead.'

'The one and only.'

Except when he conceals the fact that his father is Sir Lockley so he can do well on merit.

'Who did everything in his power to undermine you at work?'

'Indeed.'

330

Except when he decided not to tell Mr Samuel I'd tried to frame him during a fake meeting with Daniel that could have got me fired.

'OK. Good,' Sofia says. 'Just thought it was worth clarifying all that. For a minute there I thought you'd forgotten what he was really like.'

'Ha. No of course not,' I say trying to convince myself more than Sofia. 'It's just playing on my mind a bit, that's all… I mean, what if he knew all along and that's why he went on that date with me?'

Dan, who has been surprisingly quiet during the Martin-rant, puts his arm around me.

'Chances are, he has no idea it was you,' Dan says, earnestly. 'I mean, you had no idea it was him, did you?'

'No,' I say and bite my lip.

I really did have no idea at the time, but now the signs seem to be so obvious. I feel sick thinking back to the conversation I had with him at the MediaTech conference. 'Puzzle-man' hadn't stood me up after all and what happened? I told him I'd gone behind his back. All I can think about is that look of disappointment in Martin's eyes when he realised what I'd done. It was the same look he'd had when he said goodbye to me at Holywells.

I sigh.

'How could I be so blind?' I ask, only afterwards realising I'd said it out loud.

'Ah, Cassy,' Sofia says, looking very sympathetic.

'Trust you to confuse true love with hatred, eh?'

Is that really why I feel so confused?

We drop the Puzzle-man conversation after that and turn our attention to the business.

'OK,' Dan says. 'First on our first meeting agenda is… the name.'

'It's Brookes Advisory.'

'Yes, I know that was your suggestion, Cassy, but it's crap.'

'No, it isn't!'

'OK, it's crap and boring. Do you want people to think we're giving out advice on the latest doorbell technology?'

'Ooh, how about Sofia & Co.?'

The three of us begin to laugh.

–

'Is leftover pizza on the menu for tonight again?' Dan asks once Sofia has gone.

I smile weakly. The 'meeting' had turned out to take most of the afternoon with exactly none of the agenda points being completed. It was a nice afternoon though.

'You're not regretting your decision to leave Holywells, are you?'

'No. Of course not.'

Dan waits for me to say more but I don't.

'Well, something is on your mind... Is it about Martin?'

Yes.

The more I think about everything that has happened between Martin and me over the past few weeks, the more I wonder if it was me that was the chauvinistic pig and not him. What if I got him all wrong?

'Are you upset that it's him and not Prince Charming?'

'No. It's not that.'

Dan gives me a wry smile and walks over to me.

'Well then, is it because it's him and he *is* Prince Charming?'

'Don't be silly,' I say and fold my arms.

'Y'know, Sofia may not be able to tell when you're outright lying but I can.'

Dan gives me another wry smile. Suddenly I feel very hot and self-conscious.

'Why don't you just talk to him?'

'And say what? Sorry for... everything. A phone call can't fix this. Urgh. It's all irrelevant anyway... It's a silly problem... There's no solution.'

'Cassy! I never thought I would hear such words from you! A problem with no solution? That can't be.'

'Well, someone told me that I need to stop seeing everything so black and white,' I say and walk into the kitchen to make something to eat that isn't pizza.

'Why don't you make a list?' Dan calls out to me.

'I thought I only made lists when I feel helpless,' I call back.

'Well, you do feel helpless over the Martin situation, don't you?'

I guess he's right. I could make a list. I think about all the lists I made about hating Martin.

'No, I don't want to.'

'Man, you really are upset. So what are you going to do about it?'

'There's nothing I can do. Aside from making a world-wide public apology and begging for forgiveness.'

'Cassy, that's it!'

'Wow, you're right. Why didn't I think of that?'

'You did.'

'I wasn't being serious.'

'Why not?' he asks.

'How could I?'

Dan looks at me as though I'm simple. 'You know I'm starting to doubt whether starting a digital marketing agency with you is a good idea.'

'So what do you suggest, I tweet him?'

'That's exactly what I'm suggesting,' Dan says, already tapping away at his laptop. He turns it to face me. He's opened a new twitter account @_Puzzle_Girl.

'Puzzle Girl is going to tweet him and we're going to get it to go viral.'

Twenty-Seven

@_Puzzle_Girl: Puzzle-man, I know you
probably want nothing more to do with me
but I really hope you'll meet me for tea at St
Paul's on Sunday at 3 p.m.

I didn't expect that the first client of our new business
would in fact be me. Sofia, Dan and I worked tirelessly,
promoting the tweet and calling in favours with media
friends all week. The tweet has been retweeted enough
times to make it into local news and #whoispuzzleman
has been trending for the past few hours.

'Do you reckon Martin will see it?' Sofia had asked last
night.

'Everyone's seen it,' Dan had said.

'The question,' I'd added, 'is whether he wants to meet
me.'

—

It's Sunday morning and the only thing keeping me from
collapsing with exhaustion is the adrenalin and anticipation of what might happen this afternoon. Can this
be real? I, Cassidy Ann Brookes, have turned down the
opportunity to be Head of Accounts at Holywells and
resigned to take on a new entrepreneurial venture with

my best buddy Dan. I have also hung, 'dumped' and quartered Seph and have set up a date with my arch-nemesis Martin who has turned out to be none other than my Puzzle-man. No. This can't be real. Can it? The moment threatens to overcome me when another thought pops into my head. What am I going to wear?

-

'Dan, Dan, Dan! Time to get up! I need help!' I really do need help, I feel like I'm seventeen again going on my first date.

'No. You're fine, you don't need me,' Dan says sleepily from under the duvet. I don't have time to argue with him, I need to get moving.

I have my shower and blow-dry my hair. Now it really is crunch time, what the hell am I going to wear and why the hell am I so excited? Martin's seen me a thousand times. But then, this is different. Today will be a date between Puzzle-girl and Puzzle-man not a catch-up for work colleagues. That's if he shows up.

'Dan, Dan, Dan, I need you, seriously,' I call out. I can hear heavy footsteps coming up to my door.

'Here, wear this.' Dan is holding the most beau-tiful, three-quarter length, two-tone, blue-green dress. It's made of silky, light fabric and I think it's the most gorgeous dress I've ever seen.

'Where did you get that?'

'I—' Dan yawns, 'I bought it for you.'

'What? When?'

'After you metaphorically murdered Luke I figured you deserved a treat and we both know I have better taste in fashion than you.'

'Oh, Dan.'

'All right, all right, enough with the hugging. I'm going back to bed. It's 8 a.m. on a Sunday!'

'No, it's 10 a.m.'

'No, it's 8 a.m.'

'No, it's – oh crap, I screwed up the time on my alarm clock.'

'Night,' Dan calls, already halfway out the door.

Hmmm. Now what am I supposed to do for seven hours????

-

I've spent the whole morning in the City. I ended up getting here at 10 a.m. before any of the shops were even open but now, finally, it's quarter to three on Sunday afternoon.

I'm walking up Ludgate Hill towards St Paul's. My legs are a little wobbly. Actually my whole body is shaking. What if this has all been a set-up? What if all the graduates had been in the joke with Martin and they all turn up and start laughing at me?

Too late to worry about that, I say to myself, *I'm here*. It looks like there is some kind of demonstration going on. There are loads of women crowded around the steps of St Paul's all holding the same flyer.

Wait.

That's not a flyer.

It's the front page of the local newspaper and my tweet is on it.

Oh my God. They're all here pretending to be Puzzle-girl!

As I edge closer, I can see some of the women madly applying make-up. And it's not just old ladies looking for a last romantic story, there are teenagers, mums with buggies… It's insane. They're all calling out at any man that walks past: 'It's me, your mystery Puzzle-girl,'; 'I'm the real Puzzle-girl.'

Oh my God, there's a camera crew!

'Since when did a silly puzzle mystery make the headlines,' I exhale, a little louder than intended.

'O-M-G, don't you read?' asks a young girl, thrusting a newspaper into my hands. I look down at the article again. I hope Martin reads between the lines.

'Cassy!'

'Sofia! Dan! What are you doing here?'

'You didn't think we'd miss this, did you?' Dan winks at me.

'How the hell are you going to spot Martin in that mob?' Sofia asks, nodding towards the crowds of erratic women. 'It's a disaster. I mean, look at them all.'

'What, are they all here for this?' Dan says, utterly perplexed. 'And I thought it was only straight guys that were supposed to have trouble understanding women,' he says, shaking his head.

'Oi,' Sofia nudges Dan, 'there's some sad men here too. Look at him over there. Can you imagine if he was Puzzle-man?'

They both start giggling like silly schoolgirls.

'Look over there,' I say, 'that pregnant lady just attacked that poor man! And, oh my God, it can't be!'

'What?'

'It's Janet. There, look! That's Janet, the receptionist,' I say, flabbergasted. 'What the hell is she doing here?'

'Where?' Sofia says, eyeing up the crowd.

'Over there, in the blue shirt, standing at the bottom of the steps. God, I can't believe all these people are here. I just hope Martin got my message.'

'Look around. The whole of London got the message.'

'I meant understood it. The tweet was cryptic.'

'Huh?'

'Think about it. "Meet me for *tea* at St Paul's".'

'Oh, that's so clever,' Sofia says.

'What? I don't get it,' Dan says, looking very confused.

'It's the Tea café, that's where I'm supposed to meet him,' I say, my eyes already focused on the black shop sign in the distance.

'Well, we're coming too,' Dan says.

'No way.'

'Yes, we are,' Sofia joins in. 'There's no way you get to have all the fun.'

Two against one.

'Fine, but you'd better go there now before he arrives and stay out of sight.' I wait for Sofia and Dan to walk off, arm-in-arm, towards Tea before ditching the paper, not wanting to attract any attention, particularly not the media's. I do my best to act casual as I walk past St Paul's and make sure to stay out of Janet's view. With every step, my breathing gets a little heavier and the butterflies in my stomach are so strong I feel I could fly.

I'm a few paces away and I can see Dan and Sofia sitting down at one of the far corner tables for two. Oh my God. He's already here. He spots me out of the window and smiles. Suddenly my whole body is urging me closer to him. He's wearing dark denim jeans and a gorgeous burgundy shirt that brings out his complexion. I make my way over to him. What do I do now? All my introductory sentences have gone. I can't think what to say. I don't even know if my mouth works.

'Hi,' I say, quietly.

'Hello, Puzzle-girl.'

I blush, hearing him call me that feels so weird and yet fantastic at the same time. He gestures for me to sit down opposite him.

'I picked a table by the window so we could watch all your impersonators. How long do you reckon they'll stay?'

'Quite a while I reckon. I didn't know if you'd come after everything.'

Martin smiles and looks down at his lap. 'Do you really not know how I feel about you?' He looks up and I can barely breathe.

'I'd better order a drink,' I say and stand up abruptly to walk to the counter.

Ouch! I clip the edge of a neighbouring table. I manage to recover my footing and restrain myself from crying out in pain. But I'm sure he'll have seen it. I have a quick glance in the direction of Dan and Sofia. They are both quietly cracking up with laughter. I glare at them.

'G'day, what can I get ya?'

'Could I get a pot of Eternitea, please?' I take a moment to recover my nerves as I pay the waitress and walk back over to the table. Come on Cassy, get a grip, you've been on a date before… Besides, it's not exactly a date, it's just tea.

'Tea?'

'Sorry?' I say, realising I must have walked back from the counter to the table on autopilot.

'Which tea did you get?'

'Oh, Eternitea. So—'

'So—'

'Sorry, you first,' he says.

'Did you always know it was me?'

'The Boris Johnson crossword question was a bit of a clue but I wasn't convinced until I bumped into you there that day.'

I blush thinking about it.

'You've been to Bea,' I say, changing the subject. 'I'd recognise that icing anywhere.'

'Indeed, I love it in there almost as much as this place. The waitress said she didn't mind me bringing them in as long as I ordered tea.' He smiles again and I find myself smiling back. He's like a different person from the guy I've known for five years. Have I really been that blind?

'So, tell me how you managed to conjure up so many excuses to go the walk-in centre? I'm dying to know. The sexual health clinic was genius.'

'I think we might need another pot of tea before I've explained all this,' I say and we both laugh in agreement.

'It just got a bit out of hand,' I say when I've recounted all my walk-in centre antics. 'I wasn't expecting anyone to read it,' I admit.

'Well, I didn't really expect you to keep replying, although I wanted you to.' Our eyes lock together, as if they are having their own private conversation.

'Once I saw the first reply,' he carries on, 'I started doing extra voluntary work.'

'So why didn't you tell me it was you?'

'I tried at the strategy conference but you were... distracted.'

My heart sinks, I knew we couldn't avoid talking about the conference for ever.

'Martin, I am so, so sorry.'

He holds up his hand. 'Look, the way I see it, everything worked out fine. I got a new job and you got the promotion. I'm actually a bit impressed you could be so devious.'

'I'm not devious! All right maybe a little. But I do feel awful.'

'It's history and actually for the first time in years my father and I have found something we agree on.'

'What's that?'

'You.'

Martin sips his tea. Unsure whether I want to know what they think of me I decide against asking and say, 'I didn't accept the promotion.'

Martin spurts his tea. 'Excuse me.'

'Quite all right,' I say trying not to laugh.

'Was that a joke?'

'No, I quit.'

'You *quit*?'

'I'm starting my own business.'

'Huh,' Martin leans back, 'you are just full of surprises.'

'Pardon me, can I get ya anything else?' asks the waitress.

'No, thanks,' Martin says to her. 'Three cups of tea is my limit,' he adds to me once she's gone. I hadn't even noticed how much tea we'd drunk. I guess we have been here a while and it couldn't last forever but I don't want to part ways. Not just yet.

'Do you fancy going for a walk?' he asks me.

'Sure.'

'Cool. Best we ditch Sofia and Dan, eh?'

I can't stop a huge smile spreading over my face. He holds out his arm and we make our way outside. I glance over at Dan and Sofia and mouth, 'See you later'.

The late-afternoon air has a chill to it that has seen most of the Puzzle-girl wannabes go home (although there are a couple of hard-core women still standing on the steps of St Paul's). I pull my jacket tight around me and we walk at a good pace to keep warm. We soon reach the Thames.

'So, I still can't quite believe you managed to find enough excuses to keep replying to me,' he says to me as we walk across Blackfriars Bridge.

'Yes, well, it wasn't the most moral thing I've ever done,' I say, looking down at the river.

'No, perhaps not, but I'm pleased you did it,' he says and gives me a nudge. We're not holding hands, but we are close enough to feel the warmth emanating from each other and occasionally brush our hands against one another.

'What I can't get over is how wrong I was about you,' I say. 'I mean, I don't get why you act like a completely different person in the office from how you've been today.'

'I thought that would be obvious.'

'You're going to tell me you're playing the game, aren't you.'

He nods. 'People have certain expectations of what a man is supposed to be like in client relationship management. Just look at *Mad Men*. Sure you can do all right being yourself but at the end of the day partners want to promote people they can get on with. So if you fit their model of an ideal worker you'll get there faster.'

'So your entire image: a slick, rich, womaniser, was all just an act?'

'Err, not entirely. I'm not saying I'm perfect and I'm not making excuses for myself but five years of unrequited love would take its toll on most people, wouldn't you say?'

His words stop me in my tracks. He turns to face me and puts his hand on my cheek.

'I always thought you knew. I thought that's why you were so hostile towards me, because you were with Seph and you didn't want him to get the wrong idea.'

I open my mouth but no words come out.

'He knew instantly,' Martin says and shakes his head. 'He was quick to piss on his territory.'

'Why did you never say anything?'

'A man has his pride. Come on, Cassy, you told everyone within a month of knowing you that you planned to marry the guy. What would you have said if I'd told you how I felt?'

'Fair point, sleeping around does sound like a better option.' I laugh in a desperate attempt to lighten the moment. This is all so much to take in.

'I'm not proud of it.'

'I wasn't judging. The puzzle book made me realise a lot about my life too,' I say.

'Such as?'

'How much I obsess over everything. My job. Seph. I never did anything spontaneous. OK, pretending to be sick wasn't right but I think I needed it as a wake-up call.'

'So… what do we do now?' he asks.

'I should probably get home soon,' I say, avoiding the more general question to which I don't really have an answer.

'Yeah, me too,' he says, although he looks a little disappointed which gives me butterflies in my stomach again.

'Well, I might cut down here to get to Waterloo station and back to Canning Town,' I say. I can feel an itchy fear running over my body, I don't know what to do. I don't know how to say goodbye.

'OK, well, I'll go across Waterloo Bridge to Embankment so I guess we should say goodbye here then.'

'OK,' I say. I can feel him looking at me, like *really* looking at me. He's working out whether to kiss me. He leans forward slightly. I stay still. Very still.

'Well,' he says quietly and takes a step back, 'it was lovely to see you again, Cassy.'

'You too,' I say and force myself to turn away. Why didn't I let him kiss me?

'Cassy, wait.' Martin is suddenly standing next to me again, his eyes staring into mine. 'I can't spend another five years doing the whole unrequited love thing. Put me out of my misery, please.'

'I can't tell you I love you.'

'I'm not asking you to.'

'I like you. I think I *really* like you. But this is all new to me. I haven't dated someone in over seven years and I don't know if I'm even a good kisser, let alone if I'm good in—'

Martin pulls me to him and kisses me hard on the lips and every nerve in my body sparks into life.

'I'd say you're a great kisser. Let's take it from there.'

'OK,' I whisper.

'OK,' he whispers back. He smiles and goes to walk away but this time I pull him back. I kiss him again. It feels so right.

'When can I see you again?' he asks.

'Well, I'm my own boss now so my diary is wide open.'

'How about dinner tomorrow?'

I nod. I don't think I can speak without giggling.

'OK, what's your number? I'll text you the details.'

'Five years and we don't have each other's personal phone numbers,' I shake my head. 'Things could have been very different if it wasn't for Seph, couldn't they?'

'Things have a way of working out.' He kisses me again. 'Good night.' I watch, rooted to the spot, as he walks away and around the corner out of sight. The sound of my phone vibrating brings me back to reality.

> **From: Martin Mobile Sun 21:50**
> My beautiful Puzzle-girl, I can't wait to see you tomorrow night. I'll meet you at the Underground station at 8pm (if you can solve the clue that is). 'It's been a long road getting you to date me, I'll be bringing out the big guns.' Your Puzzle-man, Martin

Ha, Cannon Street, too easy. I wonder where he's taking me. Wherever it is, something tells me, I'm going to enjoy this.

Acknowledgements

First and foremost I want to thank my amazing husband, Tim Davis. None of this would have been possible without his love and support. Tim encouraged me to take up writing at a time in my life when I needed an escape. Thank you for always being there for me.

I would like to say a huge thank you to my wonderful agent, David Headley; my editor, Rebecca Lloyd; Emily Glenister and the whole Dome Press team. Thank you all for believing in *Puzzle Girl*.

Publishing *Puzzle Girl* has been an incredible journey and I couldn't have done it without the support of my friends and family. In particular, I would like to thank Alison Lawrence, for not only giving me a job in a bookshop when I was sixteen but also being my first beta reader. I would also like to thank my good friends and fellow writers, Jo Agrell, Lou Stephenson and Daniel Paoli. A big thank you to my romantic comedy expert, Rebecca Millington, for always giving me honest feedback. Thank you also to Sean Philip for his insights into the world of digital marketing. Finally, I would like to thank my grandparents, Jennifer and John Featherstone, who are always there for me.